SOMETHING POWERFUL REACHED DEEP INSIDE to pull Danny out of his body. It seemed as though he was gripped by invisible hands, then *extracted*, like a cork from a bottle. And when he came out, he could see the doorway. It hung in space directly in front of him, an unearthly luminous green triangle like nothing he had ever seen before. When you looked into it, strange shapes pulsed and writhed.

Danny felt twisted, as if somebody had taken him and turned him inside out, and he was now facing in a direction no mortal human was supposed to face. It was a hideous sensation, but while he wanted desperately to turn away, something held him firm. His fear ramped toward downright terror. There was a pounding in his ears. The writhing shapes swam closer to the surface of reality and reached for him. . . .

Despite himself, Danny stepped into the doorway.

the
shadowproject

herbie brennan

BALZER + BRAY
An Imprint of HarperCollins*Publishers*

Balzer & Bray is an imprint of HarperCollins Publishers.

The Shadow Project
Copyright © 2010 by Herbie Brennan

Library of Congress Cataloging-in-Publication Data
Brennan, Herbie.
    The Shadow Project / by Herbie Brennan. — 1st ed.
        p.   cm.
    Summary: A young English thief stumbles on, and subsequently is recruited for,
a super-secret operation that trains teenagers in remote viewing and astral projection
techniques in order to engage in spying.
    ISBN 978-0-06-175645-0
    [1. Psychic ability—Fiction. 2. Astral projection—Fiction. 3. Spies—
Fiction. 4. England—Fiction.] I. Title.
PZ7.B75153Sh   2010   2009014276
[Fic]—dc22   CIP
                                                                           AC

Typography by Carla Weise
    11   12   13   14   15   LP/CW   10   9   8   7   6   5   4   3   2   1
❖

First paperback edition, 2011

For Jacks, always

the shadow project

Danny, outside London

Danny would never have noticed the door that night if it hadn't opened a crack. It was hidden on the outside by the same wood paneling that ran along the whole length of the corridor. Cleverly hidden too, lovely workmanship. How it opened, Danny didn't know—you probably twisted a candlestick or felt behind a family portrait for a hidden button. Only he didn't have to look for anything like that, because the secret door was already open. Not much more than half an inch, but half an inch was enough.

He was expecting the door to be stiff—it looked like it hadn't been used in years—but it swung back sweet as you like, not so much as a creak. There was another door behind it, a modern door this time, brand-new and high-tech looking. There was a combination lock pad built in with some sort of sensor plate above it and a little lens above that.

Danny stared, impressed but puzzled. He knew what he was looking at, all right—high security. Very high security. You didn't just need the numbers to punch in: that pad was for a thumbprint, and the little lens above it was an iris recognition system. But what was such a high-security system doing in a   ⎵   run-down country house?

He took a step back before and   ⎵   thought struck him. Maybe the secret door led to   ⎵   vault where the owner kept his priceless art collection. Maybe the old boy who owned the house was filthy rich. Not that it mattered, because Danny didn't have the combination or the thumbprint or the iris pattern to get through a door like this anyway. But it didn't stop him from pushing it. Just a little push, not really expecting anything to happen—just the sort of thing you did if you were somebody like Danny with nothing to lose.

The door opened.

Not inward, but sideways. A sliding door, so silent you couldn't hear a whisper. And an automatic light came on.

Danny was looking into a lift.

Danny kept looking into the lift, thinking it was all too much. The thing was all sparkling chrome with mirrors built into the walls, not so much as a finger smudge on any of them. No buttons, though: no top floor, ground floor, lobby, or that sort of thing. But there was a discreet brass plaque announcing OTIS, which meant that this was an American installation, what they called an elevator. What was an American high-tech, state-of-the-art, high-security elevator doing hiding behind a secret panel in an old English country house?

There was no question of getting into it, of course. That would be stupid. No buttons. This was an automatic elevator, the sort that took you somewhere of its own accord with no way of stopping it or making it go somewhere else. All the same, he was curious. He wondered if there really was an art collection.

Danny stepped into the elevator. The door slid closed behind him. "Going down," the lift murmured in a soft American accent. It went down for a lot longer than he thought it would, a lot longer than it would take to get to a converted cellar, for example, before the doors slid open again.

Danny felt a sudden pang of fear. He was in a corridor that didn't seem to suit the rest of the house. It was modern, stark, dead straight, and painted blue. No furniture, no ornaments, no pictures on the walls. And not just a corridor. This looked like a whole maze of corridors, which definitely didn't belong here. It was as if somebody had built an entire office deep underneath the old house. But why?

Danny wished the lift would go back up again, but it stubbornly refused to move, refused even to close its doors. There had to be sensors, maybe even a hidden camera, that told it somebody was still inside. So it left him standing exposed to anybody who was down there. He had to move to somewhere less conspicuous, and he had to move fast. He was no longer in an empty country house. There might be people down here—people who set up high-security systems.

As Danny stepped smartly off the elevator, its door slid shut again, and this time it didn't open when he pushed it. Whatever he'd got himself into, he was stuck here. But where was he? What was this place? It even had light tracks along the floor, like the markers in airports that showed where you were supposed to go. Different colors seemed to lead to different places.

He turned to push the elevator door again, but nothing happened. Coming down here had been really stupid. It was one thing trying to nick a few quid from an empty house, but this place was something else. One step in and he was creeped out already. His heart was pounding uncomfortably. His hands were sweating. It wasn't just waiting for somebody to step into the corridor and spot him. It was the feeling that getting caught down here could be a lot more serious than getting caught up above. He needed to find a way back out and find it *fast*.

Danny started to move along the corridor. There were doors opening off it, which might mean places to hide but might also mean roomfuls of people. All the same, he had no choice. He stopped and listened at one of the doors before pushing it open.

The room was the weirdest thing he'd ever seen. All he could think was *execution chamber*. Two electric chairs—at least they looked like two electric chairs with their shining metal headsets and cables snaking everywhere—were set side by side in the middle of the floor. There was a pretty girl inside, about Danny's own age, dressed in a T-shirt with a fairy on it and expensive-looking designer jeans. She might have been headed for a high-class disco, only she wasn't. She was sitting in one of the electric chairs, strapped in with the steel cap on her head, not quite covering the blond hair. There were *things* flying around her: for some reason his eyes couldn't focus on them properly, but they flapped like little bats. Behind her, standing by a bank of switches, was a man who looked like Nicholas Cage, except for the color of his hair. The girl had her eyes closed, but the man was staring straight at Danny. His mouth dropped open.

Danny went cold. Nicholas was about to execute the girl!

"Hey!" shouted Nicholas Cage. The girl opened her eyes.

And right on cue, like in some really bad horror movie, Danny heard running footsteps behind him.

Danny swung around. There was a figure rushing toward him down the corridor, a muscular young black guy, Danny's height or maybe an inch taller, who looked about his own age. But his gear was nothing like anything Danny ever wore: a cream-colored two-piece suit that fit so well, it had to be tailored. He reached for Danny—who, with street-fighter instincts, kneed him in the groin.

The boy howled, jackknifed, and clutched himself with both hands. Encouraged by the reaction, Danny drew back to hit him in the mouth. But somebody grabbed his wrist, somebody strong. He spun around, thinking about repeating the knee trick, only it didn't work so well with girls, and he was definitely looking at the girl, free of her electric chair and glaring at him.

"What the *hell* do you think you're doing?" she demanded.

[2]

Dorothy, London

Ring for an ambulance, Dorothy thought. *You have to get me to a hospital, otherwise I'm going to die down here at the bottom of the stairs. So ring for an ambulance and then ring Danny on his mobile. Not that he ever answers it, but you can leave him a message, voice mail or whatever it's called, bound to pick that up eventually. Tell him his old Nan's had a bit of a turn. Don't worry him, mind: tell him the hospital is just a precaution. You can say observation, took her in for observation.*

"Oh, Jesus!" Aggie said.

Go on, you useless old fool, Dorothy thought. *Think* telephone. *Think* get help. *Don't just stand there like a headless chicken taking the name of the Lord in vain.*

"Oh, Dot!" Aggie said, which was a change from *Oh, Jesus,* but not much more helpful. Then Aggie did a strange thing. She leaned forward and kissed Dorothy very gently on the cheek. Then she stood up, slowly, painfully—Dorothy could hear her knees crack. "Don't you worry, Dot, I'll get the doctor round. You're going to be all right. You stay there and don't move."

Don't move? Don't move? *What world are you living in? If I could move I wouldn't need the bleeding doctor, would I? And never mind the doctor anyway—it's an* ambulance *I want.* In her desperation, Dorothy tried to say something—*ambulance*, probably—but all that came out was a squeak. Not that Aggie would have heard her anyway, because she was already on the move, huffing. Step—*huff.* Step—*huff. She was walking past the telephone!* What was wrong with her? Right past and into the kitchen and—Dorothy couldn't believe it—out the back door.

Suddenly the house was very quiet.

Dorothy knew what she'd had, and it wasn't just a bit of a turn, whatever she told herself. What she'd had was a stroke, same as Stanley. She knew all about strokes because she'd gone with Stanley in the ambulance and talked to the nice young doctor. That's how she knew there were two kinds of strokes. With one you got a clot on the brain, and they had to give you medicine to dissolve it. With the other you had bleeding in the brain, and they had to give you medicine to make it clot.

Could see the problem, couldn't you? Until they found what sort of stroke you had, they couldn't give you any medicine at all. Because if you had a clot and they gave you the stuff that helps clotting, they'd kill you; and if you had bleeding and they gave you the stuff that dissolved clots, it would make the bleeding worse. So the trick was to get you into the hospital and find out what sort of stroke you'd had. "Timing is everything," the nice young doctor had said.

And Aggie had gone off, silly cow. Walked right past the phone, right out of the house. Gone to feed her cat or do the Lotto. The woman was batty. It'd be funny if it wasn't so sad. Gone off and left Dorothy to die.

But talk of the devil, there she was again. Dorothy could hear the back door and the sound of Aggie's steps and heavy breathing. And then Aggie was standing over her, looking down at her, face all full of anxiety.

"I called the hospital," Aggie said.

She'd gone and done it from her own phone, Dorothy thought. *She only went and used her own phone to save me the cost of the call!*

"You're going to be fine, Dot," Aggie said.

[3]

Opal, the Shadow Project

"**A**re you going to be all right?" Michael asked. "After last night."

Opal forced her mouth to close. She'd never worked with Michael Potolo before, although it wasn't for want of trying. He'd joined the Project nearly two months ago and was absolutely gorgeous, especially the smile. They'd chatted a few times, but never for long enough. She wondered where he came from, where Mr. Carradine had found him. She wondered if he had a girlfriend.

"Yes, I'm fine." She smiled back. "What about you?"

He looked faintly surprised. "Me?"

"You know, your . . . ?" She glanced down, realized what she was doing, and looked up again hurriedly.

Michael stared at her for a moment, then looked embarrassed. "Still aching a little."

What should she do next? Offer sympathy? Ask for details? Now she was sorry she'd brought it up. "Good.

I mean, not good. Not good that—not good about the ache, but good about the little." She was beginning to blush; she could feel it. To divert the conversation onto safer ground, she said cheerily, "Well, where did they find you then?"

"Where did they find me?" He had a nice voice, and there seemed to be a slight trace of a French accent. Perhaps she hadn't put that very well. *Where did they find you?* made it sound as if somebody had been scavenging in a dustbin. "Where do you come from?" Opal asked. "Who—?" She stopped herself in time. The voice in her head was her late mother's, asking imperiously, "Who are your people?"

"Eton," Michael said. He seemed to be watching for a reaction.

For just the barest moment she couldn't think where in France Eton might be; then she realized what he meant. "Oh, the school!"

He smiled slightly. "Yes, the school."

He was a long way from Eton now, that was for sure. "Where are you staying?"

"With my uncle," Michael said. "He lives quite close to the Project."

When would he be going back to Eton, Opal wondered? But before she could ask, Michael said, "I understand you're Sir Roland's daughter?"

It was usually the first thing she was asked by new-comers. Opal nodded. "Yes. Yes, I am." She hoped he wouldn't find it off-putting: some people were very silly about these things, and Mr. Carradine's habit of describing her as a star performer didn't help. But before she could ask any more questions, Mr. Carradine interrupted, "You okay to go, Mike?"

"Thank you, yes," Michael said, a little frostily, Opal thought. He probably hated being called Mike, and frankly she didn't blame him. *Mike* wasn't anything like as dignified as *Michael*. But Mr. Carradine was American, which meant he was terribly informal.

"And *you're* okay?" Carradine asked, looking at Opal. "You must have had a bit of a shock with our intruder."

"I'm fine, Mr. Carradine," Opal said. She was curious about their intruder. "It was poor Michael he hit—he didn't actually attack *me*. Who is he?"

"We don't know yet, but he's under lock and key now, so we won't be disturbed again. I've asked George Hanover to question him. I'll have a word myself after I send you off. Meanwhile, we need to get going. Feel okay to start—the two of you?"

"What's the target?" Michael asked.

Carradine glanced at him in surprise. "Haven't you been briefed?"

Michael shook his head. "No. Should I have?"

"Neither have I," Opal put in.

"Sorry," Carradine said. "Thought George talked to you." He went over to the control panel and flicked a switch. "We've had a tip-off from Israeli Intelligence— another Elvis sighting. We need you to check it out."

Another Elvis sighting. Opal groaned inwardly. The target was the Skull, head of *Épée de la Colère*, the Sword of Wrath terrorist network. Real name Venskab Faivre, but no one ever used it since the media had come up with the nickname. At the Project they'd taken to calling him Elvis because so many people reported seeing him in peculiar places, the way nutcases insisted they kept seeing Elvis Presley. He was widely believed to be the most dangerous man in the world ever since his chemical weapon attack on New Jersey had left seven thousand people dead and an almost unbelievable eighteen thousand seriously injured. Although America had always been his prime target, he had struck successfully in Britain, India, Australia, Israel, and Bermuda. Security services throughout the world were now listing him as their number-one priority. The problem was that the U.S. government had put a $50 million bounty on his head. No wonder people kept thinking they saw him. "Where's he been sighted?" Opal asked.

"Lusakistan," Carradine said. "Near the border with China."

"Lusakistan." Opal sighed. "Like the last time. And the time before."

"Actually," Carradine said, unfazed, "Mossad thinks it's the real deal this time, hence the urgency. So if you two are okay with it, maybe we should get started."

Opal slumped down in her chair. She didn't want to complain too much or Michael might think she was a bit of a brat, and she didn't want that, certainly not on their first mission together. She grinned at him. "I'll try not to put too much strain on you," she said, then groaned inwardly at her lame attempt at a joke.

Michael looked as if he might say something, but when he did, it was only a sober "Thank you," which was not a satisfactory response at all. Annoyingly, he looked at Mr. Carradine, who nodded. Michael sat down in the other chair, then redeemed himself at once by turning to stare directly into her eyes. He gave her the smile again, then turned away. But they were still sitting close, almost shoulder to shoulder. She could smell his cologne. Normally she hated boys who used cologne, but this one was rather nice, spicy and subtle.

Carradine adjusted the helmets for both of them. The metal skullcaps were always icy cold, and their trailing filaments were irritating until they connected with the microchip implants in her scalp. She waited patiently while he made the electrical connections, then watched out of the corner of her eye while he did the same for Michael. "Comfortable?" he asked them both when he had finished.

She disliked the gel—she had to shower after every mission to get it out of her hair—but since the equipment wouldn't work without it, she just said, "Yes."

"Yes," Michael echoed confidently.

Out of the corner of her eye she saw Fran come in. Fran usually took care of operations once Mr. Carradine finished the initial setup. After a moment she heard the whine of the generator, closely followed by the distinctive tone of the Hemi-Sync. "Good luck," Michael murmured, then closed his eyes as per standard procedure. Opal did the same. There was a brief moment of disorientation, but almost at once she felt the warm, pleasant flood of relaxation as their brain waves synchronized. Opal let out a long, sighing breath. The sensation was almost as if Michael had crept into her head and was now hugging her. Not telepathy, exactly—but she could sense the close connection of his presence and his warmth. She felt as if she'd known him for years.

"Here we go," said Carradine, and he threw more switches.

He must have gotten the Hemi-Sync under control, because suddenly she could see the hazy flutter of the threshold guardians. Not for the first time, she thought they looked like little bats.

[4]

Danny, the Shadow Project

It was like being back in court, except it wasn't. More like the Spanish Inquisition. Or the interrogation room at his local cop-shop. He knew these characters well. Not by name, of course, but you could spot the types a mile away.

Take the goons by the door. Beefy. Big chests. Sharp suits just a shade too tight so you could admire their muscles. You saw the type employed as bouncers outside clubs, throwing their weight around and showing off for the girls. You saw it in the drug gangs too, minders for the pushers. And you got it with certain cops at the precinct as well, not the brightest bulbs in the sockets, but great when you wanted to break a door down or scare somebody rigid, the way Danny was now. These two stood like sentries in the doorway, faces blank, arms crossed, all ready to make sure young Danny Lipman didn't make a break for it. Flattering to think it took two of them, but that didn't make him feel any less nervous.

The ones behind the desk were familiar types as well: Good Cop, Bad Cop, only Bad Cop was a woman. Nice looking too, if she'd only crack a smile, but you could tell from the shoes you wouldn't want to mess with her. Good Cop was older, liked his food, nice open face, lazy eye, friendly grin, shapeless suit. They could both actually be cops, Danny thought. Especially the woman. He could imagine her in uniform, pounding the beat, poking her nose in where it wasn't wanted. And the man might be plainclothes gone to seed, close to retirement.

Danny tried to get his fear under control. He knew from past experience he mustn't show he was scared— that only encouraged them. But the bad news was, he really *was* scared. This wasn't like any of his previous brushes with the law. He was in some sort of huge underground complex, like nothing he'd ever seen before. This wasn't law enforcement: the cops didn't have enough money to build something this size. It was far too big to be anything but government.

Danny worried about that, worried about that *a lot*. He didn't know for sure what he'd gotten himself into, but his money was on some sort of secret agency. It was the only thing that made sense. And he was old enough to know that British secret agents weren't nice gentlemen like James Bond, whatever they said in the movies.

These characters really *were* licensed to kill and weren't afraid to do it, either. The question was, would they kill somebody just because he'd found their hideaway?

"What's your name?" Bad Cop demanded.

"Lester Thomas, ma'am," Danny told her. He opened his eyes wide and tried to look innocent. With luck she might think he was too stupid to lie.

"Where do you live, Lester?" asked Good Cop mildly.

"Sixty-eight Rigby Villas," Danny told him. It was the home of a dealer he knew. If these freaks ever came calling, they were in for a big surprise. Lester was a hard man and so were his friends.

"What are you doing here?" asked Good Cop, still mildly.

"Sir," said Danny earnestly, "your front door was open—somebody must have left it off the latch by accident—and I heard a noise inside and I came in to tell you, to warn somebody. I mean, just last Wednesday my old gran got her handbag nicked." He blinked his eyes, took a deep breath to steady his nerves, and added, "Can't be too careful."

"Is that why you assaulted Michael?" Bad Cop cut in, glaring.

That was admittedly a weakness in his story. Michael had to be the boy he'd kneed in the nuts. He stared at her with wide-eyed innocence. "You know him, then? Thought he might be a burglar."

"He's an African prince, you young—" Bad Cop started to get out of her seat, and for just a second Danny thought there might be a bit of grievous bodily harm coming.

But then Good Cop waved her back with a quiet "It's okay, Fran, the boy's just a bit nervous." Then to Danny he said, "Actually, we do know him." He had an interesting accent, a bit upper crust for a copper, but country rather than city. Danny filed that away, along with the information that Bad Cop was called Fran, probably short for Frances.

"Yes, well, he was running straight for me," Danny said. "Seemed like he was up to no good."

"The door wasn't really open, was it?" said Good Cop suddenly. He smiled a little sadly to show there'd be no hard feelings if Danny decided to tell the truth. Danny opened his mouth to tell another pack of lies, but Good Cop hadn't finished. "Or, if it was, you thought it might be an opportunity to look around, see if there was anything worth . . . borrowing?" Fran glared, but Good Cop's smile never wavered. "I understand," he said. "I know what it's like to be short of money." Danny blinked. It looked like it had been a long time since Good Cop went short of cash. "It makes you do things—on impulse—that you mightn't otherwise do. Now, you look like a decent enough lad to me." Fran snorted, but GC went on without a pause: "There's nothing missing from the house, and I know our staff handled you a little roughly, so why don't you just tell us what you did and what you saw, and maybe *we* could see our way to forgetting the whole thing."

"George!" Fran exclaimed, like she was shocked by the suggestion.

So Good Cop's name was George, but the most important words in his speech were *what you saw*, Danny thought. They were up to no good, that much was obvious, and wanted to know how much of it he'd spied. Which meant there was a chance he might get out of this with a whole skin, but he had to be careful. The thing was, he *hadn't* seen much. There'd been the girl, and God alone knew what they'd been planning to do to her, but just at the precise minute he'd seen her, they hadn't actually been doing *anything*. She was the one who stopped him from punching what's-his-name-Michael in the mouth, so unless she was Houdini, she *couldn't* have been strapped into an electric chair.

Danny considered his options. In a situation like this you couldn't assume they were stupid, couldn't pretend you'd seen *nothing*. This was a critical moment and he had to play it right. "All right, it's a fair cop. I *did* come in thinking there might be something . . . you know, some cash, lying around. But the door really was open, I swear it, and that's a big temptation when your mother—" He was going to say *needs an operation* but decided that would be overdoing it. "—has all those bills to pay. But I didn't take anything, I swear to God I didn't."

They didn't look like they were buying it. Danny said hurriedly, "Anyway, when I came down here, there was a girl getting her hair done in a room with bats flying round her head, and next thing I knew this guy was running at me and I panicked, I admit it, and I hit him. But I didn't mean any harm and I didn't take anything, not a thing." He thought of making an impassioned plea for freedom, but decided to leave well enough alone and stopped, waiting for a reaction.

Good Cop George was frowning. "Did you say 'bats flying round her head'?"

Opal, Lusakistan

There were mountains, of course, but they looked completely different from the last time. Opal stared. This was her third trip to Lusakistan, to the same part of the Pakistan border, but—

She stopped. Mr. Carradine *hadn't* said the Pakistan border, now that she came to think of it. He'd said *border with China*. She didn't even know Lusakistan *had* a border with China. So this was a different part of Lusakistan altogether, but just as rocky, miserable, and depressing as the bits she'd already seen. The mountains were all around her, a barren wasteland.

There was no sign of a camp.

Which meant nothing, of course. On this sort of mission, the coordinates were always approximate and sometimes just plain wrong. You could travel for miles before you found the exact place you were looking for. But there was a standard procedure, drummed into her by her father and Mr. Carradine. You examined the area where you landed, moving in gradually widening circles. You took your time and were extremely thorough, because even though coordinates were always approximate and mistakes were often made, the area where you landed was still the most likely place to find your target. So you searched it thoroughly before you even *thought* of anything else.

Opal moved away carefully. She was looking, basically, for signs of life—any signs of life. Once she spotted something—anything—she could investigate further. She was excited, as she always was on a mission. After nearly a year as an operative—and eight months of preliminary training—that had never faded. It wasn't the thrill of danger. When she was tracking terrorists, she felt like she was doing something really important. And her work was respected in the Project. Her success rate was the highest of all the operatives', even though many of her missions drew a blank. She suspected this one would be among them.

Despite Mr. Carradine's remark about strong intelligence, she knew the chances of finding the Skull were slim; the agencies had been trying for years without result. But she might be able to confirm he'd been here, which would still be useful. Or she might stumble accidentally on some other terrorist, perhaps even a training camp. Anything like that would be a reasonable result.

After more than an hour of diligent searching, there was still no sign of life, current or recent. She was experienced enough to spot the signs now—the unnatural clearings in the prevailing wilderness, the remains of temporary fortifications, even carelessly strewn rubbish. Sword of Wrath groups kept on the move, so few of their encampments lasted long—except for training camps, which could sometimes stand for months. They often lived in tents, like desert nomads, staying in any one spot for a day or two at most before moving on. If they had reason to think they were being tracked, they worked hard to eliminate signs of their presence. But when they considered themselves safe, they got careless. If you looked closely, you might find a spent cartridge, sometimes signs of a fire, the occasional empty Coke can (Coke got *everywhere*). Once she'd even spotted a half-written letter ornamented with a doodled drawing of a dog.

Of course her previous experience had been with low-level Sword of Wrath cells. If the new intelligence was correct and the Skull really was somewhere in the area, nobody was going to get careless, whether they thought they were being tracked or not.

Whatever the reason, Opal could find nothing. She was on the point of beginning the wider search when a thought struck her. Everything she'd done so far had been based on the assumption that they'd camped out among the rocks. What if this assumption was wrong? She looked along the face of the mountain and saw the cave at once, high up in the escarpment. There could be a dozen men in there, their ArmaLites at the ready, looking down across the terrain below. Even a single sentry would stop their being taken by surprise. You could send an army after them, and they would have melted away before it moved higher than the foothills.

Opal began to climb.

As she'd been trained, she took her time, moving slowly, alert for any movement. The light was at an angle to the cave mouth, so it was impossible to see more than a foot or so inside. Anything could be in there: terrorists, wild animals, anything. So long as they stood back, no one could see them.

It was silly, but she found she was breathing heavily by the time she reached the level of the cave. Strange how old habits got you, even in situations like this. From her present vantage point she could see a great deal farther into the cavern, and there was still no sign of life. But when she entered it herself, it was clear that someone *had* been here. The signs were in plain sight—the dead ashes of a fire, a scrap of newspaper with Arabic printing, an abandoned plastic container. But all indications were this was the litter of a single man, two at most. The cave was too small to shelter more. So not the Skull. It was unthinkable that the Sword of Wrath leader would travel alone, or with just one other companion. His survival depended on protection. The last time he'd been positively sighted, he was accompanied by a small army equipped with heavy ordnance and armored cars. What she'd found here might be an overnight for a lesser terrorist, but it could just as easily have been shelter for a goatherd.

She took a last look around, then moved outside again. If the Skull really was somewhere in this vicinity, she needed a better vantage point to find him. She looked up at the sky. There was cloud cover, but it was high, so at five hundred feet she would have a clear view for miles.

Opal launched herself from the mouth of the cave and flew.

Opal's father was carrying a coffeemaker through the kitchen when his cell phone rang. He flicked it open and glanced at the caller name. Hector—inconvenient as always. He thumbed the green handset icon and said, "Roland."

"Priory meeting on the fifth," Hector said without preamble. "Can you make it?"

"Doubtful," Roland said. "I may be in Malta."

"Do your best," Hector said. "There are some peculiar undercurrents running at the moment. They've moved the spear."

"What? From the *Kunsthistorisches*?"

"No longer on display," Hector said almost cheerfully, one of his more annoying traits at times of crisis.

"Where's it gone?"

"Hoping you could find out for us," Hector said. "Since you have the might of MI6 behind you."

Roland frowned. "I'll do my best." If Hector was right, this was not good news. "You don't think it's been stolen, do you?"

"Doubt it—there'd have been something in the papers."

"Have you checked the Austrian papers?"

"Don't speak German," Hector said without apology.

"I'll have someone take a look," Roland said. "It might not make the British papers—not sensational enough, even with the Hitler connection." He sighed. "I'll also make contact with the museum—they may just have taken it off display for a while."

Hector snorted slightly, his usual prelude to ringing off, but instead he said, "How's the boy working out?"

"Don't know yet," Roland told him. "I'm not even sure when his first proper operation's scheduled."

Hector snorted again, a little more loudly, and rang off. Roland hung up, but the phone rang again at once.

This time it was the Project.

[7]

Sir Roland, the Shadow Project

Is it the Skull?" Sir Roland asked as George led him into his office and closed the door. He didn't add *this time,* but they both knew what he meant. The agency received perhaps four or five reports of Skull sightings on a daily basis. The CIA got even more. Most of them came from cranks. But George would not have called this one in if it was routine.

George Hanover shrugged. "Mossad seems to think so. We have Opal checking now."

Roland said, "I gather there was a delay?"

Hanover looked uncomfortable. "Yes. Yes, there was. Because of the intruder."

"I want the whole story on that," Roland said. "Was this an attack on the Project?"

"We don't think so. Actually, we're certain it wasn't. I've talked to the boy, and he seems to be just a petty thief. Carradine will investigate fully, of course."

"Hardly something to shout about, is it, George? A petty thief simply walks into what's supposed to be one of the most secure sites in Britain. A young boy at that."

Hanover made a helpless gesture with one hand. "There were circumstances."

"Specifically?"

"The boy broke into the mansion. Low security, as you know: it's designed to look like an ordinary country house. Anyone could walk in and stay for a month without realizing what was going on underneath."

"*He* worked it out," Roland said.

"There's an explanation, Roland," Hanover said. "We had a power failure, hardly long enough to notice, but enough for the backup generators to cut in. Then the mains came back on and the generators turned off again. It was all just a second or two, but the surge affected the computers that run the security system. The result was that one of the elevator doors opened. Just for a second or two, as I said, but as luck would have it, our boy was on the spot at the wrong moment. He got curious and entered the lift. Then the power came back on and it took him down. Million to one chance. Would never happen again, and we caught him within minutes, of course."

Bloody computers, Roland thought. Aloud he said,

"No evidence of sabotage?"

Hanover shook his head. "Just bad luck and bad timing."

What puzzled Roland was that George was acting a shade too relaxed about the whole thing. Roland had known him a long time. Something else had happened—he was sure of it. "So the boy wandered in on Opal's mission?"

Hanover's lazy eye drifted slightly. "He appeared in the doorway, gave her a bit of a surprise, but that's about it. The Michael business—he claims he thought Michael was attacking *him*. Which, of course, he was."

Roland said, "All right, George. About the boy. Do we have a name yet?"

"Lester Thomas."

The thing was, George still wasn't looking particularly contrite. Someone had penetrated a top-security project, and the operational head was clearly working hard not to look *pleased*. "How much did he see?"

"Nothing of real importance, Roland," Hanover said. Then added, "Although it could actually turn out to be *very* important." Roland waited. Hanover leaned forward in his chair. "I think our boy could be another operative."

Roland paused. "What are you talking about?"

Hanover was openly excited now. "Frankly, Roland, it's the real reason I called you. I mean, the Skull may be out there somewhere, but we've all been down this road before, and I'd never dream of dragging you away until we had some sort of confirmation." He tapped Roland lightly on the knee. "The kid told us he saw the bats."

Roland blinked. "The threshold guardians? Without a helmet?"

Hanover nodded. "Yes."

"How is that possible?"

"Roland, you're the expert," Hanover said, grinning. "That's why I called you in. I think you should take a look at this lad. If he can do it without a helmet . . ."

Roland stared at Hanover as he left the sentence trailing. If Lester Thomas could see the guardians without a helmet, that had to mean a natural talent. Even Opal couldn't do that. The psychology experts always claimed there must be a youngster like that out there, one who could project without the implants, maybe without any artificial help at all—but for all the money spent by the Project, all the covert visits to schools, all the disguised test papers filtered into the exams, none had ever turned up.

Until now, apparently.

"You're right, George," Roland said. "Perhaps I

should see young Lester right away." He stood up. "Cell block, I assume?"

"I'll take you personally," Hanover offered, grinning smugly.

But when they reached the cell block, Lester Thomas was no longer there.

[8]

Opal, Lusakistan

What the machine did was separate you from your physical body. One minute you were in there, working your arms and your legs. The next, you were floating above it . . . and you could go anywhere in the world in a blink. But the weird thing was, even though you came out of your body, you still had a second energy body, and you never quite got used to the fact that it felt so utterly, completely *normal*. You could see your hands. You still seemed to be wearing clothes—the same clothes you had on when you left. But more than that, you continued to react to your environment to some extent. So floating high about the mountain peaks, Opal felt cold.

Hot or cold, Lusakistan was the sewer pipe of the universe.

It was like looking at a satellite photograph: a few splashes of green, a rare glint of river water, but mostly gray-brown mountains, gray-brown valleys, rock fields, and narrow, winding trails. This was not a fertile land. There were no rolling grasslands, no fields of grain, just a wilderness of rock. Life here was brutal in the extreme. Small wonder the country bred such hardy people. The tragedy was that it still housed so many terrorists, despite the American invasion and the overthrow of the old government. That war was supposed to be over, but Opal knew it was still going on. Her father was scathing about the fact that Britain had become involved, even though his job meant he couldn't speak out publicly. All the same, most of the fighting was far to the south. Here she was overlooking what appeared to be a wholly peaceful region of empty, barren wilderness.

The Israelis were probably wrong about the Skull.

She caught a movement on the ground to her left, at the very edge of her field of vision, and swung her body around. For a moment there was nothing, then something moved again. It was so far away, it could have been anything: a sheep or a goat, but also possibly a man. Or actually, no, it couldn't have been any of those things: it was too far away for something so small to show up. The terrain she was staring at was rugged—*all* the terrain was rugged—a mix of foothills and the lower slopes of mountains. She seemed to be looking toward a ridge of some sort. The flicker of movement had appeared briefly above it, but she could see nothing at all beyond.

Anything could be hiding there.

Gross movement follows thought. To reach somewhere, you had to visualize the details of your target. Opal closed her eyes and soared from her high vantage point toward the distant ridge.

[9]

Danny, the Shadow Project

Piece of cake, Danny thought. But he resisted the urge to fling his cell door open and make a run for it. The people who nicked him hadn't impressed him very much, but it never did to underestimate anybody. Especially when you didn't know exactly who they were.

He pulled the door open a crack and peered through. The place they'd stashed him had *prison* written all over it, right down to the bunk bed and the standard lock on the door. Which made him grin because a standard lock didn't last more than five minutes when you had the tools.

Crap! Should have guessed it—there was a guard! He was sitting on a seat outside, one of the security goons who'd been stationed by the door when Danny was questioned. Danny could see his profile through the crack. Ugly, short haircut, thick neck, wouldn't want to meet him on a dark night. But was he built for speed?

Danny knew how to leg it when the occasion warranted, first thing you learned as a street kid. If you were big and tough, you fought. If you were a skinny little runt, the way Danny used to be, it was speed that got you away from the other gang. Danny was bigger now, and he'd left the street gangs behind, but he still had his turn of speed. And the element of surprise.

But the trouble with legging it was, he didn't know where to leg it *to*. And there might be a second guard, out of sight. There'd been two when they were questioning him.

The guard spotted him! Danny jerked his head back, waited for a moment, then put his eye to the crack again. No, he'd been wrong—not spotted. The guard was just closing his book and standing up. Standing up and plodding off. Call of nature, probably.

Danny held back until the footsteps faded and he heard the closing of a door. Then, all thoughts of a second guard forgotten, he opened his own door, looked around, slipped out, and took off.

He was on the bus home before he switched on his cell phone.

There was a message waiting for him, a woman's voice, familiar though he couldn't place it and she didn't leave a name. Sounded a bit anxious, like she wasn't used to voice mail. The woman said, "Danny? That you,

Danny? Hate these bleeding things. Danny, if you get this, come straight home. Your Nan's been taken bad."

And that was it. No details, nothing. Danny clicked the button and stared at his reflection in the window of the bus. He'd gone cold inside.

[10]

Opal, Lusakistan

Opal dropped lightly behind the ridge like an eagle landing on a crag. Everybody kept telling her there was no way she could be seen, but she simply couldn't shake the habit of caution. The problem was that she felt solid, as if she still had a physical body, and her head kept telling her it made no sense to take chances. In some ways it was like being in a dream. Nothing could really hurt you in a dream, but you still screamed and ran when the monster chased you.

She started to walk. Everywhere was rocky and steep. In normal circumstances she would have found the terrain difficult, stumbled, maybe even fallen. But in her second body she could move without problems. She could have walked right through those rocks, right through the ridge itself, if she put her mind to it, but she found walking through things creepy and avoided doing it where possible.

She reached the top of the ridge and peered over.

She knew at once she'd gotten lucky. Stretched out across the valley below was a massive military camp, so massive it was almost a town. Opal crouched, thunderstruck. Temporary structures and tents mixed with permanent brick buildings, while on the far side of the valley several tracks and two well-made roads wound their way up to what had to be a warren of caves pushed deep into the mountain. The whole place looked like a garrison, swarming with armed men. Even as she watched, a convoy of trucks, armored cars, and a scattering of light tanks meandered along the valley floor. At one end, behind a heavily guarded stockade, soldiers were loading a helicopter with crates from a low building with a camouflage roof.

She'd found the Skull!

The moment the thought occurred, she dismissed it. Until she investigated further, she couldn't even be sure this was a terrorist encampment. Lusakistan was still run by warlords. For all she knew, she could be looking at the headquarters of one of them. She needed to get closer.

Opal glanced at her watch and found herself staring at an empty wrist. It was so irritating. Nothing could be brought on a mission except the clothes on your back, but looking at your watch was like hiding behind rocks—a habit that died hard. She focused on the main road through the camp. There was just the briefest pause—and then, with no sensation of movement, she was standing in the middle of the road itself. New smells assailed her nostrils.

There was an armored car bearing down on her, but she ignored it. From a distance the roadway looked in better repair than it was close up. It was potholed and crumbling as if made in a hurry or subjected to a lot of wear and tear. Opal looked around. This *might* be a legitimate township despite the heavy military presence, but she doubted it. The whole location looked as if it had been chosen for secrecy. There was a single, narrow entrance to the valley. The place was invisible from the lowlands, invisible even immediately below until you stumbled onto it, and as Opal had discovered, it was almost impossible to see from the air until you were directly over it.

The armored car drove through her, creating a moment of darkness and confusion. For an instant she felt disoriented, queasy; then she was back in the daylight. She began to walk toward what might have been a market square.

The place had an unpleasant smell—the sweat of unwashed men, mixed with cordite and diesel fumes, with an occasional revolting burst of cheap cologne. Almost everyone was in some sort of military uniform, mostly dusty and tattered. Everyone was heavily armed.

She hated moving through crowds, hated the way people passed through her like the armored car. There was no sensation, of course, but she found herself tensing each time it happened. It was like one of those 3-D movies where you had to wear the special glasses. When they threw the bucket of water over you, you knew it wasn't real, but you ducked anyway.

Opal had two goals. The first, and by far the most important, was to try to identify this place as a terrorist camp. She couldn't afford to make a mistake. If she did, the Allies would bomb innocent civilians. It had happened before, more than once. But never, thank God, because of one of her reports. She didn't want this to be the first.

The second goal, far less easy, was to find out whether the Skull was here. Confirmation of that would make her a legend.

There was a standard procedure for a mission like this, but she wasn't keen to apply it. It involved crisscrossing the area under investigation in a tight grid pattern, moving fast without reference to structures, people or obstacles, and all the while observing, taking note of clues. All very logical, except that Opal loathed the bewildering experience of passing through walls almost as much as she loathed the experience of passing through people. Gridding meant passing through both. All the same, it looked as if she might—

Opal stopped dead. Someone had emerged from the heavily guarded compound where the helicopter was being loaded. For a moment she simply stared at him, openmouthed, not able to believe her eyes. But there was no doubt at all. She was standing less than a hundred yards away from the tall, hairless figure of the Skull.

Sir Roland, the Shadow Project

"You did *what*?" Sir Roland exploded.

Carradine gave one of his small, crooked smiles. "Take it easy, Roland—it was the best thing, in my judgment."

Roland. Not *sir,* or even *Sir Roland.* You could always tell Carradine served a different master. It wasn't that Roland really cared about titles. But, dammit, Carradine was younger than he was, so a little respect would not have gone amiss. "Your judgment was that *letting him escape* was the best thing to do?"

Carradine nodded. "That was my call."

"You didn't think to consult me?"

"Didn't want to trouble you."

"I'm head of the Project," Roland snapped.

"And I'm head of security," Carradine shot back, as if that clinched the argument.

Because he was still irritated (read *furious*), Roland

said, "In that case, Gary, I think you'd better explain, as *head of security*, how anyone could imagine that letting the boy go was the best thing to do."

They were in Carradine's office with its uncomfortable chairs and high-tech equipment. Carradine placed considerable reliance on computers and associated gadgets. Roland hated the bloody things.

Carradine, who had parked one buttock on the corner of his desk, glanced briefly at an open laptop before he said, "Well, for one thing, our questioning got nowhere." By which he meant George Hanover's questioning: there was a bit of an edge between Carradine and Hanover, although neither let it interfere with work.

"It got us his name and address," Roland said coldly. "Enough to run a check, I would have thought."

"Both phony, I'm afraid."

Roland stared. "What?"

"Lester Thomas isn't his name, and he doesn't live at Rigby Villas."

Roland drew up one of the hideous modern chairs and sat down. He looked at Carradine. "How do you know?"

"As you say, what he gave us was enough to run a check. So I had the Department send some men around."

Roland found himself feeling even more aggrieved.

"MI6? You ordered MI6 to send some men around?" Carradine was CIA. They thought they ruled the world.

"Requested," Carradine corrected him.

Roland made a conscious effort to reel in his temper. CIA or not, Carradine had considerable experience, so presumably he did know what he was doing. "What did you find out?"

"Rigby Villas exists, and Lester Thomas lives at number sixty-eight. But Lester isn't our boy. He's a Jamaican thug in his fifties, known to the police. I think our young burglar probably knows him too—he was awfully quick with the name, and it matches the address. My guess is he hoped we'd go calling and Lester would beat us up. But he's not Lester."

"Who is the boy, then?" Roland asked.

"We don't know."

Genuinely puzzled, Roland asked, "So you let him escape?"

"Seemed the easiest way," Carradine said. "The kid had a set of professional lockpicks—"

"Are you serious?" Roland interrupted. "Where would a teenager get hold of professional lockpicks?"

Carradine smiled slightly. "The Internet, I'd think. You can buy the basics for a few dollars."

"Can you really? Good God."

"Anyway," Carradine said, "I found them when I searched him, but pretended I hadn't—he'd sewn them into the lining of his jacket, so the only way you could get to them was through a hole in an inside pocket. When I felt the set, I had the idea that it might save some time and effort if I let him use them. I put Burke on duty outside the door with instructions to take a leak if the kid managed to get the door open. Sure enough, the kid did—amazingly quickly, as well. Burke heard the door click, took himself off and warned everybody else to keep clear. When he got back, the kid was gone." He grinned. "There was only one way he could go—we locked the other doors and left an elevator operational, so he had to end up in the parking lot."

"What about gate security?"

"Templeton had orders to look the other way."

Frowning, Roland said, "You've let him walk out, and now he could be anywhere?"

Carradine's smile broadened. "Not anywhere. I bugged his jacket when I searched him. If you come around the desk, I can show you on the laptop *exactly* where he is right now."

[12]

Danny, London

Danny ran the last few hundred yards. Old man Kozak—kids all called him Kojak—came out of his front door and waved, but Danny ignored him. By the time the bewildered look settled back on Kojak's face, Danny had his key in the lock, the door open, and was shouting, "Nan? You in there, Nan?"

Danny and his grandmother lived in a terrace house, two up, two down, that belonged to the local council and was set aside for pensioners. There were a few younger souls living there, family members like Danny, but there was always a wrinkly in the house somewhere.

"Nan? It's Danny." His panic grew. Nan wasn't answering, but she was a bit hard of hearing, specially with the TV on, and she might be in the kitchen, or even out the back. *And she might be lying dead,* his panic whispered, but he pushed the thought aside.

There was nobody in the kitchen, nobody in the

living room. He took the stairs two at a time and ran into his Nan's room, which was full of junk, mainly plastic flowerpots, but empty of his Nan. He looked into the bathroom, which needed a bit of cleaning, but no Nan lying on the floor.

Danny ran down the stairs, ran through the kitchen, ran out the back door. "Nan!" he called, just stopping short of screaming it. He looked around the little yard. His grandmother wasn't here, wasn't anywhere. Somebody on his voice mail said she'd been taken bad, and now she was gone. He thought of the hospital. (Which one?) For just a moment he thought of Fanning's Funeral Parlor and hated himself for it.

"Danny? That you, Danny?"

Aggie from next door was rattling the latch, shuffling into the yard in her slippers and cardigan. She looked pale and worried, but relieved to see him. "Oh, Danny, thank God you've come. Didn't know if you would get my message."

"What's happened, Aggie?"

"It's your Nan, Danny. She's had a stroke. Came in for a little chat and found her lying at the bottom of the stairs. Put the fear of God into me, I can tell you—I thought she was dead, see? I mean she looked dead, even though she had her eyes open, couldn't see her breathing. *Sweet Jesus,* I said when I saw her."

"Where is she now? At your place?"

"Saint Luke the Physician's, Danny. They took her away in an ambulance, put an oxygen mask on her and everything. I thought I should go with her, but I wasn't family and my Tommy's on the night shift and the buses don't run this route. 'Sides, nothing I could do, was there? Don't think she even knew me, Danny. But you should go. Need to be somebody there when she wakes up."

"I'm on my way," said Danny.

Saint Luke the Physician Hospital was a sprawl of grimy buildings at the far end of Victoria Street. There was a large woman on reception who gave him a tired fake smile and asked, "Can I help you?"

Danny discovered he was sick with fear. He licked his lips. "Come to see about Dorothy Bayley." He knew he was muttering, but he couldn't seem to get his voice any louder.

It made no difference to the receptionist, who was probably well used to nervous visitors. "Dorothy Bayley," she repeated clearly, and turned sideways to flick through card index drawers. After a bit she frowned. "I don't suppose you know what day she was admitted?"

"Last night, I think," Danny said. "They brought her in an ambulance."

"Ah," said the woman. "Excuse me a minute." She reached for a phone.

Danny waited. When he couldn't hear what she was saying, he looked around the reception area. There was a young woman with a small child sitting in an armchair near the second set of glass doors. A cheery-looking old guy in a porter's uniform nodded to her as he walked past.

The receptionist was saying something. Danny turned back. "Pardon?"

"Are you a relative?" the receptionist asked him again. Her voice had taken on a kindly, sympathetic tone, which was worrying.

"Grandson," Danny told her woodenly. "Come to visit."

"The doctor will be with you in a minute," said the receptionist. "You can take a seat over there."

Danny took a seat beside a little table that was littered with old *Hello!* magazines. He didn't like this at all, didn't want the doctor to be with him in a minute. When your Nan was fine, just had a bit of a turn, they said, "She's in ward eighty-eight—go on up." When there were problems—bad, serious problems—they said, "The doctor will be with you in a minute." Doctors were too busy otherwise. Only got to see them when the receptionist didn't want to give you the bad news.

He was leafing through *Hello!*, calculating how much he could get for the ornaments on the singer's mantelpiece in the main photo feature, when he noticed a man in a white coat talking to the receptionist. His stomach sank another notch as they looked in his direction. Then the doctor was walking toward him. "For Mrs. Bayley, is it? You're . . . ?"

"Lipman," Danny said. "Danny. She's my grandmother." There was bad news. He could tell from the man's face.

The doctor sat down beside him, which meant it was even worse news. "Is your mother here?" he asked. "Or your father?"

Danny's father wouldn't be here for another five years, given time off for good behavior. God alone knew where his mother was, still with the Romanian maybe. Danny shook his head. "No." Usually it was best not to explain, not to say anything more, but he could appreciate where the doc was heading, so he added, "I'm her only living." When the doc looked blank, he finished: "Relative. In the country, so to speak."

"Ah." A pause, a deep breath, then, "I'm Dr. Miller, Danny. Your grandmother's had a stroke. You know what a stroke is?"

"Yes," Danny said irritably.

"There was substantial bleeding into the cranial aper—inside her skull, and some swelling of the brain. We've operated to relieve the pressure and also to repair the blood vessel—"

"You've operated already?"

"Yes. We had no choice. Your grandmother was in a very bad way when she arrived here." He sounded a tad defensive. It occurred to Danny that nobody had been around to sign a consent form.

Danny said, "She's going to be all right, isn't she?"

That deep breath again. Dr. Miller said, "She's still in recovery, Danny, but I think she'll be okay. Her age is against her, of course, but she looks like a fighter. I think she'll pull through."

Which told Danny they hadn't expected Nan to survive the operation. But now she was lying in a recovery room, tubes stuck up her nose. Danny knew the doc wasn't telling him everything: he could smell it. As an encouragement he said, "You think she's going to live?"

"I think so. I hope so."

Danny looked him in the eye. "But . . . ?"

The doctor shifted uneasily, and Danny could read his mind. There was good news and bad news, and the operation hadn't been the bad news. The bad news was still to come. "Look, Danny," the doctor said, "it isn't just a question of whether she lives or dies. She's not quite out of danger, but her vital signs are good, and there were no problems during the operation, no technical problems. But it was some time before she got here, some time after the actual stroke. There was a lot of bleeding. Frankly, we're worried about the possibility of brain damage."

Danny stared at him. The words *brain damage* had turned him cold. After a long moment he asked, "How bad?"

"We don't know."

Brain damage could mean you lost a bit of feeling in your hands, or a small part of your face got frozen. But it could mean something else, something he didn't want to think about. He thought about it, swallowed, then asked hoarsely, "Could my Nan turn into a vegetable? Could it leave her so she can't speak, can't move at all?"

The doctor looked away. "We don't know."

"How was she before the operation?" Danny asked.

Dr. Miller looked at him. After a long moment he said, "She couldn't move and she couldn't speak. But that doesn't mean she will stay that way. Not necessarily. We've done everything we can to minimize the damage, and we'll continue to monitor her very carefully while she's here, but she's going to need constant nursing for a time after she's discharged. Quite how long that will be I can't tell you yet."

"Can I see her?" Danny said.

For a second it looked as if the doc was going to refuse, but then he said, "She'll be moved into ward seventeen when she comes out of recovery. That's on the second floor. Why don't you go up and wait by the nurses' station? I'll look in and see how she is, and if everything's okay, you can see her for a short time: it might do her good to have someone from her family around when she wakes up." He fixed Danny with a serious look. "But you mustn't expect too much at this stage, Danny. She'll be groggy from the anesthetic on top of all her other problems. So just a few minutes, eh?"

"Okay," Danny said.

The nurses on the second floor were nice. They told him his Nan was going to be all right, found him a quiet room to wait in—somebody's office, by the look of it—and offered him a nice cup of tea. He was drinking it when the door opened and a fresh-faced young doctor in a white coat stuck his head in. "You Danny Lipman?"

"That's me," Danny said. He set his cup down and started to stand up. "See my Nan now, can I? She all right?"

The young doctor came in and closed the door behind him. "Your Nan's fine," he said. He reached out and took hold of Danny's arm, and Danny noticed for the first time that he was carrying a hypodermic needle—but by then he felt the prick near his wrist, and his legs started to feel wobbly.

"Hey!" Danny started, "What the hell . . ." Then things began to slow down. And it was almost an effort to breathe. ". . . is happening?" *I want to see my Nan,* he thought as the lights went out.

The young doctor caught him as he slid toward the floor.

[13]

Opal, Lusakistan

He looked old. The cadaverous features were deeply lined. But it was the Skull, all right, all six feet four inches of him, flanked by two bodyguards carrying automatic rifles. Opal closed the distance between them so she could look into his face. To her surprise, he had kind eyes.

The Skull moved forward, deep in conversation with a man in battle fatigues. Opal stepped back hurriedly, and he passed her so closely that she could have reached out and touched him.

Opal fell into step beside them, so excited now, she could scarcely breathe. She could hear every word they were saying and kicked herself for the fact that she couldn't speak more than a word or two of Lusakistani. The truth was she was hardly a dedicated spy. If her father hadn't been with MI6, she doubted she'd have been a spy at all, despite her special talent. Actually, if it hadn't been for her father, she'd probably never have discovered her special talent in the first place.

Amazingly, it had all started with a game. While Opal was still a little girl, her father, who was old-fashioned, read her Rudyard Kipling's novel *Kim* chapter by chapter as a bedtime story. Opal loved it. She loved the exotic locations, loved the adventure, and above all loved Kim's Game. In the book, the game was used to train Kipling's young hero for clandestine operations, and Opal couldn't wait to play it. You collected a number of articles—knives, spoons, pencils, pens, stones, coins, and so on—and laid them out on a tray, which you then covered over with a cloth. To play the game, you uncovered the tray for exactly one minute. When it was covered up again, players had to list as many articles as they could, and the one who remembered most won the game. Opal nagged her mother until she laid out a tray, then nagged her father until he agreed to play the game. Opal didn't know yet that he was a spy, didn't know he'd been trained in a modern military equivalent of Kim's Game. She just knew she could never beat him. (And typically, her father never let her win, even when she got upset.)

One evening two years ago, when he was complaining that she watched so much television her brain was in danger of rotting, she challenged him to another round of Kim's Game, convinced she was old enough to beat him now. When she didn't, he finally taught her the trick of it. Instead of attempting to remember the items by rote, repeatedly listing them in your head, you had to relax and visualize each one, along with the position it occupied in the tray. Opal tried it and found she could remember every single item. The discovery excited her so much, she decided to try something more complicated and set out to remember every single item in their cluttered living room. While she was sitting with eyes closed, imagining she was walking around the room examining each piece, something clicked inside her head and she stepped out of her physical body.

It was the scariest experience of her whole life. When it happened she actually thought she'd died. But fortunately it didn't last long. Almost at once there was a metallic clang, and she was back where she belonged, panting with panic. Her father noticed her discomfort at once, and eventually, a little reluctantly, she told him what had happened. He thought about it long and hard, but a month later, he had her sign the Official Secrets Act and told her about the Shadow Project. A week after that, she was in the Project operating room, wide awake, but with a frozen scalp, getting the micro implants that would link her brain with the psychotronic projection stimulator and allow her to leave her body to order—the device that had sent her to Lusakistan today.

With Opal just feet behind him, the Skull and his companion left the roadway to walk down a narrow alley and across a busy square. They paid almost no attention to where they were going—people moved briskly aside to let them pass, and she noticed that the bodyguards were not averse to shouldering away anyone who was too slow. But the Skull himself moved slowly. He took tiny, mincing steps for such a tall man, and she half wondered if he might be ill.

The party entered a building, and the guards slammed the door behind them. Opal passed through it without a second's thought. She already had the intelligence coup of the century, but if the Skull really was ill, that was important information in itself. A lot of people were going to be very pleased with her when she got back.

She was in a gloomy hallway and experienced a moment's disorientation, unsure where the Skull had gone. Then she passed through a second door and saw him lowering himself carefully onto a large pile of cushions. His bodyguards were behind him now, beside a hanging curtain. The man in combat fatigues was no longer in sight, but there were three other men in the room. One was a small, wizened Lusakistani in traditional robes, squatting with his back against one wall, his eyes cast toward his feet so that he seemed almost asleep. To her surprise, the remaining two were wearing well-cut, Western-style business suits. One was in his late middle age with plump features, manicured fingernails, and distinguished gray wings to his hair. The other was younger and harder with the sort of wary air about him that made Opal think he might be a bodyguard as well, although he carried no visible firearm.

"It is satisfactory, gentlemen," the Skull said in French-accented English.

"Good," said the older man. "The question of payment . . . ?" His English was more heavily accented than the Skull's, but Opal could not decide on his country of origin.

"As we agreed," the Skull said.

"In bullion," the younger man put in.

The Skull eyed him coldly. "As we agreed," he repeated. "My men load it onto your helicopter as we speak." He looked back at the older man. "Will you take coffee while we wait?"

"No," said the younger man.

"Thank you," said the elder. He glanced at his companion, who looked away. To the Skull the elder man said, "We appreciate your hospitality. It has been a pleasure doing business."

The man in battle fatigues appeared, carrying a tray with three tiny steaming cups of Turkish coffee. He served the visitors first, then the Skull. The old man in robes looked up and seemed to stare straight at Opal for a moment before allowing his eyes to drift across the others in the room.

The elder of the two Westerners sipped his coffee and said, "May I inquire what you plan to do with . . . ?"

The Skull looked up at him from under hooded eyelids. "Does this information constitute any part of our agreement?"

The other looked momentarily flustered, then covered it with a smile. "No. No, of course not. I merely—"

The Skull smiled back, thinly. "In that case, I must insist that my plans remain my business." The man in battle fatigues bent down to whisper something in his ear. He nodded briefly, then began to push himself—rather painfully, Opal thought—to his feet. "I understand the loading of your helicopter is now complete. Doubtless you will want to inspect it."

"I doubt that will be—" the elder man began.

But his younger companion cut in firmly, "As a formality, yes."

The Skull shrugged and began to walk toward the door with his slow, small steps. His older companion rose to his feet and moved across the room. He stopped directly in front of Opal, and though she knew he could not see her, she was hard pressed to suppress a shiver: for an instant he seemed to be looking deeply into her eyes. Then he turned to say something quietly in Lusakistani to the Skull.

"Something wrong?" asked the younger of his visitors at once.

The Skull shrugged. "Nothing that need concern you," he said shortly, and pushed through the door, followed by the other men.

As the door closed, the old man turned back toward Opal and raised a closed hand. "American?" he asked in English.

It was exactly as if he'd spoken to her, and while that was impossible, she took an involuntary step backward. Then the man opened his hand to show an odd medallion nestling in the palm.

Suddenly Opal could no longer move.

Danny, outside London

Danny swam slowly into consciousness. For some reason he expected to be in a hospital bed, but he was actually slumped in a comfortable chair. His head felt as if somebody had just put it through a mincer. When he forced his eyes open and persuaded them to focus, there was a man standing over him.

The man smiled and said, "My name is Harrington."

That's the smile on the face of the tiger, Danny thought sluggishly. He pushed himself upright in the seat and tried to get his mind to function. The last thing he remembered was the hospital and the young doctor coming at him with the needle. Now he was somewhere else. To play for time he said, "Won't get much of a ransom, Mr. Harrington—most of my friends would pay you to *keep* me."

"It's Sir Roland, actually," Harrington said dismissively.

"And you've probably guessed this isn't about a ransom."

What Danny guessed was that he was back in the big country house, although the room they were in was unfamiliar. He hadn't seen Sir Roland Harrington before, either, but he had the feeling His Sirship might be the Mr. Big of whatever was going on down below. Danny shifted in the chair and massaged his arm where the needle had gone in. "What is it about, then? Only I've got a sick grannie I need to be getting back to." He glanced around the room. It was furnished with antiques. There was even a log fire.

"I heard about that, Danny," Sir Roland said. "And I'm sorry. But it may be one of the things we can help you with."

Danny! So they knew he wasn't Lester Thomas. That hadn't taken long. Hadn't taken them long to find him and bring him back, either. These boys had connections. And the fact that they'd gone to so much trouble meant he was in a bigger mess than he'd thought. They *really* didn't want him talking about what he'd seen, even though he hadn't seen much. He tilted his head to one side, stared Sir Roland in the eye, and asked, "Who are you people?" Like they were going to tell him, but he had to ask.

To his astonishment, Sir Roland said, "We're a special

department of MI6—Britain's counterintelligence service. We're code-named the Shadow Project, although round here you'll usually hear it simply referred to as the Project. We're working in cooperation with the American CIA, which established the Project in the first place. Do you know what I mean by remote viewing?"

Danny shook his head. "No."

"Do you know what I mean by the Cold War?"

"Of course I do—I'm not stupid."

"It never occurred to me that you were, Danny. But you're young, and the Cold War must have ended before you were born." Sir Roland was sitting in a wing chair on the other side of the lovely big fireplace. "During the Cold War," Sir Roland began, "the CIA—"

"I know what the CIA is," Danny said helpfully, but Sir Rollie ignored him.

"The CIA received information that the Soviets were recruiting psychics for espionage work. At—"

"Psychics?" Danny interrupted again, this time seriously. "Like Madame Sosostris with her wicked pack of cards?"

For some reason it stopped Sir Roland short. "That's from Eliot," he said, and couldn't quite keep the surprise out of his voice. Another one who'd marked Danny down as an uneducated prat because he had the wrong accent and lived in the wrong neighborhood. Danny'd had a lot of that, even after his Nan scraped together the money to send him to a private school. *Especially* after his Nan sent him to private school. Some of the other boys were all right, but most of them treated him like a freak, and the fact that he was bright made no difference at all. Which was the main reason he'd decided to pack the whole thing in. If private school was bad, Cambridge had to be ten times worse. So no university for him. He was quitting. After he'd paid back his Nan, of course, which was the reason he'd gone back to thieving.

He dragged his mind back to his present problems. "That's right," Danny said. "*The Waste Land*. But it's what you meant by psychics—right?"

"Well, without the fairground connotations," Roland said, "but essentially, yes. No one believed the reports at first. The Communists were militant materialists, so occult ideas seemed the last thing likely to interest them. But the reports persisted, and the Soviets scored some spectacular successes, and eventually we—the Western intelligence services—were forced to take them seriously. So the CIA set up its own program."

"With *psychics*?" Danny let his eyebrows rise.

Sir Roland sighed. "That was exactly our attitude. And we were wrong. In any case, the initial approach was investigative. All this was CIA, you appreciate—we declined to take any of it seriously over here. But their people looked into various forms of psychism and found more or less what you'd expect—a great deal of self-deception, fraud, and nonsense. But then they stumbled on remote viewing. Remote viewing is the ability to see distant places in your mind, places you've never actually visited or read about. There were people who claimed to be able to do this on demand. You can see the attraction to an intelligence service."

Danny nodded. "It's a no-brainer. A spy never needs to leave his office. Can't get caught, either." He hesitated, then added, "If it's true."

"That's exactly it; and as it turned out, it *was* true. There really *were* people who could gather information from distant locations without, as you say, ever leaving the office. They could do it under test conditions, and some of the data they brought back checked out. Not all of it, unfortunately, but some. All you had to do was give them map coordinates. But the interesting thing was that the real stars, the one or two with high accuracy ratings, all claimed they did not do remote viewing in their minds at all, but left their physical bodies and *traveled* to the target."

"How?" Danny asked. He caught Sir Roland's blank look and added, "What did they travel *in?* Mean to say, you leave your physical body, you leave everything behind, don't you—eyes, ears, everything. So how do you see where you're going?"

"You're very quick, aren't you?" Sir Roland said admiringly. "They told us they separated out a sort of second body, an energy body something like a ghost. They traveled in that." He may have thought Danny was about to interrupt again, for he pressed on hurriedly. "The thing is, they got results. So the CIA set up a special project to train others. That went well enough, but even the best of them was never one hundred percent accurate. In fact, very few of them came anywhere near. So after a while, the emphasis moved toward trying to *understand* the remote-viewing process. The theory was that if we knew how it worked, we might be able to get it to work better. The ultimate goal was to develop electronic equipment that could trigger the experience and make it more reliable. Which was where the trouble started." He stood up suddenly. "Come with me and I'll show you."

[15]

Dorothy, Saint Luke's Hospital

You could hear everything. Couldn't speak, couldn't move, hardly breathe sometimes, but those young doctors came through clear as a bell. Now there was one talking about her condition to somebody, a nurse probably, talking about her operation and her chances of recovery as if she wasn't lying there large as life in the bed in front of them. That was the trouble. You lay there and you couldn't move and couldn't speak, and half the time they forgot you were there.

Apparently her chances weren't all that good.

"Dr. Miller seems optimistic," the female voice said.

"Dr. Miller is always optimistic," said the male voice, "but I had a look when Benson opened her up." There was the sound of breath being drawn in through teeth.

"Bad?"

"The rupture wasn't too severe, but there'd been an awful lot of bleeding. My guess is she lay for a long time before the ambulance came—before anyone found her, I suppose. I'm not sure what quality of life she'll have even if she does recover."

Mind your own quality of life, you little brat, Dorothy thought. But she still couldn't say anything, and after a while she heard shuffling sounds and a door and then a deep silence.

She was going to die here if she wasn't careful. She could see it coming in the tea leaves.

Dorothy wasn't too fussed about dying, not on her own account. Just passing over, wasn't it? She'd had proof of that often enough. Anyway, life hadn't been up to much since Stanley went. Never seemed to be enough money, arthritis played up in wet weather. Your taste went too, as you got older. But all the same, if she popped her clogs now, who was going to look after Danny? Who was going to keep him out of trouble? And there were other people who needed her. Important work, that; and she was the only one who could do it.

It was funny: Dorothy's eyes were closed, but sometimes she thought she could see the hospital room, end of the bed, bedside table (nobody had brought her flowers), tubes going from her arm up to a transparent bag of something hanging from a stand. Sometimes she could see all that, sometimes she couldn't. Mostly she couldn't. Mostly it was dark, the way you'd expect lying in bed with your eyes shut. And then you were never sure if you were asleep or awake. It was very hard to judge the passing of the time, but at some point Dorothy must have slipped into a dream because she could see Stanley standing in front of her, plain as day.

"I think our boy Danny's getting into trouble," Stanley said.

[16]

Danny, the Shadow Project

"They're remarkable works," Sir Roland said as they entered the library. "We have volumes dating back to the fifteenth, sixteenth centuries, sometimes even earlier. There's a drawer over there that contains a Roman scroll from the time of the Emperor Claudius. And they all have one thing in common—"

"They give you the creeps?" Danny suggested. He loved books, but looking at some of the titles, they were seriously weird.

Sir Roland smiled. "Well, that, certainly, but I was actually thinking of the fact that they all deal one way or another with spirits or astral projection."

"Those ones over there deal with magic," Danny said.

"Ah yes, that's true—a great many of them do," Sir Roland agreed. "But where does the magic come from?"

Danny shrugged. "Sacrificing goats?" They'd done

it in a horror movie he once saw. Actually he was feeling uncomfortable with the way the conversation had turned. The books he mainly liked to read were scientific. The irrational—magic, spirits and the like—made him uneasy.

"Or should I say, who is the sacrifice made *to*? Spirits, or gods—disembodied intelligences. All the magic, or what passes for magic, arises out of communications with entities that have no physical bodies—exactly the way our best remote-viewing operatives claimed to function."

"Yes, but it's all superstition," Danny said.

Sir Roland ignored him. "Now over there"—he pointed—"is a section on . . ."

It was getting to be like a museum tour, but Danny dutifully looked over there, where most of the books seemed new, in contrast with all the magic stuff: *UFOs: Operation Trojan Horse*; *Above Top Secret*; *The Roswell Incident*; *Alien Dawn*; *Communion*; *Abduction*; *Open Skies, Closed Minds*; a video of *UFO: The Final Warning*. . . . "Flying saucers?" he asked skeptically. If there was one thing worse than the people who wrote about magic, it was the nutters who saw little green men.

"Can you see the connection?" Sir Roland asked. Danny couldn't, but Roland was in full flight now. "Read the flying-saucer literature," Sir Roland said, "and you'll find report after report of creatures who could pass through solid walls as if they weren't there. Our remote viewers, the ones who said they used a second body, also claimed to be able to pass through solid walls."

Danny was beginning to get it—he'd have to be pretty stupid not to, and he'd been offered a Cambridge scholarship, not that it would be doing him much good. But at the same time he had no idea where it was leading. "Flying saucers come from outer space," he said. Then added uncertainly, "Don't they?"

"I don't know where flying saucers come from," Sir Roland said. "Neither does anybody else. But the point is, here was another whole body of literature that seemed to have some bearing on what the CIA was studying." He wandered again. "Now, over here . . ."

This time the shelves had a mix of old and new books. Sir Roland pulled one down entitled *Astral Doorways*, flicked through it briefly, then pushed it back. "These are all books that deal with the experience of leaving your body—out-of-body experience, it's called: OOBE for short. Quite clearly what many of these writers experienced was similar, if not identical, to what happens to our remote viewers. So the CIA shifted the focus of their entire program to the investigation of magic, UFOs, and astral projection—and it worked. They extracted enough historical information to develop electronic aids.

In fact, they were beginning to develop a whole new remote-viewing technology when word leaked out about the historical research; and inevitably it was twisted. You can imagine how the press had a field day. 'CIA Uses Black Magic in Intelligence War' and that sort of thing. A group of senators and congressmen from the Bible Belt decided this would never do at all and made such a fuss that Mr. Tenet was forced to close the Project down."

"Who's Mr. Tenet?" Danny asked.

"Director of the CIA," Sir Roland said.

"He really closed it down?" *Not the end of the story,* Danny thought.

"Well, in a manner of speaking," Sir Roland told him. "What he actually did was move the operation over here. As I mentioned earlier, we had our own interest in remote viewing at MI6 by this time, so we were happy to cooperate. It gave us access to the very latest American technology, and we here were able to share one or two of our own discoveries in the field. All in all, a potentially fruitful partnership."

Danny grinned at him. "Now you've told me all this, won't you have to kill me?"

"Only if you don't agree to join us," said Sir Roland without cracking a smile.

Opal, Lusakistan

They kept her in a wicker cage that hung from a rope looped around a hook in the ceiling of one of their buildings. It was impossible that the thing could hold her—no Project operative had ever reported anything that could trap an energy body—yet it did. Opal crouched inside, unable to stand fully upright, unable to lie down, unable to sit except with her knees pressed up against her chin. Had she been in her physical body, the pain would have been excruciating. As it was, she experienced continuous discomfort, nausea, dizziness, as if she'd just stepped off a roller coaster and couldn't catch her balance. She'd never felt so helpless in her life.

They came back after a time. The Skull glanced up at the cage, then said something in Lusakistani to the old man in robes. The old man stared into Opal's eyes and smiled coldly. "He wishes to know if you are still in there," he said in English.

How had this happened? There was nothing, nothing in her entire experience, to suggest that she could be trapped while out of her body. Throughout her training and on missions, she had cheerfully walked through walls in her second body, pushed into solid rock, stayed for hours underwater. In her second body, she was like a ghost flitting through the solid world, but no longer a part of it. She was invisible and indestructible. She should have been able to pass through the wicker of her cage like mist.

"Can you hear me?" she asked softly. Nobody could hear her. They'd told her that on her very first briefing—"No one can hear you, no one can see you." She'd proven it herself during her very first RV projection, standing inches from a woman and shouting in her ear. Since then she had moved freely through city streets without anyone suspecting for a moment she was there. Of *course* he couldn't hear her!

"Yes, I can hear you," said the old man. "But my master cannot. Nor does he see you." He turned and murmured something briefly to the Skull, who bent his head to listen.

The Skull looked up again, staring into the cage, but his eyes fluttered as if he was searching for her; and when he spoke, he was not looking directly at her, but to one side and a little above her head. "Are you American?" the

Skull asked in English.

"My master wishes to know if you are an American," the old man repeated.

"I heard him," Opal said.

"I know you did," the old man said. "But he cannot hear you. You must answer to me and I will convey your words. Are you an American?" He stopped abruptly as a cleaning woman slid silently into the room, then froze when she realized it was occupied. The old man waved his arms and shouted something that sent her scuttling away.

"Who are you?" Opal asked.

"My name is Hazrat Farrakhan, adviser to my master, Venskab Faivre, whom you doubtless recognize. He wishes you to tell him if you are an American."

"How can you hold me here?" Opal demanded. "How is this possible?"

"I am a student of *ilmu al-hikmah*," said Farrakhan.

"Who is Ilmu Al—?" Opal began, but the old man held up a sudden hand for silence.

"No more questions, prisoner. You must now answer my master."

Prisoner? It struck her with the force of a thunderbolt that this was exactly what she was. She was trapped in a wicker cage and now, incredibly, *under interrogation.* And there was nothing in her training to help her. Why train operatives for something no one believed could happen?

Should she answer? What was it they said in war movies—name, rank, and serial number? Except she didn't have a rank or a serial number. She was a Project operative, not a soldier. So what was she supposed to tell the enemy? And what would happen if she refused to answer? If she was James Bond or Mata Hari, caught behind enemy lines, she might be beaten or tortured. But to torture somebody, you had to get your hands on their physical body, and her physical body was back at the Project, slumped in a chair with a helmet on its head. So no beatings, and torture was impossible.

Just as it's supposed to be impossible to hold me in a cage. The thought brought her up short. Opal felt a chill of fear.

Did it matter if she told them she was not an American? Her nationality was hardly important. What *was* important was that the Skull should not discover she was a spy. Half the effectiveness of the Shadow Project was that no one knew of its existence. The secrecy of the Project had to be protected at all costs. What she needed was a cover story, something to convince these men she was . . . a civilian. She almost laughed aloud. An innocent, invisible, ghost of a casual visitor.

"I'm not an American," she said.

"Ah good," murmured Farrakhan, as if she'd told him something of importance. "My master does not like Americans." He spoke a few words in Lusakistani to the Skull, then turned back to her. "Why are you here?"

"Why are you here?" the Skull echoed in English. His brown eyes were locked on the cage and this time he seemed to be looking directly at her.

There were scraps of cloth and paper woven into the wicker of her cage. It was the first time she'd really noticed them, but now she saw they were covered in curious, hand-drawn symbols. Cramped as she was, she reached out to uncover one of them, momentarily forgetting that she could not actually touch anything. The fabric of the cage *repelled* her hand.

"I don't know," Opal said. "I don't know how I got here."

"Elle ne sait pas," Farrakhan repeated to the Skull in French.

"What is your name?" the Skull asked.

Did it matter if he knew her name? Opal Harrington would mean nothing to him. Unless he knew of her father's position with MI6. Even then, he wouldn't know her father had a daughter. All the same, best not to let him know her last name. She took a chance that he simply wanted a name to call her by and said, "Opal."

"Opal," the adviser Farrakhan repeated.

To her surprise, the Skull smiled. "Like the jewel," he said. "Are you a jewel, my captive?" He snapped off several staccato phrases of Lusakistani to the old man.

"My master wishes to know how you got here," Farrakhan said. "He is a patient man, but now he grows *im*patient."

One of the books Opal had read during her basic training was entitled *The Projection of the Astral Body,* written by a psychical researcher called Hereward somebody. It told the story of an American named Sylvan Muldoon, who had spontaneous out-of-body experiences throughout most of his life. He attributed them to the fact that he was a chronic invalid. He believed illness loosened his second body. She'd also read various reports of people projecting while in the hospital and after accidents.

"I was ill," Opal said. "The doctor told me to stay in bed—I had fever. I think I must have fallen asleep because I dreamed I was here, in the mountains." The dreaming business was sheer inspiration. Dreaming made her sound confused and innocent. Dreaming made it sound as if it might be safe to let her go.

"Where do you live?" Farrakhan asked.

Her accent would give her away if nothing else, assuming he was familiar with accents. She decided it was probably safe to tell him, in any case. "Great Britain."

"*Great* Britain," Farrakhan repeated with emphasis. He smiled a little.

Opal hesitated, trying to stay in character as a school-girl dreamer, then said innocently, "Can you let me out of this cage? It's very uncomfortable." She half thought of adding that she wouldn't try to escape, but decided not to press her luck.

"In Great Britain where? Is it London?"

"Yes, London," Opal said. It didn't matter anyway. The Project was located outside London.

The adviser Farrakhan turned to the Skull. "British," he said in English. "A girl who is ill and dreams she is here visiting Venskab Faivre. A girl from London. *Ce qu'elle voudrait nous faire croire.* This she would have us believe." He turned back to Opal, and the smile had left his face. "We have no more patience with such lies," he said. He made a gesture with his left hand. "Now we must learn from you the truth!"

Opal's second body convulsed as it flooded with a tidal wave of agony.

[18]

Danny, the Shadow Project

Sir Roland was serious. They walked out of the library and took a hidden lift down to the underground complex. He went through the full security bit, thumbprint, eye pattern, key pattern, and—something Danny hadn't discovered earlier—voice analysis. Danny kept staring at Sir Roland, wondering what he'd gotten himself into.

"I want you to understand exactly what our work is here," Sir Roland said. "Would you like some tea?"

The guided tour had taken them to what looked like a little canteen, deserted at this hour, but Sir Roland got them tea from a machine and carried it to the table in plastic cups. The tea tasted awful, but Danny said nothing because his Nan had brought him up to be polite when somebody was nice enough to do something for you. Besides, it sounded like nice Sir Roland might be offering him a job.

Sir Roland sipped his own tea and made a brief face

as he sat down. "I suppose the best way to put it is this," he said. "The world we live in is a lot more dangerous than it used to be. Time was when you knew where to find your enemy—Napoleonic France, Nazi Germany, Communist Russia. If they decided to attack you, there was always a warning. Troop movements, missile alerts, what have you. Not anymore."

"You mean like the War on Terror?" Danny asked.

"That's *exactly* what I'm talking about," Sir Roland told him. "International terrorism. An enemy that could be anywhere and attacks without warning. There has never been a time when intelligence—espionage—spying, if you like—has been more important to the free world. But even spying doesn't work the way it used to." He glared at his plastic cup. "This is dreadful tea. Do you want me to see if the machine has some coffee?"

"No thanks," Danny said. He wanted the man to keep talking.

Sir Roland sighed. "It used to be you infiltrated men into East Berlin, or bugged the Russian Embassy in London. You knew where to plant your bugs, you knew where to send your spies. But how do you plant a bug in a terrorist camp halfway up some mountain in Lusakistan when the people you want to spy on keep moving about like a three-card trick? Oh, we still do it, of course, but it's particularly difficult for spies to maintain their cover when it sometimes involves killing innocent civilians. Frankly, we've lost many good people. Meanwhile, the quality of the intelligence coming back has been dropping steadily. Clearly we need a new approach. Which is where our Project comes in. Are you sure you don't want a coffee?"

"No thanks." Danny shook his head.

"Mind if I do?"

"Be my guest."

Sir Roland carried back another plastic cup. "Remote viewing is definitely part of the answer. You can send an operative out quite safely. You can send him at a moment's notice. You can dispatch him—instantly—anywhere in the world. There's very little cost involved, so you can afford to check out every lead or rumor. Your man can slip past every known security system. He'll never be captured or killed. The enemy doesn't even know he's being spied on—*can't* know: remote viewing is completely undetectable." He sipped from his cup. "This is just as bad as the tea."

"Thought it might be," Danny said.

Sir Roland set the cup down. "The point is that here at the Project we can now trigger a remote-viewing experience in which the operative can be sent to specific coordinates—anywhere, without fail—in his energy body, and once there——"

Danny said nothing. He was curious about "energy body" but didn't want to interrupt. Thing was, it sounded like the job might be spying, and if Roland wanted Danny as the next James Bond, there could be room for a nice little arrangement. Danny was thinking Porsche.

Sir Roland looked vaguely uncomfortable. "Unfortunately a full, reliable projection only works for certain individuals. Very few of them are adults."

Danny had the feeling something had just whizzed past his head. "Pardon?"

"It's a question of psychological interactions with the energy body. The research shows that general mind-set influences brain-wave patterns, as, of course, do endocrine levels. Some fluctuations are fine—indeed, necessary—but fixed patterns can become counterproductive."

"Pardon?" Danny said again.

Sir Roland smiled a little. "Most adults are too set in their ways. If you want to detach the energy body, you need a mind that's imaginative and genuinely flexible. Finding that in an adult is virtually impossible, so we had to turn elsewhere. Young children are viable in the technical sense, but obviously you can't use young children as spies. So we use teenagers."

It all came together. "You want me to be a remote-viewing spy?" Danny said. "Is that what this is all about?"

"I've reason to believe you have a talent for it. Not many do. In fact, at the moment, we only have a handful of active operatives."

"How do you know I have the talent?" Danny asked.

"Something you said."

Danny waited for him to explain, then, when he didn't, tried again. "What would I have to do?"

Sir Roland shrugged. "Take the basic training. We have ways to develop a natural talent, which we can then enhance electronically. Once you're trained, you would be expected to go on missions."

"Spy missions?"

"Essentially, yes."

"Like James Bond?"

"Not quite. There are very few pretty girls, I'm afraid. But to compensate, you will be in no physical danger."

Danny said, "What's in it for me?"

A small smile played across Sir Roland's lips. "I suppose I could say it would keep you out of jail. You did break in, remember—and we caught you red-handed."

"I'm too young to go to jail. But even if I wasn't—"

"I know," Roland cut in. "You wouldn't be much

use to anybody working under duress. So let me put the proposition to you. You've been offered a place at Cambridge, which you can't afford to take up—"

Danny gaped. "How did you know that?"

"We broke into your home," Roland said.

For a long moment Danny just stared at him.

"Come on, Danny," Roland said easily. "You burgled this house, gate-crashed a top secret operation, and told us a pack of lies. What did you expect—a medal? We had to find out who you were. Apart from all other consid- erations, you might have been an enemy agent—they're using youngsters your age now. Our security chief let you escape from—"

"*Let* me?"

"Yes, of course. You didn't imagine it was that easy to walk out of an MI6 secure operation?" Roland sniffed. "Well, obviously you did, but it wasn't and it isn't. When you left the building, there was an electronic tracer in your jacket. We simply followed you home, and when you left again for the hospital, two of our operatives kept an eye on you there while a team broke into your house—"

"My *Nan's* house!" Danny snapped, outraged.

"—and searched it for incriminating evidence. You came up clean, but one of my men found your letter of acceptance from Cambridge. Congratulations, by the way. I'm an Oxford man myself, but I know how difficult it is to get into any half-decent university these days. Now the thing is, Danny, we both know you can't afford to take up the offer—" He stopped suddenly. "You haven't declined it yet, have you?"

"No." Danny's gaze had turned into a glare.

"Oh, good. Because we can help you. How would it sound if I told you the Project will fund your education at Cambridge—fees, lodging, living expenses, *plus* some decent money in your pocket—in return for a simple commitment to give the Project the benefit of your talents a few days every month? Once you graduate, there will be an offer of a full-time, permanent position with MI6 in London, with good benefits and all. What do you say?"

"No."

"No?" Roland looked taken aback. "Don't you want to go to Cambridge?"

"Of course I want to go to Cambridge," Danny said. "Honest answer—I'd *kill* to go to Cambridge. My ticket out, isn't it? You wouldn't know about it, but it's no fun growing up where I live—hard men, drug dealers, street gangs, and never enough cash. Can't go out late at night—I've been beaten up more times than I can count. But I'm not going to Cambridge and it's not the money. Well, it *is* the money, but that's not the only reason. It's not even the main reason."

"What *is* the main reason?"

Danny looked at him long and hard. He never liked opening up to people, or talking about the things that were really important to him—too much chance they'd use it all against you. But there was something different about Sir Roland, something that made you feel he could be trusted. And besides, what did it matter if Danny told the truth for once? He took a deep breath. "Know what, Sir Roland? I've been telling myself I'm fed up with school, fed up with the snobby treatment. But it's not really that—after what I've gone through at home, I can handle the toffee-noses. What it really is, is my Nan. Bad enough when I went to private school—least I could get home in the evenings—but if I swan off all the way to Cambridge, there's nobody to look after her."

"I gather your grandmother has had some sort of stroke?"

"Yes, she has. But even before the stroke I couldn't have left her. She's getting on now, must be over eighty—won't tell me—my grandfather's dead, my mum's gone off somewhere, so she has no other relatives, no money except her pension. She thinks she can take care of herself, but she can't, besides which she gets lonely on her own. Stroke's made things worse, but I'd already decided I wasn't going to Cambridge—just hadn't gotten around to telling them yet."

Roland stared at him thoughtfully for a moment. "All right," he said at last. "Supposing we agreed to look after your grandmother as well?"

Danny blinked. He hadn't seen that one coming. "I don't want her in a home," he said quickly.

"I wasn't thinking of a home," Roland said. "I was thinking of a live-in nurse, something of that sort. To keep an eye on her and keep her company. You could send her extra money from your earnings, make her a little more comfortable. And you could be with her outside term time or on the weekends you're not working for us. It's not *that* far from London to Cambridge."

"But—" Danny said, then shut up and looked at Roland. Eventually he said, "I don't think I can do this. She mightn't even survive the stroke. I can't start making decisions about the rest of my life until I know for sure what's happening."

Sir Roland said soberly, "Why not compromise— make this a two-stage affair? We could start with an interim arrangement. Your grandmother's in the hospital now and may be for some time, so you can't look after her at the moment anyway. You have a couple of months before you have to respond to Cambridge. Join us temporarily, take some of the basic training, get the feel of things, and we can work out something more permanent when your situation clarifies. Meanwhile, we can be a lot of help to your grandmother."

Sir Roland was smooth, Danny had to give him that. But was he slippery? This was the Secret Service. Once you were in, you were in. All the same . . .

"Okay, what's the deal with my Nan? The *exact* deal?"

Roland hardly hesitated. "At the moment your grandmother is in a public ward of a second-rate National Health Service hospital. If you're prepared to join us, she will be moved at once to a private clinic—one of our own, in fact—where she will receive round-the-clock nursing and the most up-to-date medical treatment. She's had a serious stroke, so there can be no guarantees, I'm afraid, but she will have a much better chance of recovery, and she will be infinitely more comfortable." He looked at Danny soberly. "I've spent far too long here—I'm supposed to see the prime minister this afternoon. Do you want to sleep on my question, or can you give me an answer now? If you do, I'll make a phone call and have your grandmother transferred right away."

"I can give you an answer now," Danny said. "I'll do it."

Sir Roland smiled and flicked open a mobile phone. He dialed, spoke softly for a moment, then flicked it shut again. "Done!" he said to Danny, and stood up.

As he did so, an alarm began to sound.

[19]

Dorothy, Saint Luke's Hospital

The Lord giveth and the Lord taketh away, Dorothy thought. *Well, we all know what the Lord took away, don't we?* And now he'd given her a headache. Funny how much you took for granted. You got a headache, you swallowed an aspirin. If you couldn't get it for yourself, you asked somebody. Only now you couldn't. So when the Lord gave you a headache, you kept it.

Look on the bright side, Dorothy thought. Apart from the headache, she was getting a bit better. Could open her eyes now. Just a slit, but couldn't do that before. Not that she could see a lot because she couldn't move her head yet, but it was still an improvement. So she lay there with her headache, looking at the brown stain on the ceiling.

There were voices in the corridor. Men's voices and another voice she recognized as the ward sister—right old battle-ax she was too. Sounded as if they were having a bit of an argument. Men must be doctors, because they weren't taking any nonsense from Sister: you could hear from the tone.

They were coming into the ward. "Well, it's most irregular," said Sister's voice severely. And a man's voice said, "If you have any further concerns, you can take them up with the ministry." Which put manners on her because she said, "No, of course not, sir." That *sir* meant she'd given in. Sister called nobody *sir* unless they were a consultant or some other big cheese. Dorothy wondered gleefully what was going on.

They were moving her out of bed! The fuss had been about her all along! She caught glimpses of white coats and uniforms as they lifted her onto a gurney. Next thing she was being wheeled along the corridor. Change of ward, obviously. At least she'd get away from that stain on the ceiling. And the smell of wee.

Except it wasn't a change of ward. They were all in a lift, going down, and now they were in the lobby going out and there was an ambulance waiting: Danny called them "white sick cars" when he was little. They loaded her into the white sick car, gurney and all, like somebody being driven away in a disaster movie. Except in the movies they drove you *to* the hospital, and she was being driven *from*. There was a young doctor sitting beside her, face blank. She wished she could ask him where they were going. Another hospital, she supposed. Probably needed her bed.

All the excitement made her tired, so she closed her eyes and dozed a little. The noise of the ambulance doors opening woke her up. The new hospital was smaller than the old one and a lot better looking. Seemed to be in the country, for one thing. Nice grounds, like a convalescent home. You could see trees and flowers and grass. And when they wheeled her through the doors, the smell was different: less antiseptic scrub and more furniture polish. And the gurney wheels didn't rattle the way they did in the last place, as if she was being wheeled over carpet, not linoleum. Maybe things were looking up.

Somebody adjusted the head of the gurney so she was propped up a bit, which was a real improvement because she could see where she was going. Which was a ward all to herself, could you believe it? Just one bed and a big color TV and a nice view of the gardens through the window.

There was a bouquet of flowers beside the bed.

There was a plump nurse with a nice smile who said, "Hello, Mrs. Bayley. I'm Cathleen and I'll be looking after you most mornings and afternoons."

There was . . . she hadn't noticed it before. There was posh music playing gently in the background.

They lifted her—*one, two, three!*—off the gurney

and into the bed, and it must have been an orthopedic mattress because the comfort was amazing, and the sheets were just washed and starched and smelled fresh, so she took in a deep breath through her nose; and as she settled into this heavenly bed, for some reason she found herself thinking of that peculiar dream she'd had where Stanley said to her, "I think our boy Danny's getting into trouble."

She hoped this wasn't another of her premonitions.

Michael, the Shadow Project

From somewhere far away, Michael Potolo could hear the singing. He stirred uneasily in his chair—

A ton appel Mali

—but the microchips in his scalp were already beginning to tingle so that he was sliding steadily away from the reality of the Project's operations room. He tried to focus. This shouldn't be happening. Today he was not projecting. Today he was acting as anchor for Opal, his mind providing the link that ensured she was locked on her target, and more importantly, that she could be called quickly back. But even without leaving his body, the anchor experience could be very peculiar.

A ton appel Mali

Pour ta prospérité

Michael knew the reason from his basic training. Years ago, a surgeon named Wilder Penfield found that if you stimulated certain areas of the brain, it caused his patients to experience past events of their lives. Not just remember them, but actually *relive* them in vivid detail, as if they were happening all over again. Dr. Penfield made the discovery when he probed a patient's brain with his scalpel, but the electrodes in a projection helmet sometimes had the same effect when set in anchor mode. The result was not always pleasant.

It was still black behind Michael's eyelids, but he was beginning to feel the backlash. Something that was affecting Opal was affecting him as well. The main characteristic was helplessness. He could no longer move and seemed to have lost all sensation. His surroundings were fading. In moments he was floating in a sort of limbo—a lonely, disembodied mind—locked in a dark universe. Dark, that was, until the memories started.

A ton appel Mali
Pour ta prospérité
Fidèle à ton destin

It was growing light and the singing was becoming louder. But now it had taken on a tinny sound as if somebody was playing a transistor radio. What was happening to Opal? Michael fought the effects and tried to force himself back to normal consciousness. Then the memories swallowed him and there was a blaze of sunshine.

A ton appel Mali
Pour ta prospérité
Fidèle à ton destin
Nous serons tous unis
Un peuple, un but, une foi
Pour une Afrique unie

Alpha Konaré was president of Mali. His distinctive voice followed the national anthem as surely as day followed night, promising better times to the people and trying to explain why the water was cut off again in Bamako. Not that Michael's father gave a damn about Bamako. His practice was in the north, about as far from the capital as you could get, in a settlement on the caravan route to Timbuktu. There was never any running water here and never had been. In most families, the women visited the water hole early in the morning to carry back pots on their heads. The water was muddy, bitter from the iron, and full of parasites. Michael's family was lucky—their supplies were brought in bulk by truck.

Abégé Potolo was a doctor. Not because he had to be, but because he wanted to be. He was, by Mali standards, a wealthy man. Michael's earliest memories were of lines of the sick at their door. Those able to pay—mostly supervisors in the salt mines at Taoudenni—handed over a few francs for an antibiotic against bacterial diarrhea or a vermifuge or whatever it was they needed. The rest Abégé mostly treated for free, although a handful sometimes traded chickens or performed some service in return.

It was one of these, a Tuareg named Suleiman, who first used the word *sohanti* in Michael's presence. Michael was only seven at the time, in the middle of his lazy stage, and spent most days keeping out of the sun while doing as little as possible. Suleiman was supposed to help out around the clinic in payment for the medical treatment that had saved him his foot, but his temperament was broadly similar to Michael's, so he was usually to be found dozing in the shade—an occupation he liked to describe as "communing with Allah." Since the amount of shade was limited, they often found themselves together.

On the day Michael remembered, they were sprawled side by side beneath the only tree in the courtyard, listening to Papa Konaré on the radio and idly watching the patients beginning to crowd in. They were mainly women, as on most days, many with babies who did not cry, or trailing large-eyed children. Because of the numbers, it would be a long wait for some, so they found their own spaces in the courtyard and squatted, patiently enduring the heat and the dust until somebody called them. The mothers shaded the babies with their bodies.

The president finished speaking, the national anthem played again, and Mansa Konkon walked into the yard. He was a small man, painfully thin and apparently of little consequence, but there was an immediate hush when he appeared. He was known in the district as a sorcerer. He walked directly to a young woman sitting with a boy about Michael's age. One of the boy's eyes was a milky gray, and there was some sort of growth on the side of his neck. Mansa Konkon grabbed his hand and tried to pull him away from the woman.

The woman screamed.

A furious dispute began between Mansa Konkon and the woman. It was too far for Michael to hear the words, but the argument seemed to be centered on the boy. Both woman and boy looked terrified, but the woman looked angry too. For a few moments it was just words, then Mansa Konkon hit her. The woman fell back in shock. Those close by began to move away, their eyes fearful. Then the woman flung herself forward and struck a flurry of blows to his scrawny chest.

Although the woman was young, scarcely more than a girl, she was as emaciated as Konkon himself. Her eyes had the feverish look of malnutrition, and she was clearly weak. Konkon, though thin, was wiry, and the blows had little effect. He simply stood there, waiting for the storm to abate. When the woman stopped, he began to chant.

The effect was electric. The boy began to struggle in Konkon's grasp like a rabid animal. The woman flung herself on her knees and caught hold of Konkon's tattered trousers in a gesture of supplication. If she'd looked frightened before, she looked terrified now.

At this point Abégé Potolo, Michael's father, emerged from the house. He was probably reacting to the scream.

Suleiman jumped to his feet at once, not wanting the boss man to see him lazing, and began to walk purposefully across the yard. Michael jumped up too, and for want of anything better to do, went with him. Michael's father walked directly to Konkon, the boy, and the woman, all of whom were closer to the house.

"Stop that!" Abégé snapped, his eyes fiercer than Michael had ever seen before. "Stop that at once!"

Konkon stopped chanting but kept hold of the boy. Abégé reached down, gripped the child, and jerked him free. *"Ce garçon est mon patient!"* he hissed, using French. "This boy is my patient!"

"My son!" Konkon screamed back in Bambara.

Abégé half turned as if to lead the boy away, and Konkon pulled something out of his pocket. For just the barest second, little Michael thought it was a weapon—lots of men carried knives in Africa, and those who could afford it carried machetes—but then he saw that it was some sort of bone or root, roughly carved into the shape of a twisted man and tied with what looked like human hair. Michael, at age seven, had not the slightest idea what it might be, but he thought it was the ugliest thing he had ever seen.

There was panic among the patients in the yard. Weak though they were, many of them began to run, dragging their children with them. Several of the women screamed. Men shouted. Even the sick, silent babies began to wail thinly.

Abégé Potolo turned again to see what the commotion was about and at once released the boy's hand. Konkon's son ran too, but not to his father. Konkon lifted the thing in his hand and pointed it directly at Abégé. The woman on her knees near Konkon's feet shouted a long drawn-out *"Noooonnn!"* Michael felt a wordless, shapeless fear.

Michael's father raised his right hand as if warding off a blow. Konkon shrieked once, dropped the carved bone, and slapped his hand to the side of his neck like someone swatting an insect. And truthfully, young Michael could have sworn he saw an insect there, some sort of locust, big and black; then it was gone and he wasn't sure he'd really seen it at all. But Konkon's knees were failing and he was sliding to the ground, while the woman at his feet scrambled away on all fours with a look of horror on her face.

Konkon hit the ground and convulsed, like a man in the grip of some fearsome epileptic fit. He drummed his head against the baked earth of the yard. Arms and legs spasmed briefly. Then he lay still.

"*Sohanti!*" exclaimed Suleiman in a voice close to awe.

It was then that Michael felt the first wave of pain.

[21]

Sir Roland, the Shadow Project

Carradine entered the operations room at a run, but all the same, Sir Roland beat him to it. He was kneeling beside the slumped body of his daughter, still held by her restraints. Beside her, Michael had his eyes open but seemed out of it. Behind her, the control panel was lit up like a Christmas tree. The chamber was filled by the wailing sound of the alarm, which sent Roland's panic soaring. He fought hard to bring it under control. It would not help Opal if her father panicked now.

"Mute that damn thing!" Carradine called, and a harassed Fran Hitchin threw a switch. The sudden silence was almost as frightening as the alarm.

"What the hell happened?" Sir Roland demanded. He was looking at Carradine, who hadn't been there, too angry to be reasonable.

"I don't know," Carradine said. He looked across. "What happened, Fran?"

Fran shook her head. "I don't know either. It was absolutely routine—all the parameters were normal."

Sir Roland had his fingers on Opal's wrist, searching for a pulse. After a moment he found one, but it was faint and erratic. "I want a medical team in here *now*."

"I'll organize that," Fran said. Anybody else would have used it as an excuse to get the hell out, but she used the intercom. Even in his extremity, Roland appreciated that.

Carradine walked across. "Excuse me, Sir Roland," he said firmly. "I need to take a closer look."

Opal convulsed. Michael groaned. Roland's whole instinct was to rip his daughter free from her restraints and hold her, but he forced himself to step back. He had to let the experts do their jobs. Carradine placed two fingers on her neck. Over his shoulder, he said, "Fill us in, Fran."

She cut the connection on the intercom. "Medics on the way," she murmured, half to herself. Then to Carradine: "Nothing to tell you, Gary. It was a routine operation until the alarm went off."

"You've sent a recall sequence?" asked Sir Roland. Of course they'd sent a recall sequence—the electronic code that should have pulled Opal directly back into her body—but he had to be sure. He looked at Opal again. Her breathing was shallow, and she was as pale as a corpse. He'd never seen anything like this happen to any of the operatives. Why now, with his daughter?

"Twice," Fran said. "Nothing happens."

"Have you run a diagnostic?"

"Running now," Fran said. "So far it's negative. I don't think this is equipment failure."

"What *do* you think it is?"

"I don't know."

As Carradine stepped away, Roland moved forward to feel for the wrist pulse again. He frowned. "Her heart rate keeps settling, then shooting up."

"I know," Carradine said quietly.

Michael groaned, even louder this time. He seemed to be in pain.

"Is he awake?" Carradine asked Fran.

"I doubt it," she said. She left the control console and moved across. "Michael?" she said. "Can you hear me, Michael?"

"What's on his EEG?"

"The alpha readings are off scale. For both of them. I'm not sure it's even meaningful anymore. Everything's runaway." She bent forward again. "Michael . . . ?"

Carradine slapped him.

"Jesus, Gary!" Fran took a step backward.

But some of the dazed look left Michael's eyes, and he turned his head as if trying to focus on Carradine.

"What's happening, Michael?" Carradine demanded.

Michael murmured something that sounded like *"Sohanti."*

The medical team arrived, headed by Dr. Hornfield. They ran directly to Opal.

"Don't unhook her!" Carradine called urgently.

Sir Roland was stepping aside for the doctors. "Why not?"

Carradine took a deep breath. "If we break the contact now, we may never get her back."

Roland said, "Has this ever happened before?"

"You know it hasn't," Carradine told him.

"I don't mean here," Sir Roland snapped. "I mean anywhere, any time. You're with the bloody CIA—have they run into this before?"

Carradine hesitated. "Not so far as I'm aware."

Roland glared at him. He smelled a diplomatic answer. Carradine was hiding something. Maybe the CIA had run into more trouble in their early experiments than they admitted. They'd sworn to Roland that the electronic process was safe, otherwise he would never have recruited Opal for the Project. Now Opal was a mindless heap slumped in the chair. He opened his mouth to push the issue when Hornfield distracted him.

"Tachycardia," Hornfield said. He had a stethoscope

poked through the top of Opal's coveralls. "Some fibrillation."

"What's that in plain English?" Sir Roland asked sharply.

Frowning, Hornfield said, "It's almost as if she's being shocked." He glanced across at Roland. "Elevated heartbeat," he explained. "Intermittent loss of rhythm—fibrillation. That's the part that worries me."

"Can you do anything?"

"I'm tempted to give her a sedative." Hornfield opened his case and began to assemble a hypodermic.

"Is that safe?" Fran asked. "She's still projected."

Hornfield shrugged. "I've never sedated a projected operative before. But I'll tell you this: we need to get that heart rate under control. She's young and she's fit, but we can't just let it run indefinitely, otherwise there's a risk of permanent damage." He looked expectantly at Sir Roland.

Sedatives acted on the brain, dampening the activity of the cerebral cortex, and as a side effect changing brain-wave patterns, the same brain-wave patterns that interacted with the electronics to make the machinery work. God alone knew what a sedative might do to someone in the projected state. It might leave her in a vegetative state or even kill her. But then so could tachycardia. Roland hesitated, but only for a moment. "Go ahead," he said.

"Michael," Carradine whispered sharply, and was rewarded by Michael's turning his eyes toward him. "Michael, get your ass in gear and tell me what is happening!"

Michael's body jerked slightly and he moaned again. But then he said quite clearly, "She's in pain."

Fran said, "She can't be in pain—she's projected."

Carradine said, "How do you know? How do you know this, Michael?"

"I can feel it. It's affecting me. It must be affecting her much worse."

Hornfield took Opal's limp left arm and slid the needle into a vein. Roland found himself holding his breath.

"Can you bear to hang in there, Michael?" Carradine asked. "I don't want to unhook you yet."

Michael gritted his teeth. "I can manage, Mr. Carradine."

"Do you know what's happening to her, Michael?" Roland asked across Carradine.

Michael shook his head. "No, Sir Roland. I have no idea what's causing it."

Hornfield said, "Her heart's stabilizing." Roland felt a wave of relief sweep over him so strongly that his knees buckled. He gripped the nearest chair for support.

"Thank God," Fran said.

Opal's breathing deepened, and while Roland couldn't be sure, he thought her color was improving a little. "Is she asleep now?"

"Yes." Hornfield poked his stethoscope again, listened for a moment, then added, "Her heart rate's back to normal."

"But we still don't know what's happened to her?"

Hornfield stood up. "Not a clue. But at least I've given us time to find out."

"How long will your sedation hold?" Roland asked.

"Several hours—probably about eight. After that I can always sedate her again, but obviously we can't keep her unconscious indefinitely."

"Diagnostic complete," Fran said. "Nothing wrong with the equipment."

"We need to find out what has happened to her," Sir Roland said.

"How?" Fran asked. "There's nothing wrong with the equipment. She hasn't reacted to the recall. There's no means of contact."

"We can send somebody out after her," Carradine said.

Sir Roland, the Shadow Project

There was silence in the chamber as they turned to look at Carradine. After a moment, Fran said, "Shall I unhook Michael?"

Carradine nodded tiredly. "Yes. He can't be any more help to her now that she's sedated."

Sir Roland said, "What did you mean, Gary? Send someone out after her?"

"Exactly what I said," Carradine told him. "Opal is out there somewhere in her second body, and clearly she's in danger. I'm suggesting that we send another operative to find out what's happened, maybe even stage a rescue."

"Second body?" Hornfield echoed. "It's a long time since I heard that term." He gave Carradine a supercilious look. "I'm not sure old superstitions will be helpful in our present situation."

"And I'm not sure a squabble will be helpful at this

stage," Sir Roland said icily. He turned to Carradine. "Send out another agent. We've wasted enough time talking. Do it *now*."

"I'll go," Michael spoke up promptly. His voice was weak and hoarse. He coughed to clear it. "I'll go," he said again.

"Ah . . . ," said Carradine.

"Oh, for Christ's sake, Gary!" Roland snapped. "What? What's the problem?"

"We don't have another agent on the premises."

"What about Michael—he's just volunteered?" Sir Roland looked across at Michael, who was out of his chair now, detached from his cap, clearly dazed but determined.

Fran said, "It's too soon, Sir Roland. Just look at him. You know how exhausting it is to work as anchor: it affects the second body far more strongly than a straightforward projection. Michael won't be ready before tomorrow evening at the earliest—better the day after. If we try to use him sooner, he could be ill for weeks."

"I'll be fine," Michael murmured. He gripped the arm of the chair to steady himself.

"We can't wait until tomorrow evening," Sir Roland said. "Is Lonny Jarrett on standby?"

"On leave," Carradine said. "In Calcutta."

"What about the other two—the girls?"

"Lynne's got flu. Christine's up north somewhere."

"Get her back."

"Yes, of course," Carradine said. "But it will take time."

"Gary, you're the one who suggested this! Are you telling me we don't have an agent to send out?"

"Not right away," Carradine said. Then he added, "Unless—"

"Unless—?"

Carradine said, "I was wondering about young Lipman. Have you recruited him?"

"He's agreed to work for us, yes," Sir Roland said, frowning.

"Is he still in the building?"

Fran said, "Our young burglar? You can't use him. He hasn't had the implants. Or the basic training."

"We think he may have natural talent," Carradine said. "We've managed without implants before."

"What about the anchor? We can't use Michael again. Not in the state he's in."

"Fine," Michael said again, swaying a little.

Surprisingly, it was Hornfield who said, "An anchor's not strictly necessary, Fran."

Fran glanced across at him. "No, but the risk factor increases. Quite considerably, I'd imagine, if we're using an untrained operative."

Carradine opened his mouth, but before he could speak, Sir Roland said, "We'll discuss the finer points later, Fran. Meanwhile, get young Lipman down here and hook him up."

"We're sending him out?" Carradine asked tentatively. "Now?"

"Of course now. Just as soon as we can brief him on what to do. Don't you imagine this is urgent?"

"What happens if . . . ?" Fran let it trail. Everybody knew what she was asking.

"He's dispensable," Sir Roland said. "My daughter isn't."

[23]

Danny, the Shadow Project

In less than five minutes, George Hanover appeared with Danny in tow. Sir Roland looked up. "Have you told him?" he asked.

Hanover nodded. "Yes."

"I'm not doing it," Danny said.

Every head in the chamber turned to look in his direction.

Roland took a deep breath, then asked coldly, "Why not?"

The girl Opal, Sir Roland's daughter, was slumped in one of the two wired chairs, clamped in like a torture victim. She seemed to have passed out, but she was still breathing. Danny said, "This wasn't the deal we had."

"I thought it was *exactly* the deal we had," Roland said.

But Danny was shaking his head. "There was no mention of sending me out tonight."

"This is an emergency, Danny," Sir Roland said.

The stubborn look stayed fixed on Danny's face. "You said I'd get training."

Fran glanced briefly at Carradine but said nothing. George Hanover put on one of his most avuncular expressions. "You don't actually *need* training, Danny. Most of it is automatic."

Carradine said, "Basic RV training is really just a question of getting used to the equipment."

"And the experience," Hanover added.

Something was going on here—Danny could smell it—and nobody was in any hurry to tell him what it was. He glanced at Fran, who seemed the edgiest of them all. "Who's my partner?"

"Partner?" Fran echoed, frowning.

"Two chairs wired together," Danny said. "Two-man trip, right?"

By God, he was quick on the uptake, Roland thought. For someone who'd only stumbled onto the Project hours before and been told the minimum about its operation, he could put two and two together. Not necessarily a bad thing, if he was going to help get Opal back. Roland came to a decision. Before any of the others could speak he said, "Usually, yes. Sometimes the experience is difficult to handle if you project without a partner. But it would be unsafe to release my daughter from the second chair at the moment, so you'll have to do this alone. We've deactivated the connection." He was staring intently at Danny. "To the second chair."

"So I'm flying solo?"

"There are very seldom any problems," Roland said. "*Very* seldom indeed."

"He the one partnered your girl?" Danny asked, nodding toward Michael.

After just the barest hesitation, Sir Roland said, "Yes."

Michael was looking like death warmed up. He could hardly stand upright, and his hands were trembling. *Something bad has happened, and they aren't telling the half of it,* Danny thought. What they were asking him to do was a lot more dangerous than they were pretending, probably a lot more complicated as well. It was one thing joining a spy outfit and playing at remote viewing— nobody could touch you if you stayed at home—but Danny was no hero. He looked at the machinery and felt a little chill run down his spine. Those seats looked more like electric chairs than ever.

Sir Roland's daughter was obviously in a bad way. Danny hadn't expected to find her unconscious in the chair—wasn't sure what he *had* expected to find, but certainly not the pretty girl he'd seen earlier slumped like an empty sack. So long as his Nan was sick, they had him, but that didn't mean he had to do everything they said. He felt sorry for the girl, but an early life on the streets taught you to look after number one. This whole deal was showing all the signs of a dangerous mission, whatever Sir Roland wasn't telling him.

Michael said, "He doesn't want to do it, Sir Roland. I can do it—I know I can."

"All right," Danny heard himself say. "Mr. Hanover says you need me. Your girl is out there somewhere and I have to get her back—is that about it?"

Sir Roland shook his head. "A little overstated. We simply need you to find out what has happened to her. If you can get her back, that would certainly be a bonus, but it's not expected. Bring us information, and we should be able to do the rest."

"How am I supposed to find her?" Danny asked.

"We can send you to her last known coordinates," Carradine said. "You don't have to do anything—that's automatic."

"And I'll be able to see her—this second body of hers?"

Sir Roland nodded. "Yes, so long as you're in your own energy body. And she can see you. But no one else can."

Fran said, "Your surroundings will seem quite normal, and so will you. Opal will seem quite solid, but she won't be and neither will you."

"What happens if she's not there?" Danny asked. "At the coordinates?"

"In that case, you'll have to look around."

"You'll be able to fly in your second body—I'd suggest you use it," Carradine said. "See if you can spot her from the air."

Danny blinked. "I'll be able to *fly*?" He looked from one face to another. "You telling me I'll be able to fly? Like Superman?"

"Leap tall buildings with a single bound," Carradine said sourly. "Danny, you will be in an *energy* body. You can do things with it you could never do in the physical. It's like being a ghost. You can walk through walls. Gravity can't hold you, so you can fly."

"How?" Danny asked him promptly. He was still wary, still *scared* if he admitted it, but the idea that he might be able to fly was something else.

"You ever fly in a dream?" Carradine asked.

Danny hesitated. "Matter of fact I have," he said. "Sometimes . . ."

"It's like that," Carradine told him. "Might take a little time to get the hang of it, but . . ."

Danny was about to say something else, but Sir Roland cut in. "Take all the time you need. We won't call you back from this mission until you signal."

"How do I do that?" Danny asked.

There was sudden silence in the chamber.

"Ah," Carradine said.

Fran said, "We haven't trained him to signal."

Danny looked from one to the other, then said to George Hanover, "That's part of the basic training I don't really need—right?"

"Maybe I exaggerated a little," Hanover said, dropping his eyes.

Sir Roland looked from Carradine to Fran, then back to Carradine again. After a moment, Carradine said, "Suppose we link the chairs again—"

"We can't do that," Sir Roland said abruptly. "Opal would have to absorb . . ." He stared at Carradine intently, letting the sentence hang.

"Not if we reroute," Carradine said firmly. "We can keep her safe and still establish a minimal linkage. Any overflow will be looped back. We're already monitoring her vital signs. If Danny makes contact, it will show on the equipment." He began throwing switches.

"Technical matters," George Hanover said to Danny, as if that explained something.

Sir Roland turned to Danny as well. "You'll have to make direct contact when you see her. Speak to her. Touch her. Something of that sort. Just make sure she is aware of you. We'll do the rest."

They were all looking at him now. After a moment, Danny finally said, "All right."

Michael pushed himself forward to block Danny's way. "Are you sure about this?" he asked.

"No," Danny said, "but I'll do it."

Michael still didn't move. "We may be talking about Opal's life here. I should be the one to go."

"You're in no state to go anywhere, Michael," Carradine said gently. "Look at you—you can hardly stand."

Sir Roland said firmly, "Let Danny use the chair, Michael."

Michael hesitated, then moved reluctantly to one side. Danny hesitated, then climbed onto the chair. Everybody was watching him as if he was going to do something stupid, like make a break for it. The slumped body of the girl was in the chair beside him, so close that he could have reached out and touched her. But then Carradine was fastening the clamps around his wrists and ankles—doing it fast, too, as if he really didn't want Danny to escape. It all felt too much like an execution for Danny's taste.

Carradine said reassuringly, "Just a precaution. It stops your body from falling out of the chair when you leave it."

"We all get strapped in," Michael said weakly. He

was obviously fading, but he didn't want to leave.

Fran came over to put the cap on Danny's head, and he couldn't shake the feeling that he was in an electric chair. In a minute somebody would throw a switch, and he'd be fried. "What's—" He coughed to clear a throat that had suddenly turned dry. "What's going to happen?"

Former Bad Cop Fran was brisk and to the point. "You don't have to worry, Danny. We're not going to do anything until you're ready. The cap establishes an electrical connection with your brain. Later on, you'll have some scalp implants to make it easier, but we'll have to run without them now. You won't feel anything—"

"My head feels cold," Danny said. Actually it felt *really* cold where the cap went on.

Fran gave him a small smile. "That's just the contact gel—it makes sure we have a proper connection. But you won't feel anything else, I promise. So take your time and get settled. Then, when you tell me, I'll switch on the power."

"Try to keep your mind a blank," Carradine said. "It helps the targeting process."

"When you first arrive," said George Hanover enthusiastically, "it won't seem any different from actually being there. The target location is Lusakistan—"

"Lusakistan?" Danny gasped in sudden panic. Nobody'd told him he was being shipped out to

Lusakistan. There was a war on in Lusakistan.

"It's all right," Carradine said soothingly. "Distance makes no difference. It's as easy—and as quick—to project to Lusakistan as it is to send you into the next room."

"It only *seems* as if you're physically there," George Hanover said, moving closer to Danny's real worry.

Carradine added, "They could fire a bazooka and the shell would go right through you. Wouldn't feel a thing."

Everybody was in on the act now, trying to reassure him. Sir Roland said, "The important thing to remember is *nothing can harm you*—nothing."

So what happened to your daughter? Danny thought.

[24]

Opal, Lusakistan

The pain was gone now, but the memory of it lingered. Opal was still panting, still gasping, still feeling the racing of her heart. Yet how could she gasp in an energy body that needed no air? How could she feel the racing of a heart that was safely tucked inside her chest nearly four thousand miles away?

Farrakhan and the Skull were gone too. The old man who'd done this to her had told her they were leaving her to *consider her position,* but she knew they had left her purely to increase her fear. It was impossible to work for MI6 without picking up some information about torture techniques—all spies got the basic schooling.

Despite what many people believed, pain was not the most effective way to extract accurate information: the best tool was *fear* of pain. An agent subjected to intense, relentless pain would say anything—anything—to make it stop, would tell his torturers what he thought they wanted to hear, but would not necessarily tell the truth. If the pain went on too long, he would pass out. If he was forced to remain conscious—and there were drugs that would do *that* trick—he would eventually go mad.

But fear was different. Fear gnawed away at your defenses. Fear was what broke you, given time enough. And there was no more potent fear than fear of pain. A good interrogator began by hurting you, badly, but always briefly, then left you so the fear of the unknown would build. Opal was feeling the fear now. It crept like liquid ice into her stomach, causing a tightness in her phantom chest, setting her heart pounding again. But she used the techniques she'd been taught, the careful visualizations, the deep slow breathing, and even though they should not have succeeded while she was in her second body, somehow they did. As the fear receded, she turned her mind to ways of escape.

It was necessary to tackle the problem methodically. She was trapped in a wicker cage. How did you escape from a wicker cage? It struck her abruptly that it was a mistake to think she was *physically* imprisoned. It might *feel* that way, but in reality she wasn't here at all. In normal circumstances the electrical field of her energy body could pass through anything solid. Why couldn't she move it now? What would contain an electrical field?

She began to examine the cage more closely, but

that proved a dead end. She pushed down a mounting feeling of despair and tried another tack—how they'd put her in the cage in the first place. She tried to recall exactly what had happened. The old man Farrakhan had opened his hand and shown her something that looked like a medallion, and—

She stopped. She had to be careful to examine what had really happened, not what she *thought* had happened. Farrakhan had opened his hand, and there was a metal disc in it. She'd assumed he was showing her something because that's what it looked like. But suppose he wasn't. Suppose the disc was a device, some sort of control, like a television remote. Suppose he'd opened his hand in order to operate it. . . .

The instant he'd pointed it at her, she found she couldn't move. A moment after that, she blacked out. When she came to, she was in the cage.

Now she was getting somewhere. The mystery was no longer a *complete* mystery. Farrakhan could see her second body, a natural talent perhaps, some sort of . . . psychism. But far more importantly, Farrakhan possessed a device that could affect her energy body. Not a medallion, not a remote control—a weapon!

She put it all in context, and suddenly the truth fell on her like an avalanche. The Skull must know about the RV program! It was the only thing that made sense.

How he knew didn't matter. The important thing was that terrorists obviously knew all about the most secret spy program ever mounted by his two main enemies, the British and Americans. More to the point, he had developed the means to counteract it. No wonder he'd never been captured.

With mounting excitement, Opal turned her attention back to the wicker cage. Now that she was no longer distracted, she found what she was looking for almost at once. Woven through the wicker, almost totally invisible in this light, were hair-thin strands of copper filament. And twisted around the rope that hung the cage to the ceiling hook was a thin electric cable.

So now she'd found the lattice and the electrical supply. It could only mean one thing. Her second body was trapped inside a modified Faraday shield! Technology so simple, it actually dated back to the first half of the nineteenth century—she'd learned all about it in science class at school. The original Faraday shield was designed to protect sensitive equipment from electrostatic charges, to keep external electrical fields *out*. The modified shield was clearly designed to keep electrical fields, including her own second body, *in*.

Farrakhan's medallion probably worked on much the same principle. Perhaps it generated an electrical field of its own, short-circuiting her energy body and causing her the excruciating pain. This was information just as vital as the Skull's whereabouts. She had to bring it back to her father without delay.

But first she had to get out of the cage.

[25]

Dorothy, the Project Clinic

She could move!

It wasn't just a little, and it wasn't gradual, either. One minute Dorothy was lying there, wide awake, bit bored, bit uncomfortable, waiting for Nurse Cathleen to come and plump her up so she wouldn't get bedsores. Next thing you knew, she'd shifted of her own accord. Just turned on her side without thinking about it, as if it was the most natural thing in the world, which it was, of course, except she hadn't been able to do it since the stroke. Hadn't been able to do a thing, except blink her eyes.

She was so excited, she turned back again, just for the hell of it. Now she was lying there a bit dizzy, a bit breathless. But she could move again! Couple of days, she could be out of here! Well, maybe not so soon, but it was a start, wasn't it?

She tried moving again, just to make sure. She

straightened her leg, then bent it at the knee. And it worked! Legs worked, arms worked, fingers worked. Everything was stiff and funny, but nothing was sore. Stroke was no joke. But this was good news. She was getting better!

Dorothy looked at the nurse's bell next to her bed, wondering whether to push it, then decided against it. The clock on the wall showed just a few minutes before nine, and Cathleen would be here at nine on the dot—said so, hadn't she? You could set your watch by her. Be a nice surprise to find Dorothy sitting up in bed, grinning.

Dorothy sat up in bed as she watched the minute hand of the electric clock. It hit the hour with a faint click and sure enough, in bustled Cathleen—nice girl, Irish by the sound of her—and Dorothy gave a little wave and said, "Argh, ooh argh argh."

Well, strap that for a game of soldiers, she still couldn't talk!

[26]

Danny, the Shadow Project

Nothing happened, not at first. He was sitting in the chair with his metal cap on, still half waiting to be executed . . . still waiting for anything, really. Then an insect flew at him, one of those big leathery things he'd seen flying near Opal that first time. He swatted it without thinking, and his arm came right out of the restraints, and before he knew it he was standing up, facing the control panel, lurking so close behind Fran that he could have reached out and tapped her on the shoulder if he'd had a mind to.

Then he glanced back and saw a boy strapped into the chair where he had been, slumped a bit like the girl Opal in the second chair. Danny wondered where the boy had come from, how he hadn't heard him. Something familiar about him too, couldn't quite place it for a minute.

Then it hit Danny. The boy was him! It didn't look like him, not really, but he had the same messy hair and the clothes he was wearing and the same beat-up sneakers. It had to be him, couldn't be anybody else but Danny Lipman, large as life. Except Danny Lipman was standing up beside the controls, watching what was going on.

Carradine murmured, frowning, "You did program the coordinates, didn't you, Fran?"

They were both staring at a digital read-out flanked by flickering needle dials.

"What's the problem?" Fran asked quietly.

I'm in two places at once, Danny thought. It made him feel sort of creepy, but in a good way. Then he wondered how his Nan was doing, and the good feeling disappeared.

"I'm not—" Carradine began, then stopped himself. "Oh, no, it's okay—I forgot to compensate for body weight. It's still set for Opal." He made an adjustment, then hit the switch a second time.

All of a sudden Danny was tumbling through darkness. It was disorientating, but not all that unpleasant, like whirling around until you got dizzy when you were a kid. Used to do it with his Nan when she was younger. Then the lights came on again, a blaze of light.

He had a glimpse of sky and mountains before swooping to earth. Then a moment of gloom, then fluorescent brightness—and he was standing at the bottom of a bed, looking at his Nan, who was lying there asleep.

First thing struck him was how small she was, tucked up in the hospital bed—it had to be, since the place had the look and smell and feel of a hospital, you could spot them a mile away. Only she looked like she'd shrunk and got older and thinner, and her skin was wrinkling like a prune and her color didn't look great. Nice sheets, though. Classy bedclothes, all tucked in hospital style so you couldn't fall out. Nice bedside table, nice TV, nice carpet on the floor, and everywhere was spotless. Which meant they'd put her into a private clinic like they promised. Thing was, how had Danny gotten here?

"I'm behind you," said his Nan without moving her lips.

The voice really did sound like it was coming from behind him—like his Nan had taken up ventriloquism. It sounded so real that he actually turned around, but there was no one there, of course.

"I'm up here," his Nan said. "But don't you worry none: I've done this before and it's safe enough."

Danny looked. Nan was floating near a corner of the ceiling, wearing her nightie and nothing on her feet. "What you doing up there, Nan?" he asked.

"Keeps happening to me," Nan said. "Mind you, after the stroke, I thought I was dead, honest to God. I fell down, then I floated up and I thought I'd given up the ghost. But it was just more of this stuff. One minute you're lying there not able to move, next thing you're floating up by the ceiling." She grinned suddenly. "Here, it's nice to see you, Danny."

"Nice to see *you*, Nan," Danny told her, beaming.

"I'm glad you can, Danny," Nan said warmly. "See me, that is. I'm glad you can hear me and I can talk to you. Can't talk at all when I'm in that thing—" She gave a disgruntled nod in the direction of the body in the bed. "When I try, all that comes out is little farty noises, couldn't even make those for a while. But I can move a bit now. You don't think I'm dreaming this, do you, Danny?"

"Nah, I'm here all right," Danny said. "Do you have to stay up there?"

"Shouldn't think so."

"Why don't you come down, then," Danny said, "and we can talk properly without me getting a crick in my neck."

Nan floated down to the floor, graceful as a ballerina. When she landed, she laughed and made a little curtsy. "What you think of *that?*" she asked. "Been a while since I've been able to move that easy, I can tell you. Let alone fly."

Danny hugged her and she felt okay, skinny, but warm and smelling of disinfectant. He hugged her again, just to show how much he'd missed her, and she hugged him back, mumbling something like *good boy* into his hair.

Then they sat down side by side on the bed, their backs to Nan's body tucked up sleeping underneath the sheets. "What happened, Nan?" Danny asked.

"They tell you I had a stroke?"

Danny nodded. "They told me that, but they didn't give me any details."

"Not much more to tell," his Nan said. "I was coming down the stairs when I had the stroke. Aggie next door found me."

"You were lucky, Nan."

"I was." She shook her head. "Brought me to Saint Luke's. Don't remember much about anything, tell the truth, except it was a bit of a dump. But I didn't have to stay long. They shifted me to this place, don't know why. Wondered if it might have been—" She stopped abruptly as if she'd been about to say something she shouldn't.

"That was me, Nan," Danny said.

She glanced at him sideways with that familiar look of disbelief. "Win the lottery, did you?"

Danny grinned. "Friends in high places, Nan." He decided not to go into it any more just now: would only worry her. Instead he said, "I want to know how you are—how you are really. Doctor said you were paralyzed, but that was a while ago."

"Well, I can move now, like I told you," Nan said. "So don't you worry none. I'm not going to die or nothing. Tough as old boots. But the doctor was right: I couldn't move, not a bit of me. Then all of a sudden I could, just like that. Makes me tired, but moving has to be an improvement, hasn't it? Be right as rain in no time, mark my words. Only thing is, it's no fun not being able to talk. Can't even ask for a bedpan when you need one." She looked at him severely. "You can laugh all you like, Danny Lipman. Still, I suppose the talking will come back eventually."

She shifted on the bed, maybe trying to reach out to him, and the strangest thing happened. Nan, who looked rock solid and real as could be, went into the body in the bed, *her* body in the bed, like a genie going into its lamp. Weirdest thing he'd ever seen. One minute she was leaning forward, reaching out to him, next minute it looked as if she was being *sucked* into the body. Went in through the top of the head, distorting and stretching and disappearing, *whoosh,* just like that.

"Nan," Danny gasped. He stared at the little old body on the bed, then looked around the room wildly, but she wasn't by the ceiling, wasn't anywhere. "Nan!" he said again, louder this time.

The body in the bed opened its eyes, then struggled to sit up. She was right: she could certainly move. She was sitting up now, looking around her like she was looking for something. "Any err aargh ooo," she said. She looked directly at him but didn't register, like she couldn't see him. Her face took on a look of panic. "Any!" she said loudly. "Any-any-any!" Like she was calling for a cat. "Oharrk us aben ar odneem." She looked crestfallen, like disappointed, worse than he'd ever seen her. Looked a bit scared too, not at all like the Nan he knew. "Any!" she shouted, almost a scream.

Danny said quickly, "I'm here, Nan. I'm right in front of you." But it was like talking to a blind woman because she kept looking around the room with the panic in her eyes. A blind deaf woman because she couldn't hear him, either. "Oh, Nan. . . ." Danny reached out to touch her face.

His hand passed through her. It was like she wasn't there at all. He could see her, he could hear her, everything seemed normal, but he couldn't touch her: no sensation at all—and his hand was pushed through her jaw, into her mouth, into her throat like a special effect in a movie. Danny stared in horror.

Something gripped his shoulders and tried to pull him back and away, but he fought against it. No way did he want to leave his Nan now, not with his hand down her throat, not without saying *sorry* and *good-bye*.

"Stop hiding on me, Danny," said his Nan. "I know

you're still there, you little—"

Danny drew his hand away and felt the tears begin to stream down both his cheeks. Because his Nan was speaking clearly. He could understand every word.

[27]

Sir Roland, the Shadow Project

"There's something wrong," Fran said quietly.

Sir Roland, who had been standing by his daughter, moved around to the control console. "What's the problem?"

Fran indicated the readout panel again. "The top figures are Opal's last known coordinates. These ones"— she pointed—"these are from Danny's projection. They should be the same."

They clearly weren't. Sir Roland said, "Perhaps he hasn't gotten there yet."

"It's instantaneous," Carradine said.

Hanover joined them at the console. "Are we certain about Opal's readout?"

"It hasn't varied since we lost her," Carradine told him.

"Perhaps that's the trouble," Sir Roland suggested. "Perhaps the tracker is giving a false reading for Opal."

"Why would it do that?" Hanover asked.

"How the hell should I know?" Sir Roland snapped tersely. "Why can't we call her back? Why do we have to send out an untrained operative to find her?"

"Sorry," Hanover said.

"That's another thing," Fran murmured.

"What?" Carradine got the question in first.

"Danny's coordinates aren't stable. At least they don't seem to be. They keep flickering."

Frowning, Carradine said, "They seem okay to me."

"They've *been* flickering," Fran told him patiently. "This readout has only been holding for the last few moments."

"Can we call him back and resend him?" Sir Roland asked.

"I'll activate a recall." Fran reached out to push a sliding control on the console.

"Good God," Carradine said. "He's resisting!"

"I didn't know agents could do that." Sir Roland sounded worried.

"They can't," Carradine told him. "Not without advanced training." To Fran he said, "Try it again."

She neutralized the slider, then pushed it up again. She turned to the others with a look of bewilderment on her face. "Nothing," she said. "No resistance, but he's not coming back." She glanced toward the chair for confirmation.

"Like Opal!" George Hanover exclaimed. He turned to Sir Roland. "This has to be the equipment. Has to be. You can't lose two operatives within a couple of hours— it's just not possible."

"Never mind not possible," Roland growled. "Just get him back." He was less worried about losing Danny than the implications for Opal. He needed to know what had happened to her, needed even more to get her back. God alone knew how dangerous this situation was, but every minute that went past increased the pressure. He felt like strangling somebody.

"I don't believe in coincidence either," Carradine said. He looked at Sir Roland. "We need to run that diagnostic."

Fran said gently. "If we take the equipment off-line, we lose contact with Opal."

"We've already done that," Carradine said. "If this is equipment failure, it makes no difference. We're not really in contact with either of them anyway."

"Sir Roland . . . ," Michael said quietly.

The others were all looking at Sir Roland. He licked his lips. "Are you sure this is equipment failure?"

Carradine said, "No."

"If it *isn't* equipment failure, we may be giving up any chance we have of bringing Opal back—or

Danny for that matter?"

"Yes."

"Sir Roland," Michael said again.

Sir Roland took a deep breath and stared at the console. He raked his hands nervously through his hair. *What to do? What to do?* After a moment, he said, "Try one more recall, Fran. For both of them."

"Sir Roland," Michael said more firmly this time. "I think you should see this—"

Someone groaned behind him.

Sir Roland spun around. Opal was moving fitfully in her chair. She convulsed and vomited onto the floor. Then she looked up and caught his eye. "Hello, Daddy," she said weakly.

28

Opal, the Shadow Project

Opal opened her eyes. She was lying in a bed that wasn't her own in a room she didn't recognize. There was a television set mounted on the opposite wall and a remote control on the bedside table.

She remembered now. After the fuss and the vomiting in the operations room as she got her body back, they'd moved her to the Project clinic. She'd told them they didn't need to, but her father had insisted. And he'd been right. She'd slept around the clock, woken to the most enormous breakfast, then slept again. She remembered the most embarrassingly thorough medical checkup by a young doctor who absolutely refused to take her word for it that everything was all right, that she should be discharged right away.

A gentle knocking at the door had woken her. She pushed herself upright in the bed. "Come in," Opal called.

To her surprise it was Michael, carrying a bunch of flowers—and she hadn't brushed her hair, or put on even the slightest smidge of makeup. She pulled herself together and smiled lightly. "Hello, Michael."

"Hello, Opal," Michael said awkwardly. He raised the flowers a fraction. "I brought you these." He looked around, clearly wondering what to do with them.

"Put them on the table," Opal said. "I'll ask the nurse to find a vase." She pressed the bell as Michael disembarrassed himself of the flowers. "I'll ask her to bring you a chair as well."

Michael perched cautiously on the edge of the bed. "How are you?" he asked.

"I'm fine," Opal told him, "I'm absolutely fine. They'll let me out soon." Which was true, she thought. Even the young doctor had been encouraging. Then, because she knew that as an operative he had the necessary security clearance, she said excitedly, "Hey, I found the Skull!"

"Yes, I know—your father told me. That's brilliant, Opal—what a coup!"

It occurred to her that she didn't know what the outcome had been. She'd only managed a few words with her father before she collapsed, and no one in the clinic had any information at all. "Did they get him? Do you know?"

Michael shook his head. "Not yet." He hesitated,

then added, "It's early days, of course." Another hesitation, then, "Are you sure you're all right?"

It was nice. She'd never had a boy bring her flowers before. "Yes, I am. Really."

"It's just . . . well, I know you got into trouble," Michael said. "There's been a lot of talk about it."

"No, I'm fine. It was . . ." She stopped, thinking about it. "It was difficult. But I'm all right." In fact, what she'd been through had been absolutely terrifying. If it hadn't been for the wildest chance, nothing more dramatic than the appearance of a cleaning woman, she'd still be in the hands of Sword of Wrath. And who knew what that frightening old man was able to do. He'd trapped her and tortured her. She could still remember vividly how her energy body had writhed and jerked and even *crackled* as the waves of agony coursed through her. At one point she was convinced she was going to die.

She didn't want to look weak in front of Michael, so she pushed the memory fiercely out of her mind. "Did you come up from Eton today?" Operatives who were still at school were usually sent back as quickly as possible. But what she really wanted to ask was whether he'd come up from Eton today specially to see *her*. The actual question was a small failure of nerve.

"Last night," Michael said. "I stayed over with my uncle."

It came out as *oncle*. She loved his accent. There was a moment's silence, then Michael asked awkwardly, "Are you going home after they discharge you? Or will you come back to the Project?"

"Father wants me to stay home for a few days," Opal said.

"Don't you want to?"

She shook her head. "Not really. He'll fuss."

"Perhaps you need a little fussing," Michael said lightly. "You've had a very difficult experience."

Opal hid a smile. "I suppose so," Opal said. *But I don't need fussing from my father.*

Out of nowhere it occurred to her she was being totally self-centered. He'd been the anchor while she was trapped. With what she had experienced, the energy could have affected him as well. He might even have been hurt. And here she was, droning on without thinking to ask him how he was. "How . . . ," she began cautiously. "How did it go as my anchor?"

He gave a shy, embarrassed smile. "I got sick."

"Honestly?"

He nodded. "Yes, I had to lie down."

Opal laughed. "That must have been horrid."

"Well, not in your league."

They filled a moment looking at each other. Then Opal asked, "When are you going back?"

"Back where?"

"To Eton."

"Not until Sunday evening. I might even leave it until Monday morning if I can catch an early enough train."

"Oh, good," Opal said. "So you'll still be here on Saturday?"

"Yes."

Should she suggest they do something together this weekend? Maybe that would sound too pushy. And besides, he probably had other plans. Hopefully with his uncle. "Are there girls at Eton?" she heard herself ask suddenly.

Michael blinked. "It's a boys' school."

"Of course. Yes, of course." She hesitated, then said sheepishly, "I meant in the town." She wanted to ask if he ever met girls in the town, but realized she was on the way to making a complete fool of herself. After a long moment, she licked her lips. "There's a hunt ball at Oakleigh a week from Saturday."

"Really?" Nothing at all showed on his face. Not a hint of interest.

But too late to back off now. "Probably a bit of a bore," Opal said casually, "but I thought I might go."

"Yes."

This was definitely not going well. All the same, she had to finish it. "I was wondering if you might like to accompany me?" When his face remained blank, she added, "As my escort?"

He hesitated. "You mean . . . like a . . . date?"

Opal gave a small shrug. Then lost the last of her confidence: "I suppose so. Technically."

To her relief, Michael began to smile slowly. It lit up his whole face. But suddenly the smile disappeared, replaced by a peculiar look.

"I'm sorry," he said abruptly. "I have to go."

Then, to her horror, he stood up and walked out of the room.

Sir Roland, London

"This isn't a secure line," Sir Roland warned.

"I'll be discreet," Hector promised. "Was it Farrakhan?"

"Definitely," Roland said. "Fits the description, and Opal claims he told her that was his name. Haven't showed her pictures yet, but who else could have done that to her?"

"Is she bearing up?"

"Opal? Yes. The medics say there's no physical harm at all. Emotionally she seems fine too, unless she's hiding it. But she *was* tortured, obviously a very difficult experience—I should never have sent her out, but I'd no idea he could do something like that. Frankly, I didn't expect her to come within a thousand miles of him. I'm afraid I assumed the tip-off would lead to another Elvis goose chase. But fortunately she seems fine. More worried about her hunt ball than *Épée de la Colère.*"

"Do you know what happened yet?"

"Not entirely. We have the broad picture, of course, but I postponed a full debriefing to give her time to recover. Not according to the book and probably a disciplining offense, but she *is* my daughter."

"She is your daughter," Hector agreed. "I'd have done the same. Any news of the spear?"

"That's why I rang. It's definitely been moved."

"Out of the *Ringstrasse*?"

"Afraid so." Roland hesitated. "Actually, right out of Austria. The museum authorities decided to feature it in a traveling exhibition of religious art and artifacts. It's currently on display in Egypt."

"Egypt!" Hector exploded. "Oh my God."

"It may not mean anything," Roland said.

"Of course it means something. It means the original has been moved as well. Which suggests somebody's been tinkering with it. My money is on Farrakhan. We've known for some time that he's the real moving force behind Sword of Wrath. This is exactly the sort of thing he would do."

Roland sighed lightly. "Don't suppose the Priory would help?"

"You know the Priory, Roland—you've been involved with us for long enough. Broader picture and all that. We don't get involved. Not even sure I should be telling you half the things I do."

"That works both ways," Roland said a little sourly.

"I know, I know," Hector said. "Tell you what, I'll have a word with the powers that be."

"Are you serious?"

"Think I am, actually," Hector said. "All very well to stand aside and claim the moral high ground, but you and I are soldiers, Roland. Things look different at the sharp end. That little creep who's running the Skull is getting help from some very nasty quarters; and with this spear thing, God knows what he might be planning. Could be time for the good guys to wade in and get their hands dirty."

"Do you think they will?"

"Probably not. Free will, destiny, collective karma of humanity—you know how they go on. But they might nudge things in the right direction. Or let me help a little if it turns out that I can. It depends what happens. And how bad it gets, I suppose."

"How bad do you think it will get?" Roland asked. His mind was on Opal.

"Bad enough," Hector said. "You've only to look at the connections."

"The Skull and Farrakhan?"

"Well, that, obviously, but I was thinking more on our own side. There's obviously a mystic link with Michael, and there may be one with Opal as well, but I'm particularly intrigued by this new boy and his association to our mediator. That's really peculiar, even in our line of work. Take it all together and you get the feeling of strange forces gathering just beyond the horizon."

"Yes," Roland muttered. It was exactly the feeling he'd been getting during the last few days. But who could you talk to? Nobody believed in Cosmic Battles anymore. Even the old concept of evil had been distorted for political ends. But what Farrakhan was up to was objectively evil. Not because he was teamed up with *Épée de la Colère*, not even because of what he had done to Opal, but because he was an occultist who deliberately tapped into dark currents, calling on evil entities. The only way to deal with that was to align yourself with the powers of good. Except, as Hector said, those powers were very hesitant to interfere. "What do you think will happen next?" he asked Hector.

"Couldn't say," said Hector promptly, "but I'd be prepared to bet you half my pension that it will involve your new boy Danny Lipman. He's in this deeper than he knows."

[30]

Danny, the Shadow Project

"What's this, then?" Danny asked. "The Project Museum?"

It was the weirdest collection he'd ever seen: cabinets and displays of African masks and jujus, ceremonial swords, Egyptian ankhs, chalices, brass discs, wands, thuribles, and a load of other religious junk, alongside—and this was the *really* weird bit—a bank of scary machines like the things they hook you up to in the hospital, a control console that must have come from outer space, and one of the coolest sound systems he'd ever seen, with speakers that were actually bigger than he was. It made the operations room with its two electric chairs look like a train set.

Fran smiled. She could smile now that she wasn't playing Bad Cop, but she was still one tough lady. Danny wouldn't want to cross her. "Looks a bit like a museum, doesn't it?" she said. "It's actually the heart of our Project."

"Thought that was the operations room," Danny said.

"That's just a feed. This is the generator. Whenever we want to send out an agent, we have one of our scientists in here crank up the psychotronic energies and pump out the infrasound. The control panel in the operations room directs what we produce in here."

"Wow," Danny said, looking at the electronic gear. Then his eyes slid across the other stuff. For some reason it made him feel uneasy. "What's all the stuff from Africa?"

"Yes, well, it *is* a strange mixture." For a moment he thought she was going to leave it there—he'd discovered they weren't big on explanations here, Fran least of all—but then she said, "We gathered it together when we were investigating magic. I expect Sir Roland told you about that?"

Danny nodded. Somehow he'd thought Sir Roland just meant books.

"We have some really interesting items." She moved to a cabinet and took out a peculiar dagger with a triangular blade and gargoyle-headed handle. "This, for example." She waved it in the manner of somebody used to handling weapons.

"What is it?" Danny asked cautiously. "Wouldn't want anybody to stick that up your nose."

"It's a Tibetan *phurba*," Fran said. "A ritual dart used to drive off evil spirits." She closed the cabinet firmly. "That's enough of the history lesson." She pulled up a chair and sat down, nodding for Danny to do the same. "Now, I want you to tell me *exactly* what happened when you projected."

Danny shrugged. "I came out of my body when you switched on the power, but I didn't *go* anywhere."

"How did you know you were out of the body?"

"Could see it sitting there."

"Have you any recall of *how* you came out?"

"How?"

"Through the top of your head, down your nose, out your ear—what?" Fran asked.

"Tried to swat an insect, and my arm came out of the restraints," Danny said. "After that I was just out. Standing there beside the chair."

"So you were aware of the insect creatures? Most of our other operatives have reported them. In the Project we call them threshold guardians: they often turn up when somebody's projecting—we don't fully understand their origins. What happened then?"

Danny shrugged. "You adjusted for weight and off I went."

"But not to Lusakistan?"

"No way," Danny said.

"What *exactly* happened?"

Danny shrugged again. "Went dark, felt like I was falling, got light, looked like mountains, then I was in the hospital with my gran." Nobody had asked him for details of his experiences with his Nan, and he hadn't volunteered.

"Looked like mountains? You didn't mention that before."

"Think I did," Danny said.

"No, you didn't." She frowned. "What were you thinking about before you went?"

Thinking about? His Nan, probably. He couldn't really remember, but he worried about her most of the time. "My Nan, I suppose."

For some reason she looked pleased. "I think I know what happened. The equipment didn't fail at all. I think the problem was that we didn't use another agent as your anchor—we took out the second chair to avoid any feedback to Opal. I think we sent you to Lusakistan all right—that was your brief flash of mountains—but without the anchor, there was no stabilizing lock. You were thinking of your grandmother. *Gross movement follows thought*—we teach that to all trainees. If you want to go somewhere, you simply focus on moving to your target—think about it, in other words. In your case that meant you went directly to your grandmother."

"But I didn't know where she was," Danny said. "I knew you'd moved her from Saint Luke the Physician's, but I didn't have the new address."

"Didn't matter," Fran said. "You locked in on the image of your grandmother. And managed to resist when we tried to pull you back. You're obviously a natural for this sort of work." She rubbed her hands together. "Well, now that we've cleared that up, let's see how much better you can get with a bit of practice."

Opal, the Shadow Project

"Whoops," the old woman said. "Wrong door—I must be getting senile." She started to back out again. "Sorry, love." She was wearing a flannel nightie and dressing gown, both of which looked as if they'd seen better days. Obviously another of the clinic's patients. A strange one.

Opal smiled. "That's all right." On impulse she added, "I was feeling a bit lonely anyway." Lonely and cross since Michael ran off like that. She was still burning with embarrassment.

The old woman reversed her direction at once. "Can't have that," she said as she shuffled across the room to sit on the edge of the bed. "Notice they don't give you chairs round here—that's to discourage visitors."

"Do you think so?" Opal asked, wondering if it might be true. It was a secret intelligence service clinic, after all, but the chair business hadn't occurred to her.

"Might be," the old woman said. She stuck out her hand. "My name's Dorothy."

"Opal," Opal told her. The old woman had an East London accent. What on earth was she doing in a clinic run by MI6?

"What you in for, Opal?" the old woman asked curiously. She managed to make it sound like a prison sentence.

Opal smiled at her again. "Just a few tests," she said. "They're letting me out this evening." She made a face and added, "With luck. How about you?"

"Me? Had a stroke, didn't I? Coming down some stairs. Lucky I didn't break my stupid neck. Right out of the blue, no warning. One minute I was right as rain, the next I was in a heap on the floor, not able to speak, not able to move. Would have been there yet hadn't been for my next-door neighbor."

It occurred to Opal suddenly that Dorothy might be an undercover agent. She certainly didn't look like one or sound like one, but that was the whole point, wasn't it? She said, "You look much fitter now."

"Thank you," Dorothy said. "Take more than a stroke to send me off. Tough as old boots. Besides, I have things to do. Going home today, same as you. Only they've hid my clothes somewhere and I can't find them. I was looking for a nurse when I came blundering in disturbing you."

"I'm very pleased you did."

"Me too," Dorothy said. Then, inconsequentially, "You're a very pretty girl."

"Thank you." It was nice to have a compliment after Michael's rejection, even if it only came from an old woman. She decided she liked Dorothy, and even though she strongly suspected she shouldn't ask, she did: "How is it you're in the clinic, Dorothy?"

"Had a stroke, dear—I just told you."

"No, I mean, how did you come to be in *this* clinic?" Opal smiled encouragingly.

"Search me, dearie. My boy arranged it all."

"Your son?" Opal asked. Perhaps he was an MI6 operative.

"Grandson," Dorothy said. "Just as well, too. I was out of it, let me tell you. Couldn't move, couldn't speak, no money to go private. It was National Health for me and no mistake. Fate worse than death. But you and me's the lucky ones, ain't we, Opal? We ended up in here. Nice place, innit? Know what I like most about it?"

"No," Opal said, bemused.

"It's clean," said Dorothy. "Everything's spotless. My room's spotless. Your room's spotless. The corridor outside is spotless. Won't find superbugs lurking in here, I can tell you." She leaned forward to stare into Opal's face, smiling slightly—then, without the slightest warning, her eyes glazed over and her mouth fell slackly open.

"Dorothy?" Opal said.

The old woman sat immobile as a statue on the bed.

"Dorothy?" Opal said again in sudden panic. She leaned forward, then began to scramble out of the bed. Dorothy was having another stroke.

Opal was reaching for the bell that would call a nurse when Dorothy said, "Beware the Devourer!" The voice froze Opal. It was deep and resonant, scarcely human, and so loud, it echoed through the inside of her skull. She spun around to look at Dorothy, whose eyes were bright again, whose mouth was no longer slack. There seemed to be some sort of halo around her head, but it was fading fast.

Dorothy pushed herself to her feet. "Best be off now," she said in her normal voice. "Need to get dressed and make myself presentable. Did I tell you I was going home today?"

"Yes," Opal said, openmouthed. "Yes, you did." Her mind was racing. What had just happened? There was something about the voice that chilled her to the bone.

Opal watched nervelessly as Dorothy shuffled toward the door. "Won't be sorry," Dorothy said, half to herself. "Nice enough place this, but there's no bed like your own bed, is there? No place like home."

Danny, the Shadow Project

Fran said, "I want to try an experiment."

Danny said suspiciously, "What you want me to do?"

"You're a bit of a natural. So I thought it might be interesting to try a new technique I've been working on."

"Sure," Danny said. "What is it?"

"Part of the gear here is a standing wave generator—I integrated it into the system just yesterday. Our specialists think it could trigger a projection without the helmet. This will be the first time we've actually tried it out. If you're game?"

Danny thought he quite liked Fran. Now that she'd dropped the Bad Cop act, her bark seemed a lot worse than her bite. He didn't know what a standing wave was, but anything that could get you out of your body without the helmet had to be an improvement on their electric chair. "Bring it on!" he said. "What do you want me to do?"

Fran looked pleased. "All I really want you to do is stand here," she said, pointing. "On the chalk mark. That's where the standing wave will generate."

"Won't I fall down?"

Fran blinked. "You're right, you might—hadn't thought of that." She grabbed an upright chair and pushed it in his direction. "Sit on that, on the mark. You should be all right." She paused, then added, "Or would you like me to tie you in?"

Danny grinned at her. "Some other time, eh? I think I'll be fine." He pushed the chair onto the chalk mark and sat down. "Where are you going to send me?"

"Nowhere," Fran said. "The coordinates are set to this room, so you should simply come out of your body and stay"—she waved one hand vaguely—"around here somewhere." She frowned suddenly and added severely, "I don't want you flying off to see your grandmother again."

"Promise," Danny said. "Cross my heart and hope to die."

Fran said. "You'll hear quite a loud sound when I switch on, like a swelling organ note. But it will keep dropping in pitch until you think it's stopped. Except it won't have stopped, just dropped below the threshold of your hearing. There's a possibility that you may be able to feel it as a vibration for a little while: some people are sensitive enough to pick that up. But once you stop hearing it, you can expect the standing wave to propagate within about five seconds."

"I'll wave to you as I come out of my body," Danny grinned.

"That would be nice." Fran smirked. "Are you all set?"

"Hit the juice!" Danny told her.

The organ note began at once and lasted longer than he expected, but dropped quickly in pitch until it was a low animal growl, then stopped altogether. Danny began to count mentally *one hundred and one, one hundred and two, one hundred and three, one hundred and*—

Something hideous hurled itself from a cabinet. It struck Danny with such force that he was flung from his chair to hurtle across the room and smash a glass-topped display. He landed bruised and dazed amid the wreckage on the floor. He had a fleeting impression of claws and fangs as the creature attacked Fran with such ferocity that it opened her arm from shoulder to wrist with a single slash. Blood spurted in a spray that fanned across the gleaming surface of the control panel. There was a scream as Fran went down, then the thing was on top of her, squatting on her chest.

Danny scrabbled wildly until his hand gripped something sound enough to support him as he climbed shakily to his feet. The thing on Fran's chest glanced around to look at him with fiery eyes. "Hey!" Danny roared. He moved unsteadily toward it.

The creature made a sound that, horribly, could only have been a laugh. There was blood all around its mouth. It climbed slowly off Fran and began to lope toward him, crouched, eyes gleaming, growling softly.

Danny's heart was racing and he wanted desperately to run, but he'd been in enough street fights to know that was the worst thing you could do. The creature was smaller than he was, about the size of an Alsatian dog, so maybe if he got his hands on it he could wring its neck. He was terrified after what he'd seen it do, almost paralyzed by fear, but he forced himself to move toward it. The thing stopped, watching him. Danny feinted to one side, then dashed forward, arms outstretched. He was feet away when the creature struck and ripped open his leg. He staggered, hit a table, and nearly fell again.

The thing rounded to attack him again, and he knew he was a goner. His leg felt on fire, and he couldn't use it anymore, couldn't run, couldn't get away, and he was starting to think if he stood still he'd likely bleed to death. After which it hit him again, ripping a wound across his throat. The creature crouched, leaped, and it was definitely laughing.

Acting of its own accord, Danny's hand reached out to grip the Tibetan *phurba* on the tabletop beside him. As the thing jumped at him again, he thrust out blindly.

There was an explosion of black light.

[33]

Opal, the Shadow Project

Opal felt wound up to the breaking point. First Michael humiliating her, then the old woman. She'd been absolutely sure Dorothy was having another stroke, absolutely sure she was going to die right there on the edge of the bed. Then the voice, so strange that she was beginning to wonder if she'd heard it at all. Now Dr. Holroyd was on his way to sign her out.

On his way to sign her out and she wasn't even dressed!

Opal swung her feet out of the bed and ran for the wardrobe. Quickly she pulled on T-shirt, sweater, and jeans, looked for her shoes, couldn't find them, found them, pulled them on while hopping on one leg, then sat down on the bed to wait.

She looked out the window, in a quandary over what to do about transportation. Should she ring for a car, or had the clinic organized one for her? She wouldn't know that until Dr. Holroyd got here with the paperwork. Perhaps her father had arranged something. She wondered if he wanted her to go home or come straight to the Project. But she didn't want to go home. She felt fine now, and she was bored after her stay in the hospital.

Bored and mad. She was angry with Michael now. No longer shocked at the way he'd positively *stomped* out just because she'd asked him to the ball, but actively furious. She suspected girls didn't ask boys out in his country—some cultures were positively medieval the way they treated women—but talk about overreacting!

She was mad at Dorothy as well. She must have done the funny voice as a joke. But it was terrifying when you didn't know the person. Especially when they said, "Beware the Devourer!" That sounded like something out of a horror movie.

Where was Dr. Holroyd? Opal was annoyed with him for keeping her waiting. She flicked on the TV and glared at some stupid soccer match.

She was anxious to go back to the Project. She wanted to find out if they'd caught the Skull and what they planned to do about that terrifying old man who'd trapped her when everybody said that wasn't possible—

Opal stopped. It wasn't a soccer match on the television, just the sports section of a news program, and they'd gone back to the main bulletin. The screen was showing an airport, Heathrow probably, with passengers disembarking from a plane. What caught her attention was Guy Manton, a friend of her father, who worked at the Ministry of Defence, shaking hands with two men at the bottom of the steps.

". . . Spiros Avramides," the voice-over was saying, "and his associate, Peter Kanska."

Then the clip finished, and they were back in the studio as the broadcaster smiled directly into the camera and said, "And now let's find out what the weather has in store for us."

Opal switched off the television, but somehow could not take her eyes off the screen. It was as if the images at the airport had burned themselves onto her brain. The plane, the passengers, the runway. Spiros Avramides and Peter Kanska shaking hands with Uncle Guy. The cameraman had been some distance away, but he'd used a zoom lens, so the faces were visible enough. Even in the second or two before the clip finished, she had no problem recognizing them.

Her paralysis broke and she scrambled for her cell phone. To hell with Dr. Holroyd—she had to get back to the Project *now*. She thumbed her speed dial for the Project, gave her code ID, and asked the switchboard to transfer her to the motor pool. She didn't recognize the voice that answered, but it didn't matter: her ID was enough to get a car dispatched to the clinic. "Priority," she said.

As she cut the connection, there was a knock on her door. Bloody Dr. Holroyd at last, exactly when she *really* didn't need him. Well, she had too much on her mind to start filling out a bunch of silly forms. She—

But it wasn't Dr. Holroyd, it was Michael. Opal stared at him. For a moment she waited for him to apologize, to tell her *of course* he would escort her to the ball, but then she saw the strain on his face, the fear in his eyes.

Michael said, "You have to come at once—something's happened. I have your driver and a car outside."

Opal, the Shadow Project

Michael didn't mention what had happened between them earlier. Nor did Opal when she saw his face. There were armed guards in the car. Their driver, Harry Byrne, was also carrying a gun, tucked into a shoulder holster. Harry *never* went armed. Nobody in the Project wore shoulder holsters.

Something horrible had happened.

Michael didn't know the details, but she realized it was serious when Harry took them through the tunnel entrance rather than the gate. And security was tighter than she'd seen it, *ever.* There were uniformed soldiers everywhere, with semiautomatic rifles.

Then they arrived at her father's office, and all she needed was a glance at their faces. Her father, George Hanover, and Gary Carradine—all three of them looked as though someone had been assassinated.

Her father walked directly toward them as they

entered the room. His face was the color of cigar ash as he said, "I'm terribly sorry, Opal. Fran is dead."

Opal stared at him as if he'd struck her. Then she decided she must have misheard. But the tightness in her stomach didn't ease. Nor did the sense of shock. She felt someone take her hand and realized it was Michael. "What?"

Her father said, "Something dreadful has happened. I'm afraid Fran is dead."

Opal said breathlessly, "What are you talking about?"

Michael said, "It's true, Opal. Fran Hitchin is dead."

"That's not possible." She didn't believe it. She couldn't believe it. But if anything, it was the sheer brutality of her father's announcement that convinced her. He'd always been that way. Bad news was something to get out in the open and deal with. He would no more have considered breaking it gently than lying. All the same, she caught her breath and said, "She can't be." Then, when her father said nothing, she said, "What happened? Was she ill?"

She heard Mr. Carradine release something close to a sigh before he said, "She was murdered."

She turned to look at him blankly. "Who killed her?"

"Danny," Carradine said.

"We think Danny," her father amended.

"It's just happened," George Hanover told her. "They were working together."

"Danny?" Opal echoed. She glanced at Michael, who was still holding her hand. Danny had assaulted Michael. But assault was a long way from murder. She looked back at her father. "Are you sure?"

Carradine shrugged. "He was the only one with her."

"But somebody from outside—"

"No signs of forced entry. Just the two of them together in the room. They were working on projection training. Fran locked the outer door—standard procedure."

George Hanover said, "We'll know exactly what's happened when we review the tapes."

Carradine said, "Meanwhile Danny Lipman is in custody."

Her father said, "But this isn't why we called you in, you and Michael."

Opal was so upset, she scarcely took in what he'd said. It was Michael who asked, "Why *did* you call us in, Sir Roland?"

Roland reached out to lay a protective hand on his daughter's arm. "We've received intelligence of a possible attempt on Opal's life."

Opal, the Shadow Project

"Who'd want to kill me?" Opal asked, bewildered. She still couldn't understand what was happening, but part of her wondered if this could have anything to do with Fran's murder.

"*Épée de la Colère*—Sword of Wrath—apparently," George Hanover said. "According to MI5."

"Sword of Wrath doesn't even know I exist!" Opal exclaimed, looking from face to face. But even as she spoke, she realized it was nonsense. Sword of Wrath was run by the Skull. And the Skull—or rather, the Skull's adviser—had caught her spying. The old man, Farrakhan, hadn't believed her story for a moment, and she'd stupidly given him both her name and her location. Admittedly it was only her first name, but that would make little difference. It might not be possible to track down a particular girl named Opal in a city the size of London if you were starting from scratch, but all you had to do was start with the premise that Opal worked for MI6—which would make sense if she was a British spy—and your job got a whole lot easier. Any good espionage service would quickly find out that the senior MI6 executive, Sir Roland Harrington, had a daughter named Opal who matched the age and description of the girl they were looking for. After that, it was only a matter of time before their agents caught up with her. "Oh my God," she breathed.

"You're in no danger here, of course," her father said, "but they *are* looking for you. The question is why?" He knuckled one eye tiredly. "I think it may have been a mistake not to debrief you straightaway."

She caught the awkward looks on the faces of the others. It was a strict rule that agents must be fully debriefed at the earliest possible moment after their return, and her father had broken it. She'd told him what happened, of course, told him about the Skull and the two men who'd visited him, told him about the old man who somehow managed to imprison her second body, but that didn't amount to a full debriefing. That would have involved days, perhaps weeks, of questioning by Carradine and his staff, the sifting through every nuance of her conversations, relentless examination of whole computer libraries of photographs in an attempt to identify the people she'd seen. There might even have been hypnosis to help her fill any blanks in her memory. But she'd been so shaky when she returned that her father had cut through all of that, sent her directly to the clinic for her tests.

Carradine cut through the silence. "Maybe we shouldn't waste any more time . . . ?"

Sir Roland stared at him for a moment, then said abruptly, "You're right. We must start this at once. It will take precedence over Fran's murder." The living came before the dead. It was an MI6 maxim.

Carradine said, "I have my people on Fran's case. They're studying the surveillance tapes and will get back to us."

"Can Michael sit in?" Opal asked suddenly. Despite his earlier behavior, she found his presence comforting.

Her father looked surprised. "Yes, if you want."

Michael said quietly, "I appreciate that, sir."

They had moved across to Carradine's office, and Opal, whose life was apparently under threat from the world's most dreaded terrorist organization, found herself thinking that the chairs here were more uncomfortable than those in any other office in the building. She sat down in one of them and looked up anxiously at Carradine.

Without so much as a glance toward Sir Roland, Carradine said crisply, "Your father has given me a broad outline of what happened to you and what you saw, but I would like to hear it for myself—everything."

He might have been about to say something more, but Opal interrupted. "Did Father tell you I saw two men with the Skull—two Western businessmen, I think—doing some sort of deal with him or something?"

Carradine nodded. "Yes."

Opal took a deep breath. "Well, I've just seen them again."

"What?" her father exclaimed.

"Where?" Carradine asked simultaneously.

"They were on *television*!" Opal said. "Just before I left the clinic. They were coming off a plane—I think at Heathrow. One's called Avramides. The other's called Kanska." She glanced at her father. "Uncle Guy was meeting them."

"Who's Uncle Guy?"

"Guy Manton," Roland said. "He's a permanent secretary at the Ministry of Defence." He looked at Carradine, then added, "Friend of the family. The *uncle* part is honorary."

There was absolute silence in the room. Then Carradine said, "Did you say Avramides and Kanska?" He reached for the laptop on his desk, typed something. After a moment, he turned the computer around to let her view the screen. "Is that one of them?"

The photograph on screen was black and white and

not particularly sharp. It looked as if it might have been taken through a telephoto lens; and possibly some years ago, because the face looked younger than the one she remembered. But for all that she had not the slightest doubt. "That's Avramides," she said.

"Christ!" Carradine breathed.

Out of the corner of her eye, she saw George Hanover look across at her father. Both had expressions of shock on their faces. Opal glanced at Michael and asked, "Who is he?" It was very clear that they knew.

Carradine took a deep breath. "Greek arms dealer. Kanska is Hungarian, his partner."

For some reason, Opal felt that he was holding something back. She caught his eye and held it. "And . . . ?"

Carradine said tiredly, "Avramides and Kanska are suspected of trafficking in nuclear weapons."

"Oh," Opal could only say, stunned.

"It's just a suspicion," George Hanover said. "We've never been able to prove anything. But Kanska has contacts in the former Soviet Union—there's a lot of nuclear material there: outdated Russian warheads and materials. The trouble is that since the Soviets collapsed, security is rubbish—and frankly, some of the governments in the smaller, poorer states aren't above making dirty little deals. It's been a massive headache for years now. But we hadn't seen it as a likely Sword of Wrath connection."

It was Michael who asked, "Why not, Mr. Hanover?"

Hanover shrugged slightly. "A question of scale. The old Soviets stockpiled what you might call conventional nuclear weapons—the sort of thing you might use if you went to war with another country. You could sell some of that stockpile to another nation state—North Korea, Iran, or where have you—but it's frankly useless to an organization like Sword of Wrath. They don't have an air force, they don't have missile silos or permanent launch bases—they're just not fighting that sort of war. The only thing that would be of any use to them is a miniaturized tactical atomic, something they could smuggle into a country and hide away in a suitcase, then detonate from a distance to take out a city. But that's a much more recent technical development, certainly not something the Soviets stockpiled. Contrary to the scare stories you read in the press, tactical atomics are very difficult to get hold of."

"But not impossible?" Michael put in. "Perhaps what Opal saw—"

Carradine cut through the conversation with just the barest hint of impatience by saying to Opal, "When you saw these men—Avramides and Kanska—with the Skull, was the conversation in English?"

Opal nodded. "Yes."

"I want you to tell me everything they said. Everything."

"Actually there wasn't much," Opal told him. "The Skull said, 'It is satisfactory,' and the older man—"

"What was satisfactory?" Carradine interrupted.

"I don't know," Opal said. "Obviously something they'd been talking about before I arrived."

"Okay," Carradine said. "So the Skull said something was satisfactory. What did Avramides or Kanska say?"

"Avramides asked about payment, and the Skull said his men were loading bullion onto their helicopter."

"Payment in gold," Hanover murmured. "The bastards were supplying him with *something*."

"Anything else?" Carradine asked.

Opal shook her head. "They had coffee after that, and Avramides said it was a pleasure doing business with him. And then he asked what the Skull was going to do with it."

"Do with what?" her father asked.

Opal looked at him. "Whatever they'd sold him."

"But there was no mention of what it was?" Carradine asked.

Opal shook her head. "No." She glanced down at the floor. "Sorry."

"It could be anything," George Hanover muttered

half to himself. "Even nuclear."

"But you said the sort of bomb they'd need would be, you know . . ." The talk of nuclear weapons was making Opal nervous. She kept thinking what would happen if a nuclear device was detonated in London.

"It may not be a tactical miniature," Hanover said soberly. "They may be opting for a dirty bomb—conventional explosive surrounded by radioactive material. Not much in the way of property damage, but widespread fallout, so the death toll would be high. Avramides could certainly supply Sword of Wrath with radioactive material."

"It's not that," Michael said bluntly.

Hanover blinked at him. "How do you know?"

"Because the men were loading gold bullion onto a helicopter," Michael said. "And it didn't sound like it was a quick job, if they were having coffee while they waited. That sort of payment is far more than you'd need for a few containers of enriched uranium."

Carradine turned to look at him with an expression of admiration. "Got it in one, Mike," he said. He glanced at Hanover, who had asked the question, and raised an eyebrow.

"Maybe it was more than a few," George Hanover said, sounding defensive.

"If it was a massive amount—enough to justify a

helicopter load of bullion—then you have to ask yourself how it was delivered. Avramides certainly didn't bring it with him, and the Skull is hiding in the middle of a war zone. You'd need a convoy of trucks, and what are the chances of their getting through without us spotting them?" Carradine tapped the casing of his laptop. "Besides, there's the threat to Opal."

There was silence in the room as everyone looked at him.

Carradine glanced from one face to the other, then said, "Put it together. The Skull discovers he's been spied on. Forget about how—that's another problem. He captures the spy temporarily, then she escapes." He hesitated, frowning suddenly. "How *did* you escape, Opal? Your father hasn't told me."

"It was ridiculous," Opal said. "They left me, and while they were away, a woman came to clean the room. She unplugged the electricity to the cage."

Carradine stared at her in astonishment, then gave the barest ghost of a smile. "Are you serious?"

Opal nodded. "She couldn't see me, of course. She unplugged the cage to plug in a funny little vacuum cleaner. I came back at once."

"Well, well," Carradine said. Then his smile faded. "In any case, you escaped. Now MI5 tells us they have information that *Épée de la Colère* plans an assassination attempt. You have to ask yourself why. Nobody goes to the trouble of sending a team to Britain just to get revenge—that's playground behavior. They have to be worried that you know something they badly want to keep secret. It's not their location, since that changes all the time; besides, they'd already moved on by the time we sent in the bombers. It's nothing obvious in their camp: everything you saw was routine military hardware. Which leaves the fact that the Skull was involved with two Western businessmen. Granted they were arms dealers, but it's hardly news to anybody that he buys arms. So it wouldn't trouble him that we'd discovered details of a conventional arms deal. Which only leaves the nuclear option. If he *is* planning a tactical nuclear strike against the States or over here, he's going to go a long way to keep it secret until it happens."

"Impressive reasoning, Gary," Hanover said. "But there's a flaw in your logic."

"Which is what, George?"

"Once they discovered Opal had escaped, they'd know their secret was out. By the time they got someone in place to kill her, it would be too late."

But Carradine shook his head. "That assumes Opal knew the men the Skull was dealing with. She didn't. It's only by the sheerest chance we know who they are. In a full-scale debriefing she might have found them in a photo lineup, but that could take several days, maybe weeks. The Skull could reasonably assume that he had time to mount an assassination attempt. In any case it would obviously be better to try than not to try. Besides, he may have had someone already in place." He looked from one face to another.

"Do you have someone in mind?" Sir Roland asked quietly.

"Young Lipman," Carradine said.

"Danny?" Opal whispered. "Why Danny?" She felt Michael's hand tighten on hers.

Carradine shrugged. "He just killed Fran, didn't he?"

[36]

Danny, the Shadow Project

They bandaged his neck and leg and put him in jail. Fortunately they locked him in the same old cell.

Danny wandered casually to the door and examined the lock. They'd taken away his lockpicks, of course . . . except for the one he'd concealed above the lintel. Danny grinned to himself. Hiding a pick was an old habit, in case he got interrupted and his stuff was confiscated. Last time he got out of this cell, he'd been so intent on escape, he forgot to take the hidden pick with him. Lucky lapse.

You had to look closely to see the way he'd sabotaged the lock. The door still closed properly, the key still turned, but if you tickled it with the pick, like *so* . . . it was even easier than the first time. All he had to do was turn the handle and step outside. But first he had to find out what guards they'd posted this time.

Danny walked back to the bunk bed and lay down.

Although his insides had settled a bit since poor Fran had switched on that standing wave, they still felt shaky and his stomach was queasy. His instinct was to ignore it and hope that it would pass. But now he began to concentrate on it. The feeling of unease grew worse.

What was it Nan always said? "What can't be cured must be endured"? Let's see how well he could endure this lot. Danny closed his eyes and fixed his attention even more firmly on the discomfort inside him. Almost at once, the shakiness turned into a vibration. Danny lay there, letting it all happen. He felt as if his whole body was shivering, but not actually moving. It didn't make sense, but he'd been here before so he didn't waste time trying to make sense of it. He waited while the vibration became almost unbearable. Then, just as he thought it was going to shake him to pieces, it stopped.

Suddenly he couldn't move a muscle. But instead of fighting, he willed himself to relax and waited for the bats. After a few minutes they arrived, flitting briefly near his head, then the paralysis vanished as abruptly as it had come, and the bats disappeared again.

Danny sat up, swung his feet onto the floor, and walked across the cell, leaving his body stretched out on the bunk.

It felt different from the way things worked with the psychotronic helmet. His second body felt a whole lot

lighter, for a start, and when he looked back at his physical body laid out on the bunk, it was positively spooky.
The thing lying there looked just like him, only dead.
He could see his chest rise and fall with his breathing,
but he *still* looked dead.

Danny turned away and floated through the wall of
his cell. If there were guards, it didn't matter: he could
see them, but they couldn't see him.

There was somebody in the corridor outside, but it
was definitely not a guard.

The gray-haired man had his back to Danny and
was dressed in robes and turban. If he was a guard, that
made him the oddest guard Danny had ever seen. But
he probably wasn't a guard, probably a visitor, or possibly an MI6 operative in disguise for an overseas mission,
although that didn't make much sense since the missions
here were all RV so far as Danny understood it, and—

The man walked through a wall, and Danny stood
there, mouth open, staring at the spot where he disappeared.

After a moment Danny's mind started to work again.
This guy was out of his body! He could project exactly
the way Danny could. But he wasn't a Shadow Project
operative—they only used teenagers. This was somebody
with special talents wandering around the Project complex, and you could bet he was up to no good. Danny's

mind raced. If he couldn't break out for any reason, or got caught and brought back like the last time, then maybe he could bargain information that somebody was spying on MI6, exactly the same way MI6 was spying on the bad guys. Danny dove for the wall and followed the stranger.

Danny emerged on the other side of the wall into a second corridor. The man had only to turn his head to catch sight of him, but Danny kept his distance and, as it happened, the man did not turn around. It obviously never occurred to him that he could be followed.

When they left the building, the stranger took to the air. Danny looked up after him with a sinking feeling. Carradine had told him about flying, but didn't explain how. What had he said? "Gravity can't hold you?" What sort of instruction was that? Danny tried to launch himself in the air and stayed firmly on the ground. He tried again, concentrating hard this time, and still nothing happened. Above him, his quarry was getting smaller in the sky. Danny imagined himself as a airplane. Nothing. The man was getting away. In a moment of mad panic, Danny tried jumping, and to his astonishment, took off like a bird. In a moment he was at the same altitude as the flying man, keeping his distance. The stranger, fortunately, still didn't look around.

In minutes they'd left the Project far behind.

Eventually they came to a run-down house along a lonely road. The man swooped in like a ghost, and Danny slid down directly after him . . .

. . . and stumbled on something that made him wish he'd never left his cell.

Opal, the Shadow Project

Gary Carradine pushed the laptop forward. "Is that the man who trapped you?"

The photograph had been taken at some sort of formal function, and most of the men in it looked like Saudis with a scattering of Westerners in well-cut suits. The Skull was in the Western group. Carradine tapped the image of the man beside him, an elderly Lusakistani with staring eyes.

"That's him," said Opal at once. She leaned forward to look more closely, but there was never any doubt. "Who is he?"

"Exactly who you said he was," Carradine told her. "Hazrat Farrakhan, the Skull's chief adviser. We've a file on him six inches thick. Sounds bizarre, but before he joined *Épée de la Colère* he was a marabout."

"What's a marabout?" Michael asked.

Carradine frowned. "It's a sort of holy hermit—we've

no exact equivalent term in the West. The Russians would call him a starets, like Rasputin. The thing is, he's a devotee of *ilmu al-hikmah*, Middle Eastern occultism."

Opal's eyes widened. "He told me he was a student of ilmu al-something. I thought it was a person."

Carradine shook his head slowly. "No, not a person."

"Are you thinking what I'm thinking?" George Hanover asked.

The phone on the desk began to ring, and Carradine picked it up. "Yes?" After a moment he said, "We'll be right up." He cradled the receiver. "Lab's finished work on the surveillance tapes." He pushed himself to his feet. "They're set up, waiting for us." As he headed for the door he paused. "Apparently we may have been a little hasty about young Danny."

The lab technicians had cleared out by the time they reached the viewing room. Roland clicked a remote control, and the screen on the wall lit up. "I'm afraid this may prove rather disturbing," he said, glancing at Opal.

Opal fumbled for a chair, only vaguely aware of Michael sliding into a seat beside her. On screen she recognized G.R. 1. The *G.R.* stood for generating room in Project jargon, and G.R. 1 was where the Project kept its collection of historical devices. At first the room looked exactly as she remembered it, everything neatly displayed on tables or in cabinets like a museum exhibit. Then her father fast-forwarded, and Fran Hitchin came in with Danny, both walking like Charlie Chaplin because the tape was speeded up. Opal felt as if she'd been punched in the stomach. She couldn't believe Fran was dead.

There was a slight picture jolt, then Danny looked around at normal speed and said, "What's this, then—the Project Museum?"

"Looks a bit like a museum, doesn't it?" Fran said. Then the picture speeded up again, the voices high and squeaky. Roland slowed it again at random. "—standing wave," Fran Hitchin said.

George Hanover frowned. "You don't think she decided on a standing-wave experiment, do you?"

"Might have," Carradine said, frowning. "See if you can find any more references, Roland."

"Do my best," Sir Roland murmured. He speeded the tape again, but in staccato bursts now, through a conversation between Danny and Fran. Only short phrases broke through ". . . threshold . . . vibration . . . wave . . ." Danny was seated in a chair in the middle of the room. Fran was by the control panel.

"Here we are, I think," Sir Roland said, and slowed the picture to its normal speed as Danny was saying: "I'll wave to you as I come out of my body." Opal noticed that he was gripping the edge of the chair, probably because he was nervous. But he didn't look as if he was about to attack Fran. He wasn't even looking in her direction.

"That would be nice," Fran said. "Are you all set?"

"Hit the juice!" Danny told her cheerfully.

The overhead camera showed Fran reaching out to the control console. The microphones picked up the low growl of an electronic organ. Beside Opal, Michael leaned forward. Danny looked around vaguely as if trying to discover where the sound was coming from. Then it stopped.

Opal gasped out loud. On the screen something struck Danny Lipman with such force that he was bowled over onto a display case. Broken glass sounded from the speakers. "Jesus!" George Hanover exclaimed.

"What the hell is that?" asked Carradine. He was leaning forward, his eyes locked on the screen.

Michael hissed something under his breath. Opal thought it might have been *demon*.

There was half a heartbeat as the creature stopped and Opal could see what it was: a gray, naked, apelike thing with vaguely feline features, clawed hands, and reddish, hate-filled eyes. It tilted its head briefly to one side as if listening, then launched itself across the room with superhuman speed. For a split second Opal thought it might attack Danny again, but it ignored him in favor of Fran. Its limbs actually blurred as it attacked her. Fran screamed and blood spurted across the room. Opal felt suddenly, violently sick and turned her head away.

"It wasn't Danny," said Mr. Hanover in surprise. "Danny didn't kill her."

Opal forced herself to turn back to the screen. Fran was clearly dead. She was lying on her back, eyes open, her clothes shredded and blood oozing from a dozen wounds. The thing was actually squatting on her chest. Then over an endless second, something almost unbelievably frightening happened. It turned its head to look toward the camera lens so that it seemed to stare directly into her eyes. Then it turned away and . . .

Opal felt her stomach convulse and retched violently. But now there was no question of looking away. She was paralyzed by the sheer horror of the scene.

"Hey!"

It took Opal a moment to realize where the exclamation came from. Then she saw that Danny had climbed to his feet and was moving unsteadily toward the beast. The thing climbed off Fran's bloody chest and loped with slow, horrid determination toward him. Even watching the security tape, Opal wanted to scream at Danny to run, but Danny didn't run. Instead, he threw himself toward it.

The sheer speed of the creature was terrifying. Danny

didn't lay a hand on it, and suddenly there was blood oozing from his thigh. He half fell backward, against a table. The thing crouched and leaped. Danny's hand came up and there was something in it, a knife or dagger of some sort. He stabbed the creature as it struck him.

The screen went blank.

"What was that?" Opal demanded. She looked desperately from one face to the other. Michael was still staring at the blank screen, his mouth open in shock.

"This is the point where the alarms went off," said Carradine.

"There seems to have been some sort of electrical discharge," Mr. Hanover volunteered. "It set off the alarms and burned out the security cameras."

"Yes, but what *happened*?" Opal demanded.

Her father shook his head. "You know as much as we do. Danny said this was what happened—something attacked them . . . some *thing* attacked them—but he was fairly incoherent and his whole story sounded utterly fantastic, so we didn't believe him."

Opal swung around to Carradine. "What *was* that?"

Carradine had the look of a man in shock. "I don't know. When my men reached G.R. 1, there was nothing there. Obviously. Otherwise we would have believed Danny."

Opal blinked. "Do you think it escaped?" She only just managed to suppress a shiver. If the creature was on the loose . . .

But Carradine was shaking his head. "There was nowhere it could go. You know the sort of security we have in the operations rooms. I think we have to assume Danny killed it."

"What did Danny say happened?"

"He said there was a wild animal and it disappeared in a flash of light. It didn't sound all that likely until now."

"Can we see where it came from?" Michael asked suddenly. The shock was gone from his face, and he was looking grave but in control. Opal admired his aplomb.

"Ah," said Opal's father. He picked up the remote again. When the screen flashed back into life, the tape had reverted to the scene where Fran and Danny entered the room. In a moment Sir Roland had forwarded it to the point just before the appearance of the creature. "At normal speed, the impression you get is that it jumps out of a cupboard. I'm going to slow it down."

He pressed the button and the picture slowed. "Hit the juice!" Danny said in a deep bass voice.

Opal's eyes were glued to the screen now that she knew where to look. Even so, the creature seemed to leap from a cupboard—a *closed* cupboard—albeit in slow motion. Then the picture reversed and the speed dropped again to frame-by-frame. There was no sound: the picture simply jerked forward one step at a time. Danny sat in his position looking vaguely uneasy. Fran's hand edged toward the controls. Opal watched the cupboard and nothing else.

Flip! It happened between one frame and the next. In the first, everything was as it should be. The cupboard was closed. Fran Hitchin's hand was on the switch. In the next, the creature was there, hanging in midair outside the cupboard. It hadn't jumped out of the cupboard at all. It seemed simply to have . . . *materialized* in the room.

There was a drawn-out moment of stunned silence; then Sir Roland said, "We'd better let young Danny go."

Carradine pulled a set of keys from his pocket and tossed them to Opal, who caught them reflexively. "Usual cell," he said.

"You want *me* to release him?"

Carradine said soberly, "He'll be less angry with you."

Michael put a hand on her shoulder. "I'll go with you."

She appreciated that, whatever his earlier behavior. The sooner Danny was released, the better. If everyone here was in shock from watching a replay of Fran's violent death, imagine what Danny must feel, having lived through it. And he'd been injured in the process. She stood up. "Yes, all right."

But when they reached the prison block, the door of Danny's cell stood open and the cell itself was empty.

[38]

Danny, Beaconsfield

There were eight men in the basement. Six were squatting at the tips of a large six-pointed star painted inside a circle on the floor. Outside the circle was a large painted triangle. The seventh was the man Danny had been following, except that he was now in two places at once. One of him sat cross-legged in the center of the circle, head bowed, looking as if he was fast asleep. His twin was gliding toward him from a closed doorway.

From his hiding place in the depths of a gloomy fireplace, Danny suddenly realized there weren't eight men at all, but seven. The moving figure was the man's energy body, now approaching its physical counterpart. He watched fascinated as the two gently blended and the man in the circle raised his head.

There was an immediate shout from the remaining six. One of them called out something in what sounded like Russian, or possibly Hungarian, but the man in the center snapped sharply, "In English! While in this country, we speak English always so that it may become our habit."

The man who had spoken looked suitably chastened. "Yes, Master Farrakhan."

But another called out at once, "How went the *ilmu khodam*, Master? Did our servant teach our enemies a lesson?"

Farrakhan's posture relaxed as he allowed himself a small, cold smile. "Most successful, Pieter. He carried one of the accursed British agents straight to hell!" There was a burst of general laughter. As it faded, the man Farrakhan added soberly, "But not the girl; and our servant was destroyed in the process."

His followers nodded solemnly one after another. They looked like hard, ruthless men, accustomed to loss.

"It is of small importance," Farrakhan was saying. "Now we know this nest of vipers can be penetrated. What we send next will kill the girl." He gave a thin smile.

What girl? Danny wondered. His mind was turning somersaults trying to make sense of what he was hearing. These goons had sent a servant to kill somebody. And Farrakhan—obviously their leader—went to find out if the murderer had succeeded. Went to the Project.

But there'd only been one killing at the Project—poor Fran—and nobody's servant was responsible for that one.

What girl? If it was somebody else in the Project, it had to be Opal. She was the only girl there at the moment. Danny frowned. Opal had been spying on the Skull—he'd overheard them talking about it. Maybe these guys were a Sword of Wrath terrorist cell. Danny watched to see which one was the servant who was supposed to sneak off and kill Opal, but nobody moved.

Farrakhan said, "Are you prepared for *ilmu khodam*? Are you prepared to call our vengeance?"

It had the sound of a ritual question and it certainly produced a ritual response. The others chanted, "We are prepared, Master." They looked excited, even frenzied, like members of a cult.

Farrakhan stood up and said, "Take your places as Officers of the Conjuration." Three of the others walked to the points of the painted triangle. There were religious symbols around the edge of that as well. Danny would have given a lot to have a closer look, but he wasn't going to risk it.

"Prepare!" Farrakhan ordered.

There was an immediate scurry of activity, and for a minute Danny couldn't figure what was going on. Two of the men sprinkled the circle thoroughly with water.

Others set lighted candles at the six points of the painted star. Someone else set up a burner and lit several blocks of charcoal with a tiny blowtorch from the pocket of his coat. He blew on the charcoal until it glowed and sparked, then sprinkled it liberally with a granular gray powder. Billows of heavily perfumed smoke began to roll across the room.

When the preparations were over, somebody switched off the electric light. With the only illumination now coming from the candles, the scene looked like a horror-movie set.

Farrakhan knelt down in his former position in the center of the circle, but turned so he was facing the painted triangle. The man he'd called Pieter, a burly middle-aged East European, took up a position directly behind him.

"Begin!" Farrakhan commanded.

The two other men inside the circle began to chant in low, sonorous voices. The sound reminded Danny of the organ note he'd heard when Fran switched on the infrasound. "Deliver thou the scribe Farrakhan, whose word is truth, from the Watchers, who would slay those in the following of Osiris."

"May the Watchers never gain mastery over me, and may I never fall under their knives!" responded Farrakhan in a high, melodious voice.

Danny watched, fascinated. The one word that jumped out at him was *Osiris.* Osiris was one of the gods in ancient Egypt. He knew that from his history lessons.

Farrakhan was still chanting. "For I know their names, and I know the being, Matchet, who is among them." He laid extra emphasis on the word *Matchet,* and as he spoke it, all six of his companions, inside and outside the circle, began a wordless howl that was the weirdest sound Danny had ever heard in his life.

As the howl died down, Farrakhan's body arched backward as he called out loudly, "It is I, the scribe Farrakhan, whose word is truth, who calls now on him who watcheth from the Lake of Fire, who feedeth on the living, who devoureth bodies, swalloweth hearts, and voideth filth, himself unseen."

The big man, Pieter, placed his hands on either side of Farrakhan's neck as if preparing to strangle him. His flat thumbs laced over each other at the base of Farrakhan's skull, where his head joined with his spine.

"His name is Devourer Everlasting," Farrakhan sang out. "He liveth in the Lake of Unt. Hail, Lord of Terror, who dost feed on the hearts of men! Come now and do the bidding of thy master and thy scribe!"

Pieter grunted as he pressed down with his thumbs so violently that Farrakhan's spine gave an audible crack.

Farrakhan himself convulsed, and his entire body jack-knifed forward so that he might have fallen on his face had Pieter not quickly grabbed him by the shoulders. Farrakhan's eyes were blank, his face contorted.

The man stationed at the apex of the triangle began to tremble violently. His eyes were unfocused too. Suddenly he clutched his throat, gasping and gurgling as if he was choking. Then, to Danny's disbelief, he slowly levitated till his feet floated a foot or eighteen inches above the cellar floor.

There was something happening inside the triangle. Out of nowhere, a roiling mist had begun to form. It swirled shapelessly for a moment, then began to take on form. A head appeared, then faded, only to appear again. The mist began to coalesce into the loose outlines of a body.

"Come, Devourer," Farrakhan shrieked. "Come to us now and feed!"

And suddenly there was something towering over the triangle. It was still indistinct, but it clawed like a beast at a window, as if trying to tear the very fabric of reality to gain access. The thing had horns and fangs and fiery eyes. It was immense, slab-muscled, and still growing. It made the creature that killed Fran look like a Chihuahua. If the thing that killed Fran was some sort of beast, this thing was the mother of all beasts. It continued to grow larger and more solid with every passing second.

Danny slid back through the wall, his heart pounding.

Opal, the Shadow Project

"Escaped again," Michael said. He stuck his head into the cell and looked around to make sure. But the cell was definitely empty.

"I don't see how he could have." Opal frowned.

Michael came back out into the corridor, biting his lip thoughtfully. "He did it before."

Opal shook her head. "Mr. Carradine let him escape last time. Daddy told me. But they took away his burglary gear after that, so I don't see how he could have. . . ."

They were walking together back along the corridor when a hand reached out of the empty guard station and dragged Opal inside. She gave a squawk of surprise and Michael spun fiercely before an urgent voice hissed, "You have to get out of here!"

"Danny!" Opal exclaimed. "Danny, they know you didn't—"

"We have to get you out of here," Danny said. "Michael can come too, if you like, only we need to get moving now before—"

"Hold on," Michael said. He reached out and firmly removed Danny's hand from Opal's shoulder.

"No, it's all right, Danny," Opal said. "You don't have to go anywhere. You're not in trouble anymore. They *know* you didn't kill Fran now. They know it was—" She stopped, suddenly at a loss. What *was* it that killed Fran Hitchin? "A wild animal of some sort," she finished lamely.

"That was no wild animal," Michael muttered.

"I'm not the one who's in trouble," Danny said. "You are. And Michael's right—it was no wild animal that killed Fran."

"Why is Opal in trouble?" Michael asked quickly.

Opal said, "Danny, I know it must have been a big shock for you when you were actually *there* and saw Fran die, and I realize—"

"Don't you ever *listen*?" Danny asked her. "I'm trying to save your life here."

"Danny—" Michael said warningly, but Opal cut in.

"How did you know about that?" she asked, staring at Danny.

"About what?"

"The Sword of Wrath plot to kill me. You weren't

there when Father told us."

"We don't have time for Twenty Questions," Danny said urgently. "I don't know if it's Sword of Wrath or the Hole-in-the-Wall Gang. I just know there's something coming after you that looks like it could eat us all for dinner."

But Opal was backing away from him. "The only people who knew about the plot were MI5 and Father, until Father told the rest of us. You *couldn't* have known about it—you were in jail."

"I don't *know* what killed Fran," Danny said. "And if you don't want—"

"You just turned up here one night, broke in, and we don't really know all that much about you, so how do we know you're not with Sword of Wrath yourself?"

"Because I'm not some bleeding nutcase who goes around blowing himself up, am I?!" Danny shouted. He got himself under control enough to drop his voice. "And you," he said, "are in big trouble if we don't get you out of this place *right now*. He said he planned to kill the girl and you're the only girl here, far as I know."

"Just a minute, Opal," Michael said, his expression worried.

"I'm not going anywhere," Opal told Danny, ignoring Michael. "Not with you. I suggest we go back and talk this over with Father and the others, and they can listen to what you have to say and decide what we should do."

"There's no time!"

"And please don't try to tell me I'm in any danger here. The Project has one of the tightest security ratings of any MI6 operation in the whole of Britain."

"So tight I managed to break in and Fran got her throat ripped out? Do me a favor, Opal. Get your head out of your backside and introduce it to the real world."

"I think we should listen to him," Michael said.

This time Opal didn't ignore him. "You think we should go with him?" she asked. "And not even take time to tell my father?"

"Yes, I do," said Michael firmly. "You can phone your father after we get out, but that is exactly what I believe we should do."

After a long, glaring moment, Opal said, "Why?"

Michael took a deep breath. "Because Fran was killed by a demon—"

"Fran was killed by a *what*?" Opal cut in.

"—and Danny is *sohanti*," Michael finished.

Opal glared at him for a beat then asked, "What's *sohanti*?"

"We don't have time for any more discussion!" Danny shouted.

But Michael reached out to grip Opal's arm. "Walk with me," he said firmly. "I want to tell you about my father."

[40]

Opal, the Shadow Project

"What happened to him?" Opal asked in a whisper after Michael finished his story.

"Konkon? He died. Actually he was dead when he hit the ground—the spasms seem to have been some sort of nerve reaction, like a frog's leg under electric current."

Opal found herself moving closer to Michael. She had a thousand questions she wanted answered and did not know where to begin. Eventually she said, "You think your father killed him?"

"I *know* my father killed him. Officially the cause of death was heart failure."

"Wait a minute," Opal said. "Couldn't it have been a virus that caused it? I mean, the whole business with your father was dramatic, but couldn't the death have been coincidence?"

"It happened again," Michael said quietly. He took Opal by the hand and started to hurry her along the corridor. The look of relief on Danny's face was palpable.

"Your father killed somebody else?" Opal exclaimed.

"No, the appearance of the little bats. I saw it myself one other time and my mother mentioned it just before he died, so I assume she saw it too. It seemed as though Father could, I don't know, *manifest* these creatures when he was in certain moods, notably very angry or upset or perhaps just tense or under threat. Sometimes the things did harm, sometimes they didn't. One of them eventually killed him."

"Are you serious?" Opal asked, wide-eyed.

"He kept a journal," Michael said matter-of-factly. "Most of it makes no mention of them at all, but toward the end he started to write about strange things happening when he was under stress and how they were getting out of control. I think he was aware of the insect things. He used an old Dogon word that translates as *pest* and clearly thought they were supernatural in origin. He was certain he had a great deal to fear from them. Then one day he died: heart failure. You may draw your own conclusions, but I believe he was *sohanti* and it got out of his control."

"These bats are what we call threshold guardians in the Project?"

Michael nodded.

"Have you told anyone?"

Michael shook his head. "Not until now. I've always been a bit—" He shrugged and looked away, as if embarrassed.

Opal stared at him but decided not to push it and asked, "You think Danny is *sohanti* too?"

"I'm certain of it," Michael said. "According to Mr. Carradine, he can see the little bat creatures when he's not out of the body. None of the rest of us can do that. I think he attracts them, the way my father did. Perhaps he will control them better than my father, use them to better effect. But whatever happens, those creatures make Danny *sohanti*—a natural magician, if you like. We must listen to him when he speaks of supernatural things."

Opal began to say something else, but stopped as Danny gripped her arm so hard that it was almost painful. "Shut up!" Danny said. He glanced at Michael. "You too. Not another word from either of you. Now it's your turn to listen. I don't know about this *sohanti* business, but I do know what I saw with my own eyes. There's a group of miserable scumbags in a cellar planning how to get you, Opal—*I saw them in my second body, same as you saw the Skull!* They're sending something, the way they sent the thing that killed Fran. Which means that if you want to chat with your boyfriend anymore, you have to do it outside this building, which is where they think it will find you. Michael, head for that door and *get her out of here*! I'm right behind you."

This time Michael didn't remove Danny's hand from Opal's arm. "I'll see if I can order a car," he said. "We can go to my uncle's place—Opal should be safe there until we decide what else to do."

Opal, the Shadow Project

"Busy day, miss," Harry Byrne remarked as they climbed into the back of the car. He looked just the tiniest bit annoyed.

"We're taking Michael home," Opal told him. She doubted he'd question the trip. Home in this instance was Blandings, Michael's uncle's place, a small manor house on about three hundred acres. It was a short drive.

Danny clambered into the car after them. "Nice wheels," he said. "Let's go." He glared at the back of Harry's head and repeated urgently, "Let's go." He reached out, squeezed Opal's hand reassuringly, then let it go.

Opal glanced at him in surprise. He was an odd sort of boy and she was growing rather fond of him, but she wasn't sure what his gesture meant. Considering the circumstances, it probably didn't mean very much.

She pushed the thought aside. She desperately wanted to know more about what he'd seen, but there was no question of talking in front of Harry. Everything would have to wait until they reached Blandings.

They huddled together in the back of the car, Opal between the two boys, as Harry pulled away. Opal's mind was racing as she tried to take in what was happening. She wanted to talk a lot more about *sohanti*, about the little bat creatures, about Danny's astonishing story, about the thing that killed Fran, but, incredibly, what she actually heard herself asking was, "What's your first language?"

"Cockney," Danny said, and grinned.

Despite everything, Opal cracked a smile. "No, yours, Michael."

"French. Mali used to be a French colony, and French is still the lingua franca."

They were almost at their destination before she realized what a clever pun he'd made.

It was growing dark by the time they reached Blandings. Opal noticed at once that the grounds were in better condition than the house, as if Michael's uncle liked gardening but couldn't care less if his home was falling down.

As they climbed from the car, Opal said, "You can go back to the Project now, Harry. We're staying overnight." Assuming Michael's uncle had no objection. It suddenly occurred to her that they were taking a lot for granted. Including the fact that Harry wouldn't start to ask awkward questions.

But all he said was, "Yes, miss," and then he drove off at once, leaving them standing in the courtyard.

"I have a key to the side door," Michael said, which suited her just fine, since it meant they could get in without disturbing his uncle. She could call her father, tell him what had happened, then plan what to do.

They walked together a little awkwardly, not saying anything, their steps crunching softly on the gravel. Since they'd left the Project, Danny had been very quiet—apart from his Cockney joke, he hadn't said a single word in the car, but she noticed that he was keeping close to her: very close. Michael hadn't said much either and the silence made her nervous, but somehow she did not have the courage to break it.

The side door was up a short flight of stone steps. They reached the top, and Opal waited with Danny in the shadow of the porch while Michael fished through his pockets for the key. He found it eventually, pushed it into the lock, then paused and looked at Opal. "I think perhaps I should tell you . . . ," he began uneasily, then stopped.

"Tell me what?" Opal asked.

He stared at her for a moment, then said, "Nothing," and turned the key.

He led them through a cluttered back hall and down a short corridor, then pushed open a door to a living room lit only by the glow of a dying log fire. When he clicked the light switch beside the door, nothing happened. "Damn!" he muttered, "Sorry." He slipped ahead of her into the room to fiddle with a standard lamp beside the fireplace. It threw a pool of light across the hearthrug, leaving the remainder of the room in gloom. "Sorry," he said again. "Uncle Hector . . ." He shrugged helplessly. "Impossible." As they followed him in, he added, "Can I get you tea? Or a Coca-Cola? Or something?" He sounded faintly desperate.

It was a pleasantly old-fashioned room with book-cases and Asiatic hunting trophies on the walls. There were oriental rugs on the floor, and one glass cabinet seemed to be full of African masks. "No thanks," Opal said. She wondered what was making Michael so nervous. The way he was acting went far beyond concern for her safety.

"Not for me either, thanks," Danny echoed. By contrast with Michael, he seemed far more relaxed now that they'd left the Project. He was openly curious about the house, wandering around and examining ornaments before he settled himself in front of a bookcase in a gloomy corner. He pulled down a book and began to flick through it.

Michael said, "Opal, actually, both of you . . ." He was sounding even more uneasy than he had at the side door. "There's something—"

"Oh, sorry," a voice interrupted. "Didn't realize we were entertaining."

Opal turned. A tweedy man with the most astonishing ginger muttonchop whiskers bustled in. "By God, a young woman as well!" he exclaimed. "About time you bagged one."

Michael's unease looked as if it might turn to panic. "This is my uncle," he said. "Colonel Hector Hamilton-Oakes. Retired. Uncle, this is Opal Harrington."

A large, warm hand reached out to shake her own. "Not Roland's daughter? Last time I saw you, you were yea high—" He held his free hand the height of a retriever from the floor. "Sitting on a horse. Bossy little thing as well. Told me to hold the reins as if I was a bloody groom. She still bossy, Michael? Well, you've changed a bit since then, that's for sure. Got a lot prettier. No wonder Michael fancies you."

"Uncle!" Michael interjected helplessly.

Uncle Hector smiled at her. "My renegade nephew offered you anything to drink? Should be old enough for gin now, I expect. Or do you prefer whiskey? Got quite a decent Scotch the other day if I haven't finished it." He moved away toward a drinks table with several bottles and a cut-glass tantalus.

"No thank you, sir," said Opal quickly.

Michael began, "Uncle, Opal and I were—"

"Mind if I do?" Uncle Hector was already reaching for an empty glass. "'Fraid I'm a martyr to gin. Habit I picked up in Africa. Tonic helps with the malaria." He poured himself an enormous gin and added a tiny splash of malaria medication. "Sure you won't? Neither of you?" He raised his glass in salute and spotted Danny in the shadows. "Good God, who are you?"

Michael said quickly, "This is Danny Lipman, Uncle."

The glass froze in midair. "Lipman? The young—?"

"Danny Lipman," Michael repeated firmly. He seemed to be making an effort to hold his uncle's eye.

"Well, cheers," Hector said after a moment. He finished a third of the glass in a single swallow and said to Opal, "It's Hector, by the way. Can't have pretty women calling me *sir*. Makes me feel like a Chelsea pensioner."

"Uncle Hector," Michael tried again, "Opal and Danny and I were—"

"Yes, I want to hear all about that. And your father, Opal—talk to him by phone often enough, but haven't seen him face-to-face in years. Sit down. Chair to the left of the fireplace is fairly comfortable. Don't touch the other one: it's got a loose spring that goes up your backside. Michael can sit there—he's used to it, and besides, it might loosen him up a bit. Danny, pull something over and sit in the light, where I can keep an eye on you; make sure you don't steal the family silver." He turned back to Opal. "You and I can have a cozy little chat. Father well, is he?"

It was hard not to like Uncle Hector, although she'd no memory at all of meeting him as a child, and her father had never spoken of him either. He was not at all what she'd expected as Michael's uncle. For one thing, he was white. "My father is very well indeed, thank you," Opal said politely, although she still couldn't quite bring herself to call him Hector.

"Delighted to hear it. Knew your mother too, before she died. She and I were a bit of an item at one time— bet you never knew that. Before she met Roland, of course. Before I married poor Djeneba, come to that."

"My mother's sister," Michael murmured, which explained things.

"Actually—" Opal said.

"Actually," Michael echoed, much more firmly this time, "Opal and Danny and I have things to discuss, Uncle."

"Don't let me stop you," Uncle Hector said as he

pulled up a chair for himself, maneuvering it close to Danny's. "Why's it so gloomy in here, by the way? Why have you only put one light on?"

"Because the others won't work," Michael said a little sourly. "I told you to get new bulbs last week. And the rest of us have things to discuss *in private*."

Something very strange happened. Sitting there on the edge of the pool of lamplight, Uncle Hector seemed to change. It was as if he was suddenly serious and more imposing. "No you don't," he said firmly.

Opal looked from Uncle Hector to Michael and back again. She felt vaguely as if she should help Michael out here, although she didn't quite know how. She was still considering what to say when her cell phone rang. Almost immediately, Michael's rang as well. They flipped them open together.

"It's the Project," Michael murmured.

"So's mine," Opal said. The momentary relief had been replaced by sudden tension. She still hadn't rung her father, and with her luck, this would be him now.

"Mr. Hanover?" Michael was saying into his phone. Then after a moment, "Yes. Yes, she is."

"Opal?" It *was* her father. Sounding serious. "Where in the name of heaven have you taken yourself off to?"

"It's all right—I'm with Michael. At his uncle's. His uncle is with us," she added hurriedly, in case he got the wrong idea. "I was just about to ring you, Father."

"How did you get there?" Not "Why?" or "What are you doing?" Somehow "How did you get there?" was typical of her father. She'd never really understood how his mind worked.

Opal said a little sheepishly, "Harry drove us." Strictly speaking, they weren't supposed to commandeer cars without permission, although Opal often did it.

But all he said was, "Is Harry still there?"

"No, I sent him back."

"And how long are you proposing to stay with Michael's uncle?"

This was the tricky bit. "Overnight . . . ," began Opal hesitantly. Her father might so easily misunderstand, but she didn't want to start talking in front of Uncle Hector, partly because of security, partly because she didn't know exactly what was going on, but mainly because no one had asked Uncle Hector if they *could* stay the night. It was so ill-mannered to take things for granted.

Michael closed his phone. He looked oddly distracted for a moment, then glanced at his uncle. Hector stood up and stepped to Opal's side. "Let me speak to him."

Opal looked at the outstretched hand for a moment, then handed him the phone without a word. Hector said, "Roland? It's Hector. They're all fine. Yes, young Lipman's here as well." He paused for what seemed an age, his face impassive, then said, "My responsibility." He closed the phone and handed it back, then turned to glare at Michael.

"It's started, hasn't it?" said Uncle Hector.

[42]

Danny, Blandings

"What's started?" Danny asked suspiciously. There was something in Hector's tone that made him nervous.

Michael turned to his uncle, "Yes, I think so."

"What's started?" Danny asked again.

"What are you two talking about?" Opal asked.

But oddly enough, it was Danny to whom Uncle Hector turned. "Has Michael told you you're a special boy?"

"What?" Danny asked blankly.

Opal said to Michael, "I didn't realize you'd discussed Danny with your uncle."

"Uncle Hector knows all about the Project," Michael said quietly. "And Fran's death."

You could see the conflict on Opal's face. Danny was pretty sure she was sweet on Michael—lot of signs pointing in that direction, no signs pointing in his own—but now she was mad at him as well, which might be good news. Besides, Michael deserved her anger; no way he should have been chatting about the Project to anyone outside.

Hector said, "I've spoken with your father." He shook his head, frowning. "The trouble is that it's out of his control."

"Somebody going to tell me what we're talking about?" Danny asked, his voice rising.

"Yes, I think that might be quite a good idea." Opal's tone was tense. She looked from Hector to Michael and back again.

Hector glanced at Michael too, then took a deep breath. "I'm afraid the majority of your Project members have no idea what they're really dealing with." He looked directly at Opal. "Your father's one of us, but there's only a limited amount he can do."

"One of who?" Danny asked.

"The thing is," Hector said, ignoring him, "some people won't believe in the supernatural even when it bites them in the backside. Try to tell them and you're labeled a nut. Doesn't matter who you are—even somebody as well connected as your father, Opal."

"I think you'd better explain properly," Opal told him coolly. Danny liked that. She couldn't be much older than he was, but she could hold her own with anybody.

Hector said, "Roland may be nominal head of the operation, but that's just because it's on British soil. It's actually a CIA project, so the real power is Carradine, however much he keeps a low profile. Since he's CIA, he follows the current party line: Sword of Wrath's the big enemy, War on Terror, all that rot. Unfortunately for the rest of us, Sword of Wrath's not the enemy."

"Could have fooled me," Danny said.

Hector smiled slightly. "Don't get me wrong, I wouldn't want to meet the Skull's men in the dark. But Sword of Wrath's a symptom, not the cause."

They were going to get a lecture on foreign policy. Danny could smell it coming. Opal probably thought so too, because she still sounded cool when she asked, "What's the cause then, Colonel Hamilton-Oakes?"

"War in heaven," Uncle Hector told them.

There was a long, embarrassed pause during which Danny did his level best to suppress a grin.

Opal didn't seem impressed either. "War in heaven?" she echoed as if she couldn't quite believe she'd heard correctly.

"My grandfather was cavalry in the First World War," Hector said soberly. "My father was a captain in the Second. Why do you imagine those wars were fought?"

Opal clearly started to lose patience because she said, "Actually we have a problem at the Project—"

Surprisingly, it was Michael who cut her short. "It's all right, Opal; Uncle Hector knows exactly what's happening at the Project. If you listen to what he has to say, it may prove helpful."

Hector took a very small sip of his gin. "They'll tell you it was politics, but politics didn't come into the First World War. Read your history books. Nobody wanted it, but that didn't stop it from happening. It's a bit easier to find superficial reasons for the Second World War—Munich Agreement, appeasement, invasion of Poland—but they don't really stack up either. Neither does the Holocaust. The German people were the most civilized in Europe and by no means the most anti-Semitic. How on earth did the Nazis persuade them to behave the way they did?" He shifted in his seat. "Neither of these wars was about what it seemed to be about. They were both about Good versus Evil, Light versus Darkness. They were about the movements of cosmic currents. Hitler was an occultist. So was the Kaiser. They both allowed themselves to become channels for some particularly dark powers. In effect there weren't two world wars in the twentieth century. There was one great spiritual conflict that manifested on Earth in 1914 and again in 1939. But it didn't stop in 1945. It manifested again in the Korean War and the Vietnam War and the Pol Pot regime in Cambodia and ethnic cleansing in the Balkans and two Gulf Wars and God knows how many civil wars in Africa." His eyes flickered back and forth between Opal and Danny as if willing them to believe him. "It's still going on today."

"Good versus Evil?" Danny said. "Right." He glanced over at Opal. "One way of looking at it."

Hector gave a thin smile. "This isn't about viewpoint, Danny. Sometimes the hidden powers manifest of their own accord. It's as if they take over people and involve them without their even knowing it. But sometimes particularly evil people tap into the powers quite deliberately to further their own ends. It may have happened with the Kaiser. It certainly happened with Hitler." He glanced from face to face, then went on soberly, "It's happening again now with the Skull—or at least with his chief adviser, Farrakhan."

The name brought Danny up short. "You know about Farrakhan, then?"

Hector said, "The Skull's political, pragmatic, but Farrakhan's no politician, not by a long shot. Before they teamed up, Farrakhan was a marabout, a sort of hermit, living in the mountains. He claims to have spent time studying *ilmu al-hikmah*—Middle Eastern occultism. We believe he specializes in *ilmu khodam,* the art of summoning spirit servants."

Out of the corner of his eye Danny saw Opal lean

forward suddenly in her chair. There was an image in his head of the thing that had killed Fran, another of the towering shape he'd seen in the cellar. Was that what Hector meant by a spirit servant?

But Hector was still talking. "Farrakhan's a natural psychic as well as an occultist. He knows about things like astral projection—they probably call it by some trendy initials in the Project, do they, Michael?"

Michael nodded. "RV for remote viewing. Or OOBE."

"Out-of-body experience," Hector sniffed. "But whatever you like to call it, Farrakhan's one of those rare individuals who can see your second body while they're still in the physical. He found out that the Americans were using astral projection in their intelligence work— probably spotted an agent in his second body. We believe he brought that knowledge to the Skull, managed to convince him it was more than mystic flimflam, and used it to get his current position of power in *Épée de la Colère*. I'm fairly sure Opal was the first agent they actually captured. They must have been furious when she escaped."

"These spirit servants," Danny said. "Do they have teeth and claws?"

Hector stared at him. "Some of them."

Opal said, "How do you know all this?"

"The problem," Uncle Hector said, "is that the CIA

and even our own intelligence services have begun to take an interest in areas that don't properly concern them. Astral projection is a very ancient spiritual practice—it can be used to access different levels of reality. But the CIA never looked beyond using it for spying. They don't believe there *is* anything beyond that. They operate with a very dangerous mix of ignorance and arrogance. They think because they've developed some electrical technologies, they know all there is to know. They're not aware of the hidden realities."

Michael said, apparently in answer to Opal's question, "Uncle Hector is a member of the Priory of Mons."

"What's the Priory of Mons?" Danny asked.

"An organization that has studied spiritual technologies since the early Middle Ages," Hector told him.

"He means a secret order of magicians," Michael said. "Like you, Danny, Uncle Hector is *sohanti*."

Danny, Blandings

They moved into the library because Uncle Hector wanted to consult a book. Danny stood wondering if his head was going to explode. Problem was, he didn't know what he wanted to focus on first. He wanted to find out more about the Priory of Mons. He wanted to talk to the other two—still not sure about Hector yet—about Farrakhan and that creature in his triangle. Everything was overwhelming. But at least Opal was safe here: that was the main thing.

Unless Farrakhan tracked her down.

A scary picture popped into Danny's mind, clear as a Spielberg movie. There was Farrakhan in his second body, strolling through the Project walls and halls. There was Opal's father, Sir Roland, hanging up the phone. There was George Hanover beside him, hanging up *his* phone. "It's all right—she's with Uncle Hector," says Sir Roland. "Yes," says George, "you mean Michael's uncle

Hector Hamilton-Oakes, who lives at Blandings, just twenty minutes south of here, and Michael's with her and so's young Danny—no worries there, then." Danny could see Farrakhan pricking up his ears.

Maybe it was time to bring up current problems. Danny said loudly, "Farrakhan sent the thing that killed Fran. I don't know what it was, but he's sending something worse after Opal. A lot worse. I saw him call it up in some sort of black magic ceremony while I was out of my body. Called it a Devourer." Well, there it was. If they wanted to phone the men in white coats, now was the time to do it.

He looked at Opal, who was staring back at him with open disbelief on her face. "Did you say 'Devourer'? The old woman in the clinic warned me about a Devourer!"

Danny frowned, wondering what she was talking about, as Hector, who had his nose buried in a leather-bound book, said, "I know."

It irritated Danny. "No you don't," he said sharply. "I'm the one who knows. Rest of you wouldn't *believe* what I saw, trust me."

Hector glanced up and said mildly, "It's a war, Danny. It's always been a war. Between people like us and people like them. The bit you see is just a puppet show—the Skull and his suicide bombers, the politicians and their armies. It's Farrakhan and his ilk who

237

pull the strings—or rather the forces behind them. 'For we wrestle not against flesh and blood, but against principalities, against powers, against the rulers of the darkness of this world, against spiritual wickedness in high places.' Read your Bible. Ephesians six, verse twelve. Never truer words spoken." He looked down again, as if embarrassed, then added, "We've known about Farrakhan for some time—and his spirit servants. The techniques he uses are old Egyptian. The Egyptians were the most knowledgeable magicians of the ancient world. Farrakhan has studied their methods. Old magic, very dark. Once Michael told me Opal had actually seen him, we knew it would only be a matter of time before he mounted an attack on the Project."

"We?" Danny asked. "You and Michael?"

"The Priory," Michael said. "Uncle Hector means the Priory."

"I think you'd better tell us more about this Priory," Opal said.

She was looking at Michael, but it was Hector who answered. "I suppose since you're under threat from the Powers of Darkness, you deserve to know you've got some friends among the Powers of Light." He took a deep breath.

"Uncle—" Michael interrupted warningly.

"It's all right, Michael," Hector said. "They're Project

operatives. They know how to keep a secret. Besides, if they did tell anybody, who would believe them?" He grinned, then turned back to Opal. "I'm afraid it's rather a complicated story. Have you ever heard of the *Fama Fraternitatis*?"

Opal shook her head. "No."

"It was a document published in Germany in 1614. Caused a sensation at the time because nobody knew who wrote it. It told the story of a man named Father C.R.—it stands for Christian Rosenkreutz—who went on a pilgrimage to Jerusalem and was subsequently instructed by the sages of the East in the most ancient esoteric wisdom. He studied alchemy, physics, mathematics, magic, and the Kabbalah. When he returned to Germany, he and some others established a secret Christian fraternity, the Fraternity of the Rose Cross. Members—or brothers, as they called themselves—were instructed to use their knowledge to heal the sick free of charge, wear no special clothing or insignia, keep their membership in the Order a strict secret, and meet together once a year in what the document called the House of the Holy Spirit."

Opal frowned. "Are you saying that was the origin of this Priory you belong to?"

"Not quite," Hector said. "The real Priory of Mons dates back about five hundred years earlier. It was secretly established by the Knights Templar based on some unbelievably ancient scrolls they discovered in the Ark of the Covenant."

This is getting batty, Danny thought, *even for Uncle Hector.* He opened his mouth to try to bring the conversation back to the problems at hand, but Opal beat him to it. "The Ark of the Covenant that's mentioned in the Bible?" she asked. "The thing God used to communicate with Moses?"

Hector nodded. "The holiest relic in the whole of the Old Testament—and an artifact of great power. The Israelites used it to slaughter their enemies when they were wandering in the wilderness. It disappeared when Jerusalem fell to the Babylonians in 586 BC, but the Templars found it hidden in a cave under the Temple Mount. It contained scrolls dating back to a lost prehistoric civilization with information on spiritual techniques of amazing efficacy in the service of the Light. The Templars used them to found the Priory of Mons."

Intrigued despite himself, Danny said, "Where does the Fama Whatsit come in?"

"It was important that the Priory remain a secret," Hector said. "Unlike the Powers of Darkness, which often work through politicians and popes and other influential people, the Powers of Light are pledged not to interfere with humanity's free will, so any work they do is subtle. And the Priory *did* remain a secret for five hundred years. But then one of our members went over to the Dark Side and threatened to expose its existence. So the Priory issued the *Fama Fraternitatis* to divert public attention. There was just enough truth in it to keep scholars busy—Christian Rosenkreutz really existed, for example: he was one of our late medieval friars—but subtly slanted to send them looking in the wrong direction. So the *Fama Fraternitatis* sparked off a whole occult Rosicrucian movement, and the real Priory managed to stay hidden. When our Dark Brother told his story, everyone assumed it was a variation on the Rosicrucian theme and ignored it."

"And my *father* is a member of this Priory?" Opal asked incredulously.

"An Outer Member," Hector said. "Which means he is sympathetic toward our ideals and is permitted to attend certain meetings, but he plays no part in policy decisions. What he does do, of course, is keep us informed on matters of interest—his position with MI6 is ideal for that."

"Look," Danny said, "the history lesson is all very interesting, but can we get back to what's happening today? That old boy Farrakhan is sending something very scary after Opal. Do you think she'll be okay here?"

It was his biggest worry, and he was beginning to think Uncle Hector might actually know the answer.

But Uncle Hector said soberly, "Nobody's safe anywhere. Fran was only a trial run. But even Opal is just the beginning. Farrakhan will aim to wipe out the entire Project, now that he's discovered it. Farrakhan will hunt down Opal; and he'll find her eventually, make no mistake about that. But before he does, he will kill everyone else associated with the Project—everyone."

"My father's at the Project," Opal said.

Hector added, "Unless somebody stops him."

There was a long silence in the room; then Opal said, "How do we do that?"

"I'm not sure *we* do," Uncle Hector said. "I think it may be up to Danny."

"Hey, wait a minute—" Danny said.

"You're *sohanti*, Danny," Michael told him sharply, as if that explained something.

Danny rounded on him. "Listen, I never even *heard* about *sohanti* until you told Opal about your old man. But even if I am, it just means I attract bugs. Farrakhan is into *devils*."

"Is it really a devil?" Opal asked, looking at Hector.

"Near enough, I'm afraid. Not exactly Satan and his minions—that's Judeo-Christian mythology—but the old Egyptians had some very nasty lines of communication into the dark side." He turned another page of the book. "Ah!" With the book still open, he swung it around and pushed it toward Danny. "Is that what you saw?"

The illustration was an old black-and-white woodcut, crudely done, of something ripping the arm off a naked man as casually as a child might pull the wing off a fly. Badly drawn or not, Danny had no doubt what he was looking at. "That's it."

Opal and Michael leaned forward to look. Opal said tightly, "What is it?"

"It's called a *matchet*," Hector said. "A creature of Isfet, who was the Egyptian god of darkness and chaos, the great opponent of the light. *Matchets* were believed to live in a lake of fire and feed on human hearts. The Egyptians used to call them the Everlasting Devourers and the Lords of Terror. Nasty buggers. Very difficult to control—even black magicians shy away from them. Farrakhan must have used the Spear of Destiny. He took a dreadful risk."

"What's the Spear of Destiny?" Danny asked.

"It's supposed to be the spear that pierced Christ's side while he was hanging on the cross," Hector said. "Also known as the Spear of Longinus after the Roman centurion who used it, or the Holy Lance. One of the reasons Hitler annexed Austria in 1938 was to steal it—the lance was in the Imperial Treasury of the Hofburg Palace at the time. He believed he could use it to channel spiritual power to aid him in his conquest of Europe."

"Thought he lost the war," Danny said. "Leastways that's what my old Nan always told me."

"Fortunately for us all, he had no idea how to use the lance. Unfortunately, Farrakhan does."

"Hold on a minute," Danny said. "Let me get this clear. You're saying Farrakhan now has the spear that Hitler stole from Austria? How did he get it?"

"It went back to Austria after the war. It's now in the *Kunsthistorisches Museum* in Vienna. Or at least it was. At the moment it's on loan to a museum in Egypt. That's how we knew Farrakhan must be up to something on the inner levels. Everything that exists on the physical has a mirror image on the astral plane, which is a whole different reality. The spear's physical location is affected by what's happening to its astral counterpart. The fact that it's moved as far away as Egypt shows there are major problems and gave us a clue to what was happening. Hitler's mistake was believing he needed the physical spear. Farrakhan knows better. He has been manipulating the astral lance that stands behind the physical spear." Hector closed the book and peered again at Danny. "When did you see Farrakhan call up this thing?"

"About . . ." Danny frowned and calculated. "An hour ago. Maybe more."

"Well, that's a bit of good news, anyway," Hector said. "It will be several hours before it manifests completely in our reality. Which gives *us* time to get our ducks in a row."

It occurred to Danny the old boy was enjoying this.

"What we need to do," said Hector, "is tackle the source of the problem. No use attacking the physical manifestation of the Devourer—you can't kill a thing like that. We need to capture the Spear of Destiny."

"You're sending us across to Austria? Oh, no, I forgot—you're sending us to Egypt."

"Come on, Danny, stop pretending you're the village idiot. I told you it's not the physical lance we need—what we need is its astral counterpart."

The *village idiot* crack irritated Danny hugely. Hector talked a lot, but he wasn't really saying anything. He kept dropping in terms that meant nothing to anybody outside this crackpot Priory he belonged to. But Danny kept his cool. "And where do we find the astral counterpart of something?"

"On the astral plane," said Uncle Hector, as if that should be obvious.

Danny still managed to hold his temper, although he did sigh loudly. "What's the astral plane?"

Hector smiled slightly. "It's another level of reality, much like the one you're used to. The astral plane reflects our world, so some of our structures appear there the way they do here. Where I'm sending you will look similar to Ancient Egypt, since that's where Farrakhan is using the astral lance."

"Hold on," Danny said. "You're going to have to do better than that. There's another reality that's just like ours, and things that are happening in our reality are also happening in *that* one?"

"More or less," Hector said. "The spear that exists in the astral plane isn't the same spear that exists in the Austrian museum collection—it's a *reflection* of that spear. And the two are linked, so what happens to one affects the other. If we're to beat Farrakhan at his own game, we need to take control of the astral spear. Which means you have to take a little trip."

"Let's get this clear," Danny said. "You want me to take a trip to this different reality? To the astral plane?"

"Not just you, Danny. One of the things we've learned about the astral plane in the Priory is the rule of three. Certain operations there require at least three people to complete successfully. I'm hoping Opal and Michael will agree to go with you."

Opal simply stared at him, but Michael said, "You can count us in, Uncle Hector."

Always gung-ho, Danny thought. "Why us?" he asked.

Hector said, "Because only those who can leave their bodies are able to reach the astral plane."

"Will it be dangerous?"

"It will be for Farrakhan," Hector said grimly. "Once you get the spear, his Devourer will turn against him. I expect that will be the last our world will hear of him. With luck it might even get the Skull too. But stopping the world's leading terrorist has to be worth a bit of risk, right?"

"I think if you're asking us to undertake this," Opal said soberly, "the least you can do is tell us what the risk is to us." Clearly she was as suspicious as Danny that Hector seemed to be avoiding the question, for she asked bluntly, "Could we die trying to get this spear?"

Hector shook his head. "You leave your bodies behind, exactly as you do on a mission for the Shadow Project. I'll make sure to keep them safe and sound." He tugged at his jacket. "Now, if you've no more questions, we need to get moving."

Opal continued to stare at him. It was the same thing she'd been taught in Project training: you leave your body behind, so nothing can harm you. Everybody had subscribed to that theory until Farrakhan trapped her in a cage. But there was no point in arguing with Hector now. There was a job to be done, even if it was dangerous. "So how do we get to this different reality?" she asked him. "How do we reach the astral plane?"

"Let me make a phone call, then I'll show you," Hector said.

[44]

Opal, Blandings

Opal wasn't sure she liked this: they were going down steps to a cellar. She still wasn't completely comfortable with Michael's uncle, even if he did know her father. And what was the phone conversation with her father all about? All the talk about black magic had made her feel uneasy and out of her depth.

They entered a candlelit room that appeared square, but when you looked at it one way, it was round, then you turned your head and it was square again. The optical illusion must have had something to do with the circular zodiac painted on the ceiling—looking up was like looking into the night sky.

In the center of the room was what had to be an altar, but nothing like Opal had ever seen in church. It looked as if it had been made by stacking two cubes on top of one other, then draping them in black silk embroidered with mystic symbols. In the center of the altar was a large quartz crystal, mounted on a wooden base so it pointed up toward the ceiling. Around it, set near the edges of the altar, were a yellow dagger, a stubby red rod, a blue chalice cup, and a peculiar wooden disc divided into four differently shaped segments.

There were four chairs in the room, one set against each of the walls, facing inward to the altar. On the wall above each chair was a painted symbol underneath an inlaid mirror. Opal's eyes flicked from symbol to symbol: a yellow square, a blue circle, a silver crescent, and a red triangle.

"What is this place?" she asked. Everything about the room screamed *occult* and *witchcraft* and *black magic.* She couldn't imagine that Michael would allow his uncle to put her in the way of unnecessary danger—and if Hector was telling the truth, her father approved—but it still looked like something you might read about in the tabloid press.

"Used to be a private chapel," Uncle Hector remarked. "The Priory helped me convert it."

Into what? Opal wondered.

Danny said, "Nifty bit of crystal, Colonel. Must be worth a lot."

Hector said, "It's a power source. Something the Priory learned from the scrolls. Apparently the lost civilization used crystals the way we use electronics."

"What's it powering here, then?" Danny asked.

Hector said, "Any of you ever watch *Star Trek*?"

They looked at him blankly.

"Star Trek," Hector repeated. "Television series. If you've watched it, you can think of this as the transporter room. Only instead of beaming you up to a spaceship, it will send you into another reality."

Opal looked around. After a moment she said, "How?"

"It's simple enough," Hector told her. "You can't visit the astral plane while you're in your physical body any more than you could walk into somebody's dream. But when you're out of body, there are astral doorways you can use."

Opal frowned. "I've never seen an astral doorway when I've been out of my body." Except, she suddenly realized, she wouldn't know what an astral doorway looked like if it fell on her.

"I don't suppose you have," said Uncle Hector. "How to activate the doorways is a very well-kept secret, but fortunately one known to the Priory—it was among the spiritual techniques preserved in the Ark of the Covenant. It's a question of turning you in a particular direction while you're out of body. The direction doesn't exist in our physical reality, so you wouldn't normally know where to look for it. What the crystal does is turn your energy body in the right direction once you've projected. In effect, it opens an astral doorway. Instead of wandering round the physical world like a ghost, you enter the astral plane."

"You haven't told us what we're supposed to do when we get there," Danny pointed out.

"Hunt the spear," said Hector promptly. "I'll make sure you're sent to the right area—I can do that by calculating the coordinates of the physical spear. But the location won't be precise. The astral plane isn't an exact mirror of our reality, and you're going to find that a lot of things work quite differently there. So I'm afraid your first job will be to find out exactly where Farrakhan is keeping the astral spear."

"And do what?" Danny asked. "Bring it back here?"

Hector smiled thinly. "Wrong reality. But once you have the spear, Farrakhan's power over the Devourer will be broken. So all you have to do is put it somewhere safe—by which I mean somewhere he can't get it."

Michael said, "Don't you think we should get started, Uncle Hector?"

"Okay," Danny said. "What do we do?"

Hector looked relieved. "I'd like each of you to take a seat. Danny, I want you to sit in the south, under the red triangle. Opal, you go to the west—" He pointed. "Michael, you're in the north, as usual, over there with the yellow square." He waited while they sat down, then said, "What I want you each to do is look in the mirror on the wall directly opposite. The chairs are placed so all you'll see there is a reflection of the symbol above your place. They're elemental symbols—earth, air, fire, and water. By balancing them correctly, we can open your astral doorway."

"I thought we were supposed to go out-of-body," Opal said. The symbol reflected in the mirror opposite her was a silver crescent.

"Yes, you are," Hector told her.

"You don't have any helmets," Opal said.

For a moment Hector looked blank. Then he said, "Oh, you mean the sort of gear they use at the Project? We've gone a very different road in the Priory. Our emphasis has been on influencing the human mind in much more subtle ways. We would never dream of simply ripping the second body out of the physical, as happens in the Shadow Project. The ancients knew there were far more natural methods available, and we have inherited their wisdom. Just concentrate on the mirror symbol until it changes color. Once it does that, it'll pull you out of your body. Then you just walk through it. That's all you have to do—no electronics at all." He took a deep audible breath. "Any questions?"

Danny said. "Are you coming with us?"

"Can't, I'm afraid," Hector said. "I'm no teenager anymore. But even when I was, nothing seemed to shift me out of my body."

"So who's going to sit in the fourth chair?" Danny asked accusingly. "You said there had to be a balance of four elements for this thing to work."

"That would be me," said a new voice from the door.

Opal turned to find they'd been joined by an elderly woman carrying a handbag.

"Cripes, Nan," Danny gasped. "What are you doing here?"

[45]

Dorothy, Blandings

*H*ector *is looking good,* Dorothy thought. *Always was a fine figure of a man.* She turned to Danny, who was opening and closing his mouth like a fish. "Come to keep you out of mischief, haven't I?"

"Dorothy!" Hector exclaimed warmly. "Thank you for coming so quickly."

Danny looked shaken. "But how did you get here, Nan?"

"Taxi," Dorothy told him briskly. She glanced at Hector. "He's waiting outside for you to pay him."

"What? Oh yes—yes, of course. I'll see to that right away." He walked off.

Danny said, "Thought you were still in the hospital, Nan."

"Sent me home, didn't they? Right as rain now. Ready to do a bit of work for Hector." Dorothy watched Hector's receding back, surprised at how fond she still felt after all these years. "Come on, Danny, introduce me. Not ashamed of your old Nan, are you?"

Danny closed his mouth at last, then grinned. "Nan, this is Opal—she's a knight's daughter. And this is Michael Potolo from Mali, and he's a prince. Told you I had friends in high places, didn't I?" He turned to them and his grin widened. "This is my Nan—Dorothy Bayley. Isn't she lovely?"

You could see the other two didn't know what to make of her, but they both got up and came across. The girl shook her hand and said, "How do you do, Mrs. Bayley?" and stone the crows if it wasn't the girl she'd met at the clinic.

The girl didn't recognize her, of course, now that she had her clothes on and her hair brushed and a bit of makeup hiding the wrinkles. Both kids shook her hand, mannerly as could be.

But then Danny had her by the arm and was pulling her back out of the door into that gloomy bit of hallway before the stairs, out of earshot of the others. "What are you *doing* here, Nan?"

"Told you—come to keep you out of mischief."

"No, listen, Nan, this is serious. You know the old boy or what?"

"The colonel?" She hesitated, wondering how much to tell him, not that her private life was any of his concern. "Sure, I know him. Wouldn't be here if I didn't, would I?"

"I know that, but *how* do you know him?"

"Think you're the only one with friends in high places?" Dorothy grinned. "You and your knight's daughter and your African prince."

"Come on, Nan, what's going on here? How do you know Uncle Hector?"

Dorothy said, "*Colonel* Hamilton-Oakes was my Stanley's commanding officer when we was in Aden. Got to know him then, didn't I?" She hoped he wasn't going to ask how.

But all Danny said was, "I didn't know that."

"Before you were born," Dorothy said.

"Doesn't tell me what you're doing here."

"Hector found out I was psychic."

Danny stared at her. "You're not psychic, Nan!"

"Course I am," Dorothy said flatly. "You remember: I used to go to the Spiritualists after Stanley died."

"Yeah, but that was just a bit of comfort, wasn't it? Because you missed him."

"No, it was because I kept *seeing* him!" Dorothy said. "Still do. I went to the Spiritualists to find out if they could make sense of what was happening. But I was psychic long before that, *long* before. Used to see things when I was a little girl."

"You never told me about that," Danny said accusingly.

"Well, you don't, do you? Not a thing you talk about. Don't want people thinking you're bonkers. Only Hector found out while we were in Aden, I sort of let it slip in the heat of the moment, you might say. Thing is, Hector's interested in stuff like that, always has been. He's a Theosophist or a Freemason or something like that."

"Priory of Mons," Danny growled.

Dorothy smiled at him. "Oh, he's told you, has he? Wasn't sure if he'd come clean—they're very secretive in the Priory. Anyway, Hector got quite excited when he found out what I could do. Wanted me to join, but I wouldn't. Tell the truth, at that time I thought it was just a lot of rich blokes with too much time on their hands. I'd have been well out of place with Lord This and Sir Henry That—but I said I'd work as their medium if they liked. Made me take an oath of secrecy, and Hector's been my contact ever since. Calls me up when they need me. Never thought he'd call me in on one of your daft schemes."

"It's not one of my daft schemes," Danny said quickly. "This is serious business." What he meant was *dangerous*, whatever Hector said, but he didn't want to worry her.

Dorothy said, "Well, don't you worry about that,

then. I'll look after you, same as I've always done."

And Danny, bless him, looked at her with that wide-eyed, serious look he got sometimes and said, "Nan, this could be dangerous! There's a sort of devil that *kills* people."

"Well, it's not going to kill *me*." Dorothy smiled at him reassuringly and winked. "Tough as old boots, me."

[46]

Opal, Blandings

"Are you all sitting comfortably?" Hector asked in a polite voice that was presumably meant to lighten the atmosphere. The old woman, Danny's grandmother, was in the east and seemed completely calm by all appearances. For some reason she looked vaguely familiar.

Opal nodded. "Yes." Hector himself was in the center of the strange room now, to one side of that peculiar altar.

"Then I'll begin," Hector said brightly. He dropped the smile and the bantering tone as he went on, "Look in the mirror on the wall opposite you. Can you see the symbol above your chair reflected in it?"

"Can't see a thing," Dorothy said. "You'd make a better door than a window, Hector."

"Sorry," Hector said quickly, and moved to stand near the door. "That better?"

"Yes, I can see the mirror now."

"The rest of you all right?"

There were mumbles from Michael and Danny that might have been assent.

"The technique is simple enough," Hector said. "The paintings above your heads are the elemental symbols of the quarter you're sitting in—*tattvas*, the Hindus call them. Stare at your symbol in the mirror until you see a sort of halo form around it. That's not magic, just an optical reflex. The symbol will also change color—that's optical too. Once you get that, you'll be drawn out of your body. Just relax. You're all experienced in astral body work or remote viewing or whatever the Project calls it. So let it happen. When you come out of your body, you'll find that the symbol you were watching has grown to the size of a door and is floating in the air in front of you. It's automatic and it means the crystal has turned your second body in the particular direction I was telling you about earlier. Once—"

"When the symbol is floating in front of you like a door, will it be its original color or the color it changed into after the halo business?" Danny asked.

"The color it changed into," Hector told him. "Now when all this happens, you simply *go through* the symbol doorways—"

"How do you get them open?" Danny asked.

"They're not *actual* doorways," Hector said. "They're

symbolic doorways. You don't have to open them. All you have to do is pass through them. Just move forward and pass through them."

"Then what?" Danny asked, not in the least put out by Hector's irritated tone.

"Dorothy will be your guide at that point," Hector said. "She'll help you get your bearings on the astral plane."

There was a long silence, then, "You've done this before, Nan?" Danny asked.

Dorothy looked at him soberly. "Learned it a long time ago."

"Can't believe you never told me this before," Danny muttered.

"Certain things have to be kept secret." Michael's eyes were glittering. Opal found his comment just the tiniest bit irritating.

It couldn't be any worse than flying off to Lusakistan, Opal thought. Probably much the same. It had to be similar to out-of-body work. Her father used to say that in the olden times, people like magicians and alchemists worked out-of-body the same way Project agents did, but called it by different names.

"There's nothing to worry about," Michael said. "Just remember we all experience these things differently."

Danny rounded on him. "Why, have you done this before?"

"No," Michael admitted.

"Then how do you know?" Danny demanded.

"Uncle Hector told me. He knows what he's doing."

Which remains to be seen, Opal thought. She wondered why Danny was so snappy with Michael, but maybe it was just their situation. Certainly the whole Priory of Mons thing made her uneasy. Probably it was not as romantic and spiritual as Hector made it sound—she simply could not bring herself to believe in scrolls found in the Ark of the Covenant. But it was clearly a secret organization that got up to some very odd things. And that was where her difficulties started. Her experience with MI6 had taught her that secret organizations were rarely what they claimed to be. She watched the silver crescent in the mirror opposite, wondering if it could really take her to another level of reality, and wondering what it was going to be like if she really did get there.

She glanced across again at Michael, but he had closed his eyes now. Danny, despite the instruction to relax, was leaning forward in his chair like someone watching a tennis match. His grandmother, Mrs. Bayley, had a vacant look on her face.

Opal looked back at the opposite wall. In the mirror a halo formed around her crescent symbol.

[47]

Danny, Blandings

Something powerful reached deep inside to pull Danny out of his body. It was nothing like the time they used the helmet on him at the Project. It seemed as though he was gripped by invisible hands, then *extracted*, like a cork from a bottle. And when he came out, he could see the doorway. It hung in space directly in front of him, an unearthly luminous green triangle like nothing he had ever seen before. It was about six feet high—a lot taller than he was—and floating without support in the air. When you looked into it, strange shapes pulsed and writhed.

Danny felt twisted, as if somebody had taken him and turned him inside out, so he was now facing in a direction no mortal human was supposed to face. It was a hideous sensation, but while he wanted desperately to turn away from that doorway, something held him firm. His stomach revolted, and for a moment he was sure he would throw up. His fear increased to downright terror. There was a pounding in his ears. The writhing shapes swam closer to the surface of reality and reached for him. Danny tried desperately to back away. Nothing in the universe would persuade him to step into that doorway. It led, he knew deep in his heart, to the darkest pit of oblivion.

Despite himself, Danny stepped into the doorway.

Opal, Blandings

Opal was intrigued by the crescent. The points were upward, like a boat. Or like the pictures of the Isis headdress in the coffee-table book they had at home. The caption said it represented the moon, but she'd never seen a crescent moon on its back like that.

She reached out to touch the crescent, then hesitated. It occurred to her that she was out of her body now, but there had been no sensation of leaving it, none of the sensations she associated with the psychotronic helmet. She glanced behind her, just to make sure, and there she was, seated in the chair, her head bowed a little, her eyes half closed. No one had strapped her in, but contrary to Project theory, she didn't seem to be falling down. What she could see of her eyes were vacant, as if she was in a trance.

Opal turned back toward the floating crescent. Hector had mentioned that it would change color, and so it had, but not much. The silver had transformed into a luminous grayish bluish . . . soᴛt of silver. But the thing had grown enormous since she glanced away from it. It floated in the air before her and, strangely enough, she thought she could hear the sound of running water.

Fleetingly she wondered again how much Uncle Hector *really* knew, how much he wasn't telling them. Then she bowed her head and stepped into the crescent.

Michael, Blandings

Michael felt nervous but excited. He was still in his physical body, but the doorway, a massive glowing purple square, was already beginning to manifest in front of him. He glanced around at the others. A thief, a grandmother, a girl. Some team fighting for the Powers of Light! But, of course, matters of *sohanti* were not the way those at the Project believed them to be. Magic was never a question of brute force or weaponry. Magic was a matter of the human heart.

And not only magic . . .

He glanced at Opal again. She was one of the loveliest girls he'd ever seen. He'd noticed her the day he joined the Project, found himself wondering how he could get to know her. And now that he *had* gotten to know her, he wanted to know her better. Wanted to . . .

He pulled his mind back to the task at hand. Some

situations could only be endured. There were many things in life he wanted but couldn't have.

The doorway solidified and Michael slipped from his body to pass through it.

[50]

Danny, the Astral Plane

It was the same, only different.

Danny didn't know what he expected from astral reality, but this wasn't it. He was standing on the edge of a desert, near the pylon gateway of a walled city. The place looked solid as the rocks its stone was quarried from, and the temperature felt pleasantly warm. A reddish sun hung low in the sky beyond some distant dunes. It was a bit of a surprise to get here—he hadn't really believed the doorway business or whatever Hector said—but apart from that, it was much like the out-of-body experiences he'd had before. It felt as if he'd been sent off to North Africa.

What *was* strange was the light. Even though it was still daytime—that big sun definitely hadn't set—there was an ultraviolet tinge across the scene and a hint of the flatness you got when you saw a landscape under a full moon. If you weren't careful, you could talk yourself into thinking there was something creepy going on.

Which there was. He could see that the minute he looked at the others. He knew them, all right, but they didn't look the way they normally did. Opal's hair had changed color and her face filled out. Still pretty, but more approachable now; and he liked that. She had nicer clothes, too: a long linen dress thing that came down almost to her ankles and clung a bit along the way. Michael seemed older and a bit thinner. But the thing was, his clothes were almost gone. He was wearing sandals and a sort of linen kilt. Looked good in it, too—nice body tone; Danny noticed to his disgust that Opal was surreptitiously eyeing his muscles.

But the big difference was his Nan. Shouldn't have recognized her at all, but he did. She wasn't old anymore. Well, not *as* old. Still on the wrong side of forty, but her hair was gray now where it had been mostly white. Looked a whole lot fitter. She was wearing a short white tunic thing and all the blue veins had disappeared from her legs.

He realized suddenly that they were all staring at him. "You look different," Danny said.

"*We* look different?" Opal echoed. She gave him a big, wide grin. "You should talk!"

His Nan did a strange thing. She produced a little mirror with a flourish that would have done justice to a conjurer, then stretched it so that he was looking at a full-length reflection of himself: taller, darker, and a lot more handsome than he'd been half an hour ago. Like Michael, he now seemed to be wearing just a kilt. Like Michael, he now had a muscular body. Danny blinked. "How did you do that?" He wasn't sure whether he meant the mirror trick or the way he looked like a film star.

"Didn't do anything, me," Dorothy said. "Most people look different on the Astral. More like their real selves, their *inside* selves. It's a dreamworld, see? You know how you meet up with people in a dream and you know them right away even though they don't look a bit like they do in normal life?"

Danny wasn't sure he did. "Naw, Nan, I meant the mirror. How did you do that with the mirror?"

"You can do stuff like that here once you get the hang of it," Dorothy said. "Remember what Hector told you— it's another reality. The laws of physics aren't the same. Might look like some old corner of our world, but it isn't. Take a squint at that flower."

Danny looked. There was a paved roadway leading to the pylon gate. Beside it, just a step or two from where he was standing, there was a small clump of grass and a bright red flower, something like a poppy. "What about it?"

"Look normal to you?"

Danny stared. "Looks normal to me, Nan."

"How do you think it grows? And the bit of grass, come to that?"

Opal said suddenly, "It's growing out of sand." She took a step forward, then stopped. "But that's—"

"That's impossible," Dorothy finished for her. "Can't grow flowers without soil. Might get a bit of rough grass to grow in sand if you were very lucky and had the right conditions, but not a nice green clump like that, and definitely not a flower. Take a closer look at it, Danny."

Danny hunkered down to peer at the flower. "No scent," he said.

"Not many flowers have perfume here," Dorothy said. "In fact I'm not sure *any* of them do. No bees either, so I suppose they've got nothing to attract. But that's not it. Get in a bit closer than that, pretend you're a telescope or something. Look right into the middle of it."

Danny glanced at his Nan, then bent forward. As his face approached the flower, something happened that was even weirder than the mirror business. His whole field of vision opened up. For a split second it seemed as if he was zooming in, not like a telescope but a microscope, deeper and deeper into the heart of the flower, then into a universe of swirling atoms that comprised the flower, then into a network of luminous filaments that made up the atoms, floating and linking and breaking apart in the black depths of space itself. The sensation made him feel like he was falling, nauseous and dizzy, so that he jerked back abruptly.

The flower was just a flower. Growing out of desert sand . . .

"See the spiderweb, did you?" Dorothy asked.

Danny looked at her stupidly. "Spiderweb?"

"The threads. Nice shining threads. Did you get that far?"

"Yes," Danny said. "Yes, I did." They were beautiful.

"You can do that with anything here," Dorothy said. She glanced at the other two and smiled. "Any of you can. Just get up close and personal and you can see right into anything—flowers, the sand, the stonework in that wall, anything you like. Thing is, if you can get down deep enough to see the spiderweb like Danny did, you can change stuff once you get the hang of it. That's how I made the mirror out of thin air, 'cause even thin air has atoms in it and every atom has the threads."

Danny muttered, "Cool!" He looked at Dorothy. "Will you teach me, Nan?"

"Course I will, sweetheart. But not just now, eh? Better deal with this lot first."

Behind them, the city gates were swinging open.

51

Michael, the Astral Plane

The creature moving through the city gates was familiar from tribal drawings. The creature moving through the city gates was a Nommo. Michael stared at it in wonder as old memories flooded back.

When Michael became a man, he underwent a tribal initiation that linked him to the spirits of his ancestors and revealed the royal mystery of his family name. The initiation was an important ceremony: the Dogon considered it the most important of his life and one that confirmed him as a prince of his people.

His father took him far to the south beyond the ancient trading capital of Timbuktu to a village on the banks of the Niger. There the elders locked him alone in a darkened hut for five days and nights without food or water. He emerged disorientated and curiously cleansed. He looked for his father, but his father was not there.

The women of the village escorted him into the bush and left him. For a further three days he survived on roots, leaves, and a handful of berries which gave him such violent stomach cramps that, hungry though he was, he threw the rest away. The elders found him on the night of the third day, sleeping in the fork of a tree. They gave him something to drink that turned everything in his field of vision a moonlit blue, then took him to a clearing where the entire tribe drummed and danced until dawn.

With the rising of the light, he was taken to another hut—it may have been back in the original village but by now his perceptions were so clouded he could not be sure—for circumcision with a flint knife. Then he was granted instruction. The drugged drink of the day before must still have been in his system, for there was surprisingly little pain or bleeding from the circumcision, and he was able to listen to his instruction without too much distraction. It was given by three priests so old that there was not a single black hair on their bodies.

They told him how, in ancient times, the Nommo descended from the sky in a ship that sailed on fire and thunder. Since the Nommo could not live on land, one of their kind, named Oannes, made himself a deep lake and lived there, emerging to teach men hunting and women weaving. In times of hardship, he fed the Dogon with his body and slaked their thirst with his blood. When he could feed them no more, they nailed him to a tree so that he died. But after three days, he rose from the dead and flew back in his fiery ship to the world from whence he came.

Michael could still remember the dread he experienced when the three priests explained that the Nommos' home was a world that circled the great star Sirius, called in the Dogon tongue *Po Tolo,* the original form of Michael's family name. The coincidence of the name made him feel as if the universe had turned to look at him, placing him at the center of attention and handing him responsibilities he was ill equipped to handle.

He had the same dread feeling now.

The Nommo was the size of a small whale but resembled nothing he had ever seen on earth. The upper torso was vaguely humanoid, although the head was not, and the creature had legs of a kind, and feet. But the lower body was that of a great fish, ending in a fishlike tail. It floated upright in a huge, transparent tank of greenish water dragged on a wooden sled by a team of Dogon priests.

The Nommo stared out at Michael with enormous, jet-black eyes.

52

Opal, the Astral Plane

Opal straightened, still annoyed by her inability to look into the full depths of the flower, but what was happening now dragged her mind from the problem completely. Once, years ago, her father had taken her to some state function at Canterbury Cathedral, where she'd watched entranced as priests in splendid robes processed along the center aisle swinging thuribles of roiling incense and chanting softly to a background drone of organ notes. But what she saw then was nothing to what she was seeing now. The priestly procession was huge— perhaps close on a thousand men. The robes were cloth of gold, reflecting redly in the setting sun. Soft organ notes underscored the rhythm of a single drum.

The procession was headed by Jesus Christ.

Opal had never seen such a beautiful man: and beautiful was the word that came to mind. He stood more than six feet tall, dressed in the flowing white robe of an ancient Judaean. Brown hair poured in a shining torrent to his shoulders. His beard was full, his skin fluoresced, his sheer presence radiated warmth. His sandaled feet appeared to float above the ground.

Jesus looked at her benignly with his soft, blue eyes.

Danny, the Astral Plane

Danny blinked. Moses was standing in the gateway. At least, Danny thought it must be Moses. He looking just like Charlton Heston, for one thing, with his gray beard and long locks of gray-white hair. He even carried a great wooden staff and the same stone tablets tucked underneath one arm. Except it couldn't be Charlton Heston, because he was dead. But it couldn't be Moses either, because Moses was dead as well, far longer dead than Charlton.

All the same, the characters with him were carrying the Ark of the Covenant.

Danny knew for sure that had to be the Ark. He'd had the description read to him years ago at Sunday School. The box itself was covered in gold plate. So were the rods used for carrying it and the rings they fitted into. There was a gold chair on top with golden cherubs spreading golden wings. More to the point, the whole thing writhed and crackled with static electricity.

But if that was the Ark of the Covenant, the character up front had to be Moses. It was Moses' lot that made the Ark and carried it around half the Middle East before the Philistines or somebody nicked it. So maybe the astral plane was where you went to when you died, not heaven or hell after all. You'd have thought old Hector might have mentioned it.

Moses casually turned his staff into a serpent, stroked his beard, and stared with deep-brown eyes at Danny Lipman.

Danny, the Astral Plane

Dorothy walked over to the creature at the gate. "Hello, Harry. Up to your old tricks again?" she said.

"What's happening?" Danny asked. Opal was standing like someone in a trance, a look of bliss on her face. Michael had a look of terror on his.

"Harry's not his real name," Dorothy said. "Tell you the truth, I can't pronounce his real name—Hari-something-or-other-Indian, leastways it sounds Indian to me. What are you seeing, then?"

"Moses," Danny said. He hesitated, then added, "And the Ark of the Covenant."

"Nice touch," Dorothy said admiringly. "Very clever." She poked the immobile Opal. "Who is he from where you're standing, dear?"

"Jesus Christ," Opal breathed.

"Well, he's not," Dorothy said. "What are you seeing, Michael?" Then, when he didn't answer,

"Michael! I'm talking to you!"

Michael snapped out of his paralysis and said, "One of the Nommo."

"What's that when it's at home?"

Michael said carefully, "It's part of my country's religious tradition. Gods who came from the sky to teach mankind."

Danny, who could *still* see Moses, whispered, "What is he—a shape-shifter?"

"Naw," Dorothy said. "If he was a shape-shifter, we'd all see the same thing, wouldn't we? He's what's called a Lord of the Flame. Everybody sees him different, like pictures in the fire. What you see depends on your religion." She grinned suddenly. "'Spect you couldn't see him at all if you were an atheist."

Frowning, Opal said, "What do you see, Mrs. Bayley?"

"That would be telling," Dorothy said. "And it's Dorothy. Or Dot."

"What's he want?" Danny asked quietly.

"He's come to help us," Dorothy announced. She dropped her voice. "We've got Hector to thank for this. He has some peculiar contacts through that Priory of his."

It occurred to Danny suddenly that living on the astral plane was like waking in a dream. The whole place had a dreamlike quality about it—the way you could look down into a flower, the tricks his Nan played with that mirror, meeting up with Moses straight down from the mountain. But at the same time it didn't shift around the way dreams did. They were still outside the pylon gate, the road was still there, the flower was still there, growing in impossible sand that still stretched out endlessly around them. And he was awake. He *knew* he was awake.

"We've come to get the Spear of Destiny," Dorothy said. "You going to point us in the right direction, Harry?"

The biblical figure before Danny suddenly erupted into a towering pillar of flame that gradually transformed itself into humanoid form. He should have been impressed, but he kept thinking—*Flame on!*—it looked like something you'd see in *Fantastic Four*. The heat radiation was immense. Danny glanced at the others and deduced from the angle of their necks that they were seeing what he was.

"Thy adversary has hunted by the Lake of Unt," rumbled the Lord of the Flame. "With the spear he has pierced the Everlasting in the Shenlu Chamber. Have care when you release him."

Not one word of it made any sense whatsoever to Danny.

Opal, the Astral Plane

They halted for the night in the desert, their surroundings flat and silent, illuminated by a blue-white moonlight that somehow appeared without a moon. They had walked for what seemed like hours, but Michael got antsy about stopping. "Do we have time for this?" he demanded.

They all turned to look at Dorothy, the one who seemed to know how things worked around here. Dorothy said, "We got time. Besides, we need to sleep to get us to the lake."

"Lake?" Danny frowned.

"Unt," Dorothy told him.

But Michael still seemed anxious. "Uncle Hector said it would only be a matter of a few hours before the Devourer could manifest in our reality. We've been here for at least two hours already."

Dorothy said, "Don't fret yourself, Michael. Time

runs slower here for some reason. Varies a bit, but you can usually rely on a day to an hour, and we ain't been a day here yet. We got time to do the job. Only we need to be fresh. And us girls need our beauty sleep, don't we, Opal?"

Opal said, "Aren't we a bit exposed for sleeping here? There's no shelter and we've no sleeping bags." She hesitated, wondering if Dorothy might produce sleeping bags the way she produced a mirror, then added, "And mightn't there be scorpions or creepy-crawlies? I mean, you always get scorpions in the desert, don't you?"

Dorothy smiled. "Just you sit down on the sand and dig a little hole."

"Pardon?"

"Like you were going to build a sand castle. You can dig with your hands. Go on—humor me."

Opal glanced suspiciously at Dorothy, but crouched down and cautiously pushed one hand into the sand. She struck bedrock at once. "It's not very deep."

"Keep going," Dorothy said. "Clear a bit of a space."

Opal pulled back a thin layer of sand. "That's not bedrock," she said. "That's not rock at all." If anything it looked like polished metal, or even plastic.

"Nobody ever believes it unless they see it," Dorothy said smugly. "This looks like the desert and feels like the desert when you're walking, but it's not the desert. It's not real. None of this is real, not the way you think. Not this place, not the city, not Hari-what's-his-name."

"Then what are we doing here, Nan?" Danny asked.

Dorothy gave him a look. "Saving poor old Opal and a lot more besides. Real or not, what happens in our world depends on what happens here, always has done, always will do, apparently." She smiled at Opal. "So you don't need to worry. You just get some sleep, and when you wake up, there we'll be in Unt, ready to do what we were sent for."

"You said that before, Nan." Danny frowned. "You said we had to sleep to get to Unt. What you mean by that?"

"Sleep's the fastest way to get to different places here," Dorothy said.

"How does that work?"

She shrugged. "Beats me, but then I can't even set a DVD player. Just one of the differences with this place. There are lots of them. Won't get any colder, for example, even though it's a clear night. No creepy-crawlies either. Or scorpions or snakes or any of that sort. Won't find superbugs lurking around here, I can tell you."

"Wait a minute!" Opal said suddenly. "I met you in the clinic, didn't I? That *was* you, wasn't it? I'm so sorry I didn't realize it before. You seem so different now!"

Dorothy grinned. "Wondered if you'd remember.

No need to apologize—I scrub up a lot better than the way I look traipsing around in my nightie. But you know me now, and that's a good thing—shows we were all meant to be together, doesn't it? Me and Danny, you and Michael. Sort of fated, know what I mean? You get a lot of that in this line of work—fate. Hector always calls it destiny. Amounts to the same thing, I suppose. Makes you feel somebody up there's looking after you, although you do have to mostly fend for yourself, in my experience."

Michael lay down first. "Well, if this is the fastest way to get the job done . . ."

Danny stared at him for a moment, then squatted down nearby, but didn't stretch out. "Nan . . . ?"

"Yes, Danny?"

"You know your way around this place."

"Maybe I do and maybe I don't," Dorothy said. "Been here before, if that's what you mean, but it's different every time. Bit like dreaming. You never know where you'll turn up next."

"But we *aren't* dreaming, are we?" Danny asked, voicing an earlier thought.

"Don't think so. What you do in dreams doesn't make much difference to what happens when you're awake. What you do in this place definitely changes things back home. I can tell you that for a fact."

Danny said, "Hector told us we can't die here—is that true?"

"You sure that's what he told you?" Dorothy said.

Danny frowned. "I think so."

"What he actually said was that he would look after our physical bodies," Michael put in, glancing at Dorothy.

"Not the same thing, is it?" Dorothy remarked. "Actually it's tricky. The astral body you're in now can't be killed, Danny—that's true. But it can be hurt, all right—hurt badly—and that can affect the link with your physical body. If it goes too far, the link will snap. You'll still be alive on the astral plane, but on the physical, your heart will stop." She trailed off with an expressive shrug.

"You mean I *can* die, whatever Hector said?"

Dorothy gave him a worried look. "Depends what you mean by dying, doesn't it? You won't be dead here. Just . . ."

"Not able to get back into my real body!" Danny exclaimed. "You'd think Hector might have mentioned that!"

"Uncle Hector had other things on his mind," Michael said defensively. "Besides, we aren't going to get hurt here." He hesitated, then added, "If we're careful." He looked at Danny. "So we've really nothing to worry about."

"Nothing to worry about?" Danny exploded. "Depends what else slipped Uncle Hector's mind, doesn't it? *Conveniently* slipped Uncle Hector's mind."

Michael flared at once. "Listen, Danny—" he said angrily.

"Now, now, boys." Dorothy moved quickly between them. "Let's not get silly about this. I think Hector might just have been trying not to upset you."

Or maybe just making sure we agreed to do the job, Danny thought. He glared at Michael but said nothing more.

Dorothy said, "You and me can lie down over here, Opal, away from the boys. They'll snore. Men always snore. So we'll just keep well away."

Opal lay down, but despite Dorothy's promise, found she couldn't sleep. Her mind was racing. She was worried about her father, of course, worried about Farrakhan, worried about the Devourer, worried about the job they were supposed to do in this weird place, but more than anything else, she kept thinking about Michael.

She lay on her back in the sand, staring up into a starless sky, listening to the faint sounds of the two boys snoring. She'd been so certain he liked her, so sure of the signals he was sending. In fact there'd been times when she'd caught him staring at her. But then he would unexpectedly turn cold. "Can't sleep?" Dorothy asked quietly beside her.

"How did you know?"

"Could tell from your breathing. You worried about your prince?"

Opal sat bolt upright and looked down at her. "You couldn't tell *that* from my breathing."

Dorothy gave her little grin. "Saw the way you look at him. You two an item?"

Opal subsided a little. "I wish."

"Maybe he's just shy," said Dorothy. "Why don't you ask him out? Girls can do that now, not like my young days."

"I tried that," Opal grumbled.

"Said no, did he?"

"Yes. I mean yes, he said no."

"More fool him," Dorothy sniffed. "You're a lovely girl. He don't know what he's missing."

"Thank you," Opal said, lying down again.

"What did he say when he said no?" Dorothy asked. "I mean he didn't just say no, did he? Must have said why."

"He just ran off," Opal said, her voice rising at the memory. "I mean, walked away as if I'd offended him or something. I have no idea why."

"Cheeky bugger," Dorothy said.

They lay in silence for a while. Eventually Dorothy

said, "You still thinking about him?"

"Yes."

"It's this place," Dorothy said.

"What is?"

"The astral plane. Stirs up your emotions."

Opal said, "Do you have a thing for Uncle Hector, Dorothy? Speaking of stirred emotions."

"Noticed that, did you? It was a *long* time ago."

Despite everything, Opal smiled a little. "I'm not sure he's entirely over it."

"You think so?" Dorothy sounded pleased.

Opal finally fell asleep soon after that. The next day—if it could be counted as a real day in this place—they woke up by the Lake of Unt.

[56]

Danny, the Astral Plane

The Lake of Unt was a sea of flames. It was set in a wasteland of black volcanic rock (the desert had completely disappeared) interspersed with boiling mud pools and glowing, thready lava streams. Danny opened his eyes to find Dorothy already awake and standing silhouetted against the fiery glow. He looked around. "How did this happen?"

"It's this place," Dorothy said without looking around. "Very obliging at taking you where you want to go."

"This is it?" Danny asked. "This is the lake where Farrakhan has stashed the spear?"

"Should be." Dorothy still hadn't turned around. "Danny, I want to talk to you about something." She sounded serious.

He pushed himself to his feet. The others were still sleeping. Michael was flat on his back, his mouth partly open. A little distance away, Opal was curled up like a rolled prawn. "What is it, Nan?" He moved to stand beside her and the heat from the fiery lake struck him like a furnace.

"You got offered a place at Cambridge, didn't you?"

It took him completely by surprise. "How did you find out?"

"Hector told me."

"How did *he* know?"

"Sir Roland at the Project mentioned it. Doesn't matter. I know about it now. You going to go?"

"To Cambridge?" He shook his head. "No . . ."

"Why not?" Dorothy asked sharply.

"Can't afford it."

She turned to glare at him. "Don't you lie to me, Danny Lipman. I'll find the money, same as I did for your private school. Or I expect your precious Shadow Project might give it to you since they seem to want you so much. Want you even more if you had a decent education. Course, they don't know what a lying toad you are."

Danny grinned at her sheepishly. "It's not just the money, Nan. I wouldn't fit into a place like Cambridge. Full of toffs."

"You'd fit, all right. Got the brains for it—that's all that counts these days. It's me, isn't it?"

Danny gave her an innocent look. "What you mean, Nan?"

"You know rightly what I mean!" She snorted. "You don't want to leave me on my own."

"Course I don't want to leave you, Nan. I love you."

This time it was Dorothy who shook her head: slowly, with pursed lips. "Don't give me that! None of your soft soap. You don't want to leave me because you think I can't look after myself—that's really it, isn't it?"

"Nan," Danny said seriously, "you're not getting any younger."

"Neither are you!" Dorothy snapped. "I want to tell you a couple of things, Danny—you listening?"

"Yes, Nan."

"First thing is, *nobody's* getting any younger. Not me, not you. One of these days you're going to look in the mirror and find you're middle-aged. I know you don't believe it now, but you will. You want to look back then and think, 'I wasted everything I had, never got a decent education, now I'm just an ignorant twit with no future and no prospects'? You want to think that? You want to think you had the chance and threw it away? Next thing is, you don't owe me, Danny. You don't owe me nothing—"

"Yes, I do, Nan," Danny interrupted. "You're the one who brought me up."

"No, you bloody don't!" said Dorothy with force. "That's what one generation does for the next—brings them up. It's just what you do. What else are you *supposed* to do?" She took a deep breath. "And the *next* thing—"

"That's three things," Danny said, grinning. "You said you wanted to tell me a couple."

"Don't get smart. The next thing is I want you to look at me. Go on, look at me."

"I'm looking at you, Nan," Danny said.

"No, look at me properly. Step back and look at me. What do you see?"

Funny thing was, she looked even younger than she had yesterday. The gray had gone out of her hair and it had taken on a reddish tint, although that might just be a reflection from the flames. But the biggest change was in her face and body. She was still his Nan, but she hardly looked much more than thirty—and a fit thirty at that. "What you telling me, Nan?" Danny asked quietly.

"That's how I am inside," Dorothy said. "Astral plane does that to you. Shows the way you are inside. Longer you stay, the clearer it gets. That's why you're taller here, and stronger. That's why Michael's starting to look like a bit of a hero when he's so quiet on the outside. That's why Opal doesn't look as pretty as usual—poor thing's not as confident as you might think. Me, I'm younger. Inside I got the feelings and the energy of a woman half my age. *And* I'm tough as old boots. I don't need you looking after me, Danny, throwing away your chance to get a decent education."

Danny said, "Shouldn't we wake up the others?"

"They'll wake up when it's their time. That's another thing about this place. Are you listening to me, Danny?"

"I'm listening, Nan," Danny said.

"I don't need you looking after me. You hear that?"

"Yes, Nan."

"And I want you to stop thieving, Danny. You thought I didn't know about it, but I do. I want you to go to Cambridge. I'd be *proud* to have my grandson studying at Cambridge. You hear that too?"

"Yes, Nan," Danny said. "I hear you."

Behind him, Michael groaned and sat up. Opal stirred as well, then propped herself on one elbow. They looked around at their new surroundings. Michael seemed a lot less perplexed than Opal, whose face had taken on a look near to astonishment.

Dorothy's fierce glare softened into the fondest of fond smiles. "You're a good boy, Danny, really."

Michael said briskly, "Now everyone's awake, I suppose we'd better get on with the job of rescuing the spear."

It was a relief not to be talking about Cambridge.

Danny said, "Any idea where to find it?"

"Shenlu Chamber, according to the Flame Lord." Michael turned to look over the fiery lake.

"Know where that is, do you?"

Still staring out across the lake, Michael said, "I think it might be over there."

Danny followed his gaze. Through the fire and the smoke he could see a blackened island of rock jutting perhaps twenty feet above the surface of the lake. "That's where we find the Shenlu Chamber?"

"I think so."

"How do we reach it?"

Michael said, "We swim."

Danny grinned, then looked at Michael's face and realized he was serious.

[57]

Sir Roland, the Shadow Project

Sir Roland Harrington was in the upstairs library when he heard the sound of gunfire. He ran to the window and looked out cautiously, standing clear of any line of fire. The floodlights had come on, a possible sign of trouble, but from the angle he was at, he could see nothing amiss. He was debating whether to shift to a more vulnerable position when the firing stopped.

Roland stood stock-still. The Project complex with its offices and operations rooms lay directly underneath the old house, which served as a disguise. The main entrance to the Project, with its massive provisions lifts and personnel elevators, was hidden in the grounds, away from prying eyes, carefully disguised in its own right, and permanently guarded. At any given time there were ten men in combat gear stationed in the bushes, armed and ready to give warning of anybody approaching too close to the entrance tunnel and even, if necessary, to act as a temporary front line of defense. These perimeter guards were issued with Belgian M249 SAWs, a particularly vicious light machine gun. Roland couldn't be sure, but the burst of gunfire sounded as if it might have come from a SAW. If he was right, it meant the guards had fired on someone. The question was why.

Standard procedure required perimeter guards to remain hidden unless there was a clear and present danger of the tunnel entrance being discovered by an intruder. Even then, they were required to alert the guard contingent within the complex itself, then attempt to head off the intruder without use of lethal force if at all possible. Only if personally attacked, or in face of a direct attack on the Project complex, were they authorized to open fire.

Roland felt himself chill. Was the Project under threat?

Even though no shots seemed to have hit the house, he dropped to his knees below the level of the window and crawled to the library table, where he used the coded phone to put through a call to George Hanover.

"Where the hell are you?" Hanover asked at once. "We're under attack."

Christ! Roland thought. "What's happening, George?"

"Not sure yet." He must have checked the location

button on his console because he added, "Get down here, Roland. We can't guarantee the security of the library."

Roland cradled the phone and headed for the lift. George was there to meet him when he emerged. "Carradine thinks it's Sword of Wrath," George said without preliminary.

Of course it was Sword of Wrath. It had to be. No other organization had the resources. "Brief me, George," he ordered shortly.

"Seven men down and the possibility of other casualties."

Seven men? One brief burst of gunfire and they'd already lost *seven men*? "What do you mean—*possibility*? Don't you know?"

"Seven guards at the entrance barrier are dead—we have that on CCTV. But none of our frontline boys are answering their intercoms. Whoever's done this certainly got past them."

There were ten frontline men concealed in the grounds. They couldn't all be dead, not all of them. The Project simply could not have lost seventeen men in a matter of minutes. But they weren't answering their intercoms. . . .

They were running down the corridor as Roland said, "Where's Carradine now?"

"Security control center. He'll bring you up to speed there."

The Project's security control center was dominated by a bank of closed-circuit TV screens looking down on tables packed with communications equipment manned by a small team of operatives. Roland's eyes swept across the images that defined virtually every inch of the Project, but he could see nothing amiss.

"There's a camera out in the entrance tunnel," Carradine told them.

"Why?"

"Stray bullet, I think. One of ours."

"How many of them are in there?"

Carradine looked pained. "Not sure, Sir Roland."

So it was *Sir* now that the pressure was on. "Why not?"

"Nothing's showing on the surveillance tapes. The outer perimeter men were concealed, of course, but we've definitely lost two that I know of, and frankly I think we've probably lost the rest," Carradine said. "One of our men heard gunfire and went to investigate. He reported back that two of the boys were dead—Ron Wheeler and Bill Griffin."

"Jesus!" Roland breathed. "Griffin's got a wife and children. Gunshot wounds?" Details could help them estimate how many enemies they were facing.

But Carradine was shaking his head. "That's the odd thing: he said it looked like a knife attack. Or a machete."

"Wheeler and Griffin, weren't they armed?" George Hanover asked.

"Of course they were armed," Carradine said a little testily. "Standard-issue M249s."

"So how did anybody get close enough for a knife attack?" Roland asked.

"Beats me," Carradine said sourly. "There's—" He hesitated.

"What?" Roland asked at once.

Carradine suddenly looked tired. "There's one peculiar detail. The chest cavities of both men had been opened and their hearts removed."

"What!" George Hanover exploded.

It's started, Roland thought. *Thank God Opal got out.* Aloud he said, "What about the men at the barrier? Same pattern?"

"Not sure. They're lying facedown. I told our main Project contingent to hold back until we know exactly what we're facing. There are reinforcements in the tunnel."

"What do the tapes show?" Roland asked impatiently. The whole entrance area was under constant CCTV surveillance. All Carradine had to do was press a button to find out exactly what had happened.

"That's what I started to tell you," Carradine said. "Nothing's showing on the tapes. Routine footage of the barrier, then you can just about hear the distant gunfire—Wheeler and Griffin, presumably—then you have the guards' bodies, but nothing in between. We know one of the entrance guards called in a gunfire report and went to investigate, and from the position of the bodies, some of the others must have left their posts, but there's no footage of what actually happened."

"That has to be sabotage," George Hanover said, frowning.

"Thank God we're not short of manpower," Carradine said. "If this is typical Sword of Wrath, they'll be able to field six, a dozen men at most. Our boys will clean them up in no time. I've issued orders to try to take at least some of them alive—might get some useful information."

"This sort of frontal attack *isn't* typical of Sword of Wrath, Gary," George said. "You sure it's not a cover for a bomb?"

Carradine said, "We're on top of that. I've strengthened perimeter security and locked down the main house. Once we sent the troops out, we sealed the tunnel this end—those are bombproof doors, you'll recall. There's nothing getting in."

"How about a detonation in the tunnel itself?" George asked.

Carradine pulled a sober face. "Messy. Very messy if it's near our troops. But it's not going to do any real damage. Frankly, I'm not too worried. Their objective has to be the Project. A bomb in an underground entrance tunnel doesn't hack it. No disruption of our work and no propaganda value. If they are carrying a bomb, they'll want to get it inside; and they won't get it past our boys to reach the elevators—there are more than eighty troops in that tunnel now. Even if they did get past them, they can't get through the doors—six inches of solid steel. And if they did, they'd still have to fight their way across the car park to the elevators."

"Unless it's the tactical nuke we talked about," George remarked quietly. "The one we think the Skull might have bought from his friendly neighborhood arms dealers."

For just the barest second Carradine looked taken aback, then he shook his head. "Oh, no, George, that's one thing I don't think we need to worry about. If they *do* have a nuke—and frankly our investigations so far don't confirm that—they're not going to waste it on us. They'll want a high-profile target. It'll be New York or Washington or London. We're too far out here to do the job."

Roland said, "Are you armed, Gary?"

Carradine blinked in surprise. "Sorry?"

"Armed. Personally armed. Are you carrying a weapon?"

"Sure," Carradine said.

"What is it?"

For some reason Carradine looked vaguely embarrassed. "Colt M1911."

"Cowboy weapon," George Hanover murmured.

"Semiautomatic, actually," Carradine said.

Roland said forcefully, "I'd like you to issue one to George and myself, then come with us to the tunnel. I want to inspect those bombproof doors."

"Listen, I'm really needed here——" Carradine began, then caught Roland's expression and amended hastily, "Yes, of course, Sir Roland."

The subterranean garage was full of soldiers. "Called out the whole army, did you?" George said to Carradine.

Carradine shrugged. "Backup for the reinforcements. Why take chances?"

Roland strode toward the bombproof doors that now sealed the exit tunnel. He'd never seen them closed before, and from close up they supported Carradine's confidence: they looked designed to stop a tank. "Six-inch solid steel?" he said to Carradine.

"Could be more," Carradine said. "Enough, any-way."

There was a sound for all the world like a sonic boom, then the great doors bulged inward.

58

Opal, the Lake of Fire

"Swim?" Opal echoed. She scrambled to her feet. "In that?" She looked out across the Lake of Fire, then turned to Michael in bewilderment.

"How else can we get to the spear?" Michael asked.

"Fly," Opal said at once. "We can fly now that we're out of body."

"That's right," Danny put in. "You must have done it, Michael. You've had more OOBEs than me."

Opal said, "Look." She took off gracefully and swung out in a broad arc above the surface of the lake, then returned to land lightly at Michael's side. "We can do that."

"I think perhaps not," Michael said. But he hardly seemed to be paying attention. He kept staring out across the lake as if looking for something.

Frowning, Danny said, "Why don't you want us to fly, Mike?"

"Because if the spear is guarded, that's exactly what they'll expect," Michael said. "They'll expect us to come swooping in like amateurs."

"Who will?" Opal asked. She stared at him intently.

"Farrakhan's guards," Michael told her. "They'll expect us to fly."

"He's right," Dorothy said. "Don't think Farrakhan would leave the spear unguarded, do you?"

"The thing is, Nan," Danny said, "even if there are guards, it doesn't matter. Try to swim in that, and we're dead before we've gone a yard."

Dorothy sighed. "Haven't been listening, have you? None of you, except Michael. Didn't I tell you things aren't the same here? Didn't Hector tell you, as well? What did he say? Different laws of physics? This isn't your world or my world, Danny. This is a dream world. This is the astral plane. Things don't work the same way here as you're used to. That lake isn't even hot."

Danny looked out across the fire again. "Hot enough for me," he said. He could feel the waves of heat rolling over him across the thin strip of intervening shore. There was sweat on his face and body, had been since he'd woken up.

Michael said, "Only as hot as you think it is. Haven't you worked that out yet?"

"Haven't I worked *what* out yet?" Danny glared at

him. "Know what, Sunshine, I'm getting a bit fed up with Mr. Know-It-All!"

Michael glared back. "And I'm getting a bit fed up with your stupidity. Why don't—"

"Who you calling stupid? You think maybe—"

But Opal spoke up suddenly, interrupting them both. "Michael, are you trying to tell us we can *control* that fire?"

Dorothy shook her head. "No, he's trying to tell you that you can control *yourselves,* which is what you two boys need to do. Can't go squabbling between ourselves when there's work on hand." She stared them both down, then said, "Listen, this world reflects our world like a mirror. Only not exactly. Distorting mirror, you might say, like we saw in that fun house up in Blackpool, Danny. It's not *real* the way we know real. What you see and feel here depends on what's going on inside your head. You accept fire at face value and it'll burn you, sure enough. But you don't have to."

"Accept fire at face value?" Danny asked.

"Accept *anything* at face value," Michael said.

"Good rule for the rest of your life, that," Dorothy added.

"I don't understand you," Opal said.

"In my country, they used to say, 'What you see—it's not what you think,'" Michael said. "That's true here.

You feel hot in this place, don't you?"

"Course I do," Danny said.

"I don't," Michael told him. "You see me sweating?"

Danny stared at him. Now that he came to mention it, Michael wasn't, while Danny was sweating like a pig. "No."

"It's what you chose to *believe*, Danny," Michael said. "If you take this place at face value, it'll kill you, but if you don't believe in the heat, it can't harm you. In my country there are witch doctors who can kill people by pointing a bone at them. But the bone doesn't work on Europeans, didn't work on the French when they occupied Mali, because Europeans don't believe in it."

Danny took a step back from the edge of the lake. "Wait a minute," he said, "this isn't some superstitious bone thing. You're telling me I can stick my head in the fire and I won't get my face burned off so long as I believe the coals are ice cubes?"

"Not in our world, obviously," Michael told him patiently. "But in *this* world, yes. Look, Danny, you remember those insect things we talked about—the *sohanti* insects you saw flying around Opal when she was out of body?"

"Yes," Danny said uncertainly. He couldn't see what this had to do with—

"Call them," Michael said.

"What?"

"Call them," Michael repeated. "Go on—call them now." Danny stared at him. "Go on," Michael urged.

Danny stared at him a little longer, then said, "Okay." He closed his eyes as if concentrating. After a moment he opened them again. "You see? Nothing happen—" Then he ducked abruptly as three of the batlike insects swooped to circle his head and flew off again. Michael grinned broadly. "Coincidence," Danny muttered.

"*Sohanti,*" Michael said.

After a moment, Danny said, "All right, suppose you're right. Big difference between calling a few bugs and risking our lives in—"

Dorothy said, "Oh, for God's sake—" and dived into the flaming lake.

For perhaps half a second, Danny stood stunned, then, "Nan!" he screamed and dived into the fire himself. The water was cool. There were flames all around him, he was swimming in fire, but the water was cool. In a few seconds he was swimming beside his grandmother. "Sorry about that," Dorothy said, "but we were running out of time."

Behind him, Danny heard the splashes as first Michael, then Opal dived into the fiery lake. It took them all less than seven minutes to swim to the island. "You really think there will be guards, Nan?" Danny asked a little breathlessly. He needed to get more exercise—it was galling that his Nan outswam him, even if she was using a much younger, fitter body on the astral plane.

Dorothy squatted on the rocky apron. "Might be, might not," she said, shaking her head. "But I didn't want you to fly and I couldn't tell you why back there."

Michael and Opal were walking out of the water. Liquid fire flowed off their bodies, but not even their hair was singed.

"Tell me now, then?"

Dorothy glanced at the other two, then said, "You had to experience that. No use just hearing how tricky this place is. Michael already knows that, but you had to find out for yourself. You just keep that in mind and you'll be all right."

Danny said, "Okay, Nan, point taken. What happens now?"

"What happens now is that the three of you retrieve the spear."

Danny picked it up at once. "You're not coming with us?" He felt relieved but puzzled. His grandmother wasn't the type to back out of anything.

Michael and Opal arrived beside them in time to hear the tail end of the conversation. Michael said, "Farrakhan used a triangle to trap the beast, from what you told us, so there can't be more than three of us in the Shenlu Chamber."

Danny was finding him more irritating by the minute. "How do you know stuff like that?" he demanded.

Michael shrugged. Dorothy said, "Michael's quick on the uptake, Danny."

Danny flushed and said, "Don't suppose you know where we can actually *find* this Shenlu Chamber, do you, Mike?"

Michael ignored his tone and nodded toward a rock face. "My guess would be over there," he said mildly. As they turned to follow his gaze, a cave mouth opened in the rock.

After a moment, Danny said, "That wasn't there before."

"You just didn't see it there before," Michael said with just the barest hint of an infuriating grin.

"Or them either," Opal whispered suddenly.

Danny went cold. Michael had been right about Farrakhan's guards as well.

[59]

Roland, the Shadow Project

"**C**lear the parking lot!" Sir Roland shouted. "All your soldiers—get them out of here."

Carradine was staring paralyzed at one of the steel doors. It bore the imprint of a giant hand. With talons.

"Get them out of here!" Roland yelled. "You too, George. And you, Gary."

Carradine's paralysis broke. "What the hell *is* that?" he whispered.

"Get the bloody men out!" Roland hissed. "And get yourself out with them. This isn't an ordinary attack." He'd only suspected before, but he was certain now.

"Rollie," George said, his eyes wide, "there are men out there in the tunnel—"

"The men in the tunnel are dead!" Roland snapped. "And you'll be following them if you don't do what I tell you. Along with the rest of the men here." Not that he knew what he was going to do himself. What could he do—throw holy water at the damn thing? But it was important to get the rest of his men to safety: the doors weren't going to hold for long.

There was another sonic boom as the doors exploded inward.

60

Danny, the Lake of Fire

They were like something out of the Arabian Nights: muscular, bearded men in turbans, wielding scimitars. A dozen of them were racing toward the little group, with more streaming from the cave mouth behind them.

"Djinn!" Michael breathed.

"What do we do now?" Danny asked nobody in particular.

"Hold our ground," Opal said grimly.

"In case you hadn't noticed, they have swords and we don't," Danny said. "We don't have *any* weapons. Plus, there are a lot more of them than there are of us."

"What you see, it's not what you think!" Michael shouted. But then the first of the djinn were on them.

Instinctively Danny stepped between the first attacker and his Nan, but then the rest were upon them and he had no time at all to do anything except fight for his life. The nearest djinn swung his sword in a high, sweeping arc aimed at Danny's head. But Danny dropped to one knee as the sword whistled past, then bounced up again like a rubber ball and kicked out hard at the djinn's right leg. For an instant he was seized by the horrifying thought that the djinn might not be solid, that it might be a creature of smoke like the thing that came out of Aladdin's lamp, but his foot connected with a satisfying thud—and the djinn, caught badly off balance, went down heavily.

Danny glanced around, still looking for Dorothy, but he was in the middle of a melee now, a jumble of moving, thrusting bodies, and was unable to see any of his friends. Two of the djinn closed in to grab him, but Danny was smaller and more agile than either of them and dodged aside. From his new position he caught a glimpse of Opal, who was surrounded by sword-swinging djinn yet moving with such fluid grace that none of them seemed able to lay a finger on her. She was so beautiful that Danny felt a pang of jealousy about Michael, not that a knight's daughter was likely to look twice at Danny anyway. But then the moment passed and he was fighting for his life again.

He struck two more of the djinn, fighting low and dirty, and had the satisfaction of seeing them go down. He was still desperate to find his Nan, make sure she was all right, but more and more djinn were piling into the fray. Why had Nan told them to hold their ground? It would have made more sense to run from this lot, run fast. But too late for that now.

He heard the singing whistle of a sword just before it struck him in the upper arm, cutting deep. Danny screamed and clapped his free hand to the wound, as blood seeped through his fingers. The pain was mind-numbing. He twisted away as his assailant drew back his scimitar for a second blow. Then he saw Dorothy, down on one knee, trying desperately to protect her head with both hands. A djinn stood over her, sword upraised. Despite his wound, Danny hurled himself forward and head-butted the creature in the stomach. To his satisfaction, it jackknifed forward and dropped its sword.

"I'm getting you out of here!" he gasped at his Nan and seized her arm. His grip made bloody fingerprints on her skin.

Dorothy staggered to her feet, and now he could see she too was injured: there was a gash across one side of her face. He tried to pull her away from the battle zone, but they were surrounded now and the djinn were closing in. From somewhere beyond the sea of waving swords, he heard Opal scream.

Then, out of nowhere, Michael was beside him, miraculously wielding a captured sword. "Call the bats!" he shouted.

Danny looked at him stupidly. "What?"

"Call the bats!" Michael repeated. He was actually fencing with the djinn, and doing it well. They fell back, leaving a space around the beleaguered trio.

The bats? "I can't!" Danny shouted. His eyes darted from djinn to djinn in panic.

"Yes, you can! You've already done it once!" Michael shouted back. "I'll hold them off until you do."

Why did he want the bats? Danny spun around, dragging his Nan along with him. The djinn may have fallen back, but they were still surrounded. *Oh, God,* Danny thought. He closed his eyes and tried to call the bats, but there was no way he could concentrate.

"Hurry, Danny!" Michael shouted.

A black-bearded djinn dashed forward and snatched Dorothy out of Danny's grasp. "Nan!" Danny screamed. A blood mist of fury swept across his vision. He wanted a sword desperately. Something seemed to snap inside his head.

The bats came. They flew out of Danny's mind in a rustling, squeaking cloud, hundreds, thousands more of them than had ever appeared before. They swarmed like giant bees.

The djinn vanished. It was like some mad conjuring trick. One minute they were there, the next the rocky landscape was empty. Even the bats were gone. Danny grabbed for his Nan and hugged her. The slash on her face was gone. He glanced at his own arm and found it completely healed. Opal was walking toward them, also unharmed, a look of relief on her face.

"What you see, it isn't what you think," Michael said, and smiled broadly.

After a moment Danny said, "What happens now?"

Michael's smile faded. "I suppose now we brave the Shenlu Chamber in that cave."

"After you," said Danny quickly.

Michael gave a Gallic shrug and walked toward the cave mouth.

61

Michael, the Shenlu Chamber

Michael found himself back in the courtyard of his father's clinic, his stomach knotted with dread. It was morning time, but the lines of sick people had already formed, some standing, some squatting, all waiting patiently. Michael saw the young woman and the blind boy, just where he remembered them that day so long ago. Suleiman was there as well, standing by Michael's side. "There he is now," Suleiman said.

Mansa Konkon looked just as he remembered too—small, thin, sinister, unsmiling. There was the same sudden silence as he walked into the yard.

"Are you ready?" Suleiman asked, as if it mattered whether Michael was ready or not. His time had come now, and there was no escape.

Michael thought it might happen as it happened before, but instead of walking to the boy, Konkon walked directly toward Michael. "I have come for you," Konkon said. He reached out and gripped Michael's arm at the wrist. His fingers looked like the talons of a bird.

The young woman screamed.

Michael's insides turned to water. He wanted to pull away and run, but could not work his body. "Father," he whispered, his voice no more than a croak.

"Your father can't help you now," the Tuareg Suleiman told him.

From the transistor radio, the voice of Papa Konare said, "Nothing can help you now."

"Except . . . ," Suleiman added. He stared casually upward into the cloudless sky.

As happened before, Michael's father, Abégé Potolo, strode from the building. "Stop that!" he commanded. "Stop that at once! *Ce garçon est mon fils.*"

Michael felt a flooding of relief. *This boy is my son.* His father would rescue him whatever Suleiman said. But Konkon was shaking his head. "Not yours," he said, "but mine."

"Ah," said Michael's father, and walked away.

"You must kill Konkon yourself," said Suleiman matter-of-factly.

"I can't," Michael whispered. He had never, ever felt so afraid.

"You can't," Konkon confirmed. He smiled then for the first time, and Michael could see that he had filed his teeth to points so that they were like the fangs of a serpent. Konkon pulled his sorcerer's bone from his pocket.

"You must kill him before he kills you," Suleiman said.

"I can't," Michael repeated. His body was still paralyzed by fear.

Strangely, it was Konkon who said, "You must conquer your fear." Or perhaps it was the voice of Papa Konare or Uncle Hector or his father.

None of them understood, of course. They thought he was afraid of Konkon. But Michael wasn't afraid of Konkon: he was afraid of what he had to do to defeat Konkon.

"If you don't do it," said Suleiman, "you will die."

As Michael's father reached the door of his clinic, he called back over his shoulder, "If you don't do it, Opal may die too."

Konkon smiled his serpent's smile and raised the bone.

From somewhere a woman's voice shouted a long drawn-out *Noooonnn!*

The thought of Opal dying turned Michael's blood to ice. Somehow he fought his fear and raised his right hand as if warding off a blow. Konkon shrieked once, dropped the bone, and slapped his neck to swat the creature that appeared there. Then the little sorcerer slid down to the ground, spasmed, and lay still.

"You are *sohanti*," Suleiman whispered triumphantly in Michael's ear as the sun began to darken and the scene around them faded.

[62]

Opal, the Shenlu Chamber

Opal glanced at Dorothy, then stepped into the cave.

Michael was squatting on the floor of the cavern, a wary look on his face. Opal glanced around, but there was no sign of the spear they'd come for, no sign of guards, no sign of anybody except Michael and herself. "Are you all right?" she asked at once.

"I thought before we did anything else," Michael said, "I should tell you why I couldn't take you to the ball."

Silence hung between them like a cloud. Opal began to feel strangely frightened. As the silence lengthened, her fear grew. Eventually she asked, "What was the reason, Michael?" Her voice was barely audible.

Michael said coolly, "Because you're so ugly."

Opal's throat tightened and her heart began to race. "What?"

"I could not bear to be seen with you," Michael said.

"It was as simple as that." He shrugged, then added, "Sorry."

"I'm not—" Opal began.

"You're not really all that fanciable," Michael said. "Quite a nice figure, I suppose, but nothing special." He shrugged again. "Perhaps ugly is too strong a word. Perhaps I should just have said *plain*."

The fear was almost overwhelming now, but beyond it tears were welling up into her eyes. "Why are you talking like that, Michael?" she whispered. She felt as if her heart was being ripped from her chest.

"Because it's *true*," Michael said. "See for yourself."

He must have learned that trick Dorothy did, for she found herself looking into a full-length mirror. Her breasts were too small and her legs were too short and her bottom looked fat. But he was right about her face as well. She really did look plain, with limp blond hair and a mouth that was too wide and eyes too far apart. It was astonishing that she'd ever thought someone as handsome as Michael might be persuaded to like her.

The fear was tearing her apart. It wasn't just Michael. No boy would want her, not now, not ever. She was too plain, too . . . nothing! She felt overwhelmed by her lack of—

"Better go now," Michael said. "I just thought you should know." He strode away.

Opal couldn't tear herself away from the mirror, couldn't stop examining her miserable face and frumpy figure. She was loathsome. She had grown too fat, her skin was dry and flaking, her eyes dull and lifeless. What she saw frightened her, disgusted her. Tears began to roll down her cheeks, but she still couldn't tear herself away.

A figure appeared behind her in the gloomy depths of the mirror, dark and very indistinct. A voice said, "You must conquer your fear." Dorothy must have come in. Or perhaps it was her own voice.

But Opal couldn't conquer her fear. All she could do was stand there and stare into the mirror. All she could think was how plain and flat-chested and fat she'd become. In the mirror, her face was changing.

It was now no longer plain but—just as Michael said at first—positively ugly. She felt herself slide toward the floor, sobbing as if her heart would break.

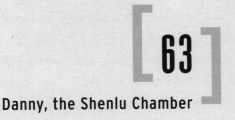

Danny, the Shenlu Chamber

Danny walked into a bedroom.

Somehow his Nan had managed to get there before him, for she was lying in the bed with the covers pulled up to her chin. Her eyes were very large and he didn't like the look of her face. The skin was pale and translucent, stretched tightly across the bones of her skull. Her lips had thinned and cracked, probably as a result of swimming in the fiery lake. Even though it hadn't burned them, it was dry and hot and Dorothy was getting on a bit. Funny thing was, she looked as old as he remembered her in their own world. The young, fit body she'd had on the astral plane seemed to have disappeared.

"What are you doing, Nan?" he asked. The large eyes turned toward him, and suddenly he felt very much afraid.

"I'm dying, Danny," his Nan said. Her breathing was

labored, and her voice wheezed and crackled when she spoke.

"No you aren't, Nan," Danny said a little desperately. "Tough as old boots you are."

"I'm dying," Dorothy repeated. "I didn't tell you what this place does for you." She pushed down the covers and he saw that her body was not simply wasted, but rotted. The bare arms, protruding sticklike from her nightdress, looked as if they might crumble away at any moment. The huge, pain-filled eyes locked onto his own. "I'm dying," she said, "and it's all your fault!"

Danny looked around. The other two, Opal and Michael, were nowhere to be seen, even though they'd both walked in before him and—as far as he could see—there was no other way out. He felt frightened to the point of panic. His Nan couldn't be dying, not now when they needed her most—but through it all he kept remembering something she'd told him over and over when he was growing up: the only thing to do with fear is face it.

"You have to leave, Danny," Dorothy said. "It's the only thing that will save me. You have to forget all about this business and go home. You have to do it now."

"Can't do that, Nan," Danny said. He couldn't, either. Opal and Michael had gone on. They were relying on him to make up the triangle.

"You *must*," Dorothy insisted. "I thought at first you could hack it, but now I know you can't. You have to go back."

Danny stared at her, and suddenly the fear that was knotting his stomach started to drain away. "You're not Nan."

"You're not up to it, Danny," said the thing in the bed. "All you're really good for is a bit of thieving. Can't even face the thought of Cambridge, can you?"

"Shut up," Danny said.

"Hit a nerve, have I? You can pretend all you like you aren't going because of me—that's noble, that is. But the real reason is you're not up to it. Oh, you're bright enough, I'll grant you that, but not university standard. And you don't have the breeding. You go to Cambridge and they'll soon show you up."

This was definitely not his Nan, nothing remotely like his Nan. "Tricky," she'd said when she was talking about the astral plane, and this was as tricky as it got. Because what Farrakhan had done was set this place up to show you your own fears.

Who knew what Opal and Michael must have faced, but what Danny was looking at was his Nan's death, all mixed up with the heap of guilt he had about not looking after her well enough. That and the way he always felt he wasn't really good enough. Not for

Cambridge, not for anything.

Only thing to do with fear was face it.

"I'm off now," Danny said abruptly. "Onward and upward." As he walked forward, his environment dissolved, starting with the Nan-thing lying on the bed.

Danny, the Shenlu Chamber

Both Opal and Michael were waiting for him near the mouth of a cavern. "What did you get?" Danny asked.

Michael seemed to understand at once. "*Sohanti,*" he said. "I've always been afraid I might be *sohanti* like my father." He paused and looked at them. "Afraid I might kill people and then kill myself."

"What about you, Opal?"

"I'm not sure I want to talk about it," Opal said.

Danny shrugged. "That's cool." He wasn't keen to talk about his own experience, either.

But Michael pushed, "What fears did you face, Danny?"

Danny took a shuddering breath and said, "Been frightened Nan might die." He hesitated, then added, "Bit of trouble with self-confidence as well."

Opal's eyes opened wide in astonishment. "*You?* Lacking confidence?"

Danny grinned self-consciously. "The way I come across is mostly bluff."

Opal stared at him for a long time, then said abruptly, "It was my looks."

"What was?"

Opal said, "It's a stupid girl thing. I was afraid I wasn't . . ." She seemed painfully embarrassed. "You know . . . pretty."

Danny said spontaneously, "But you're gorgeous."

Opal smiled. "Thank you, Danny. I'm not sure you don't need glasses, but thank you all the same."

Danny shrugged. "Not just me. Michael thinks so too—see that from the way he looks at you."

Now Michael was looking mortified. He turned his head so he wouldn't have to meet Opal's eye. All the same he said, "I think you are very beautiful, Opal."

Opal said, "It's a girl thing. I know that. Most girls think there's something wrong with the way they look." She was staring at Michael. "I also know it's not true, sort of, but that doesn't stop me from feeling afraid. It's stupid."

"Most of our fears are stupid," Michael said. "Even imaginary." He frowned. "But how clever of Farrakhan to use them against us."

Danny said, "So what happens now? Is this the *real* Shenlu Chamber?"

They turned to look at the dark entrance of the cavern. "I assume so," said Michael.

"You don't think there are any more traps or guards or anything of that sort?" Opal asked.

"Difficult to say."

"So . . ." Danny said. "We just walk in, do we?"

"I think we should hold hands." The two boys turned to look at Opal in amazement, and she flushed. "I don't know if the fighting is over, but I think we should present a united front."

"Works for me." Danny reached out and took one of her hands. After a moment, Michael took the other. Together, the three of them walked into the darkness.

They saw the creature at once, hung from a massive wooden cross in the gloom at the back of the cavern. It was pinned to the structure by a spear that pierced its abdomen. It looked for all the world like a giant bear, but with curiously human features. It stared at them with huge, dark, soulful eyes and whimpered.

"What is it?" Danny whispered.

Opal said, "I think that's our Devourer."

It was nothing like the demon he'd seen in Farrakhan's ritual. "That's not what I saw," Danny said. He couldn't take his eyes off the beast. The pain it must be suffering was indescribable. He wanted to set it free.

"Poor thing," Opal said, as if echoing his thought.

"I think Opal's right—that is the Devourer. Things look different here," Michael said.

"I don't care if it is the Devourer," Danny said. "We can't leave it there—it's hurt."

Opal nodded. "We have to take the spear out. It's in so much pain."

"If I'm right, it may attack us," Michael said.

Michael had a point there, Danny thought. Even if the creature *wasn't* the Devourer, it must be half crazy with pain. It would attack the moment it was free. Any injured animal would. All the same, he couldn't just leave it there to suffer.

"I think this is how Farrakhan controls the Devourer," Opal said suddenly. She glanced at Danny. "This is what it's really like, but before he calls it into our world, he tortures it on the astral plane so it's savage and wants to kill people."

"That's why he needed the Spear of Destiny," Michael said. "It's the only thing powerful enough."

"So we *have to* take the spear out," Opal said, then hesitated. "Even if it does attack us."

Danny looked up at the massive body. Despite the impaling spear, it gave the impression of almost bound-less strength and power. Suddenly he felt very much afraid. "It won't just attack, it will kill us." There was no way they could pull out the spear and get away before the creature savaged them.

Opal said, "I'll do it—the poor thing must be in agony."

Michael said quickly, "It's all right—I'll do it. You two leave now, and I'll release it when you've gone." A trickle of sweat rolled down his temple, and Danny realized Michael was just as frightened as he was. Danny felt a surge of admiration.

"I don't want you to do it," Opal said firmly. Of the three of them she seemed the least frightened; or if she was, it didn't show. "I'll do it," she repeated. "I'm very fast. I'm sure I can get away before it attacks me."

Would it really be possible to pull the spear out, then make a run for it? Danny wondered. He fought down his fear and shrugged fatalistically. "I'll pull the spear out." He grinned at Opal. "I've got more experience than you of running away. Usually from coppers. But it's a good idea that the two of you get away first."

"I don't think anybody's going anywhere," Opal said. "The spear's right through into the wood. I think it will take the three of us to pull it out."

They looked at one another. Hanging above them, the beast on the cross moaned slightly. Its eyes were closed now, as if it was barely conscious. Perhaps it would be too weak to attack them, Danny thought. But he knew that was nonsense. Helpless though it looked, this thing was the inner essence of the towering demon figure he'd seen Farrakhan conjure in the cellar. It had all the demon's power, all the demon's rage. Once it was no longer pierced by the Spear of Destiny, it would be on them like an express train. *How did I get myself into this?* Danny wondered.

Then Opal stepped forward to grip the shaft of the spear. She glanced at Michael, who moved without hesitation to overlap his hands across hers. *Now's the time to get out of here,* Danny thought. But he didn't. Instead, he joined his hands with the others on the shaft.

Despite Opal's doubts, the spear withdrew easily from the creature's flesh.

[65]

Sir Roland, the Shadow Project

It was pandemonium. The steel doors that had sealed off the tunnel lay twisted and shattered. Eight broken bodies lay in the tunnel entrance, their blood splattered on the walls, their chest cavities ripped open. Rifles were scattered across the floor, bent out of recognition by the beast. Some soldiers panicked and fled. Others formed ranks and, despite Sir Roland's shouted orders, stood their ground and opened fire. A hail of bullets struck the Devourer, but the creature kept coming.

George Hanover cursed and dropped back. Carradine stepped forward, assumed a shooting-range stance, and opened up with his semiautomatic. He seemed to be aiming at the creature's head, but if his bullets hit, they made no more difference than the body shots of the soldiers.

Roland drew his own gun, not because he thought he would do any better than Carradine, but as a symbol of authority. The situation was almost out of control, and

339

he had to do something before he lost it completely. He moved beside Carradine and said quietly into his ear, "Stop shooting, Gary."

Carradine looked at him in surprise but did as he was told. Roland turned and gestured to George Hanover. "Get the men out," he said firmly. "All of them. Use the service lifts. Firepower won't stop it, and if we keep trying, we'll only have a bloodbath."

Hanover asked suspiciously, "Do you know what this thing is, Rollie?"

Their only hope was retreat into the complex—retreat or rout: it was no time for fine distinctions. The creature had smashed through bombproof steel doors, but even so, it could not possibly get inside the Project complex. Once they had the men safely down below, they could disable the elevators and heighten security. Nothing could reach them, provided they moved fast. Roland took a deep breath. "Get the men out," he said again, "then go to Code Purple."

Carradine stared at him, stunned. "*Nuclear* alert?"

Roland nodded grimly. A Code Purple nuclear alert would seal the entire complex against a tactical nuclear attack. The metal shielding was nearly four feet of special titanium alloy, coated with lead for the radiation. It was approximately thirty times stronger than the massive steel doors that had just shattered, designed to withstand an atomic detonation. Not even Farrakhan's beast could break through that.

Hanover said, "You know we'll have to notify the prime minister?"

"Tell him it's a drill," Roland ordered. "We need breathing space to figure out what to do."

The thing reached the first rank of soldiers who'd stood their ground by the tunnel. It attacked the nearest man and began to rip into him. "My God!" Carradine exclaimed. He looked as if he might be sick.

"You want me to tell him about—?" George Hanover glanced toward the beast.

"Tell who?"

"The prime minister."

"Oh, for God's sake, George!" Roland exploded. "Tell him what you like. Just get the men out of here. While it's distracted."

Some of the soldiers in the squad by the tunnel had already broken ranks to start a disorderly retreat, but to Roland's horror, reinforcements were emerging from the bowels of the Project behind him. Carradine ran toward the squad commander, shouting orders. Hanover started to move back toward the elevators, then stopped. "What are *you* going to do, Roland?"

"Move it, George," Roland snapped. "You're an older man than I am—I'll follow you in a minute."

Hanover turned without a word and ran. He wasn't fast, but he was fast enough. Roland spun around and saw to his relief that the rest of the men near the entrance were now retreating, Carradine with them. Roland was terrified that Farrakhan's creature would launch another attack, but for the moment it was squatting on the bodies of the men it killed, ignoring the others while it feasted. "Quickly!" Roland shouted. He began to run toward the elevators himself. The last of the soldiers and Carradine disappeared through the elevator doors but held them open, waiting for him. He was only moments away when the beast attacked again.

He could not believe how quickly it could move. The thing was like a charging bull, an express train. Roland's heart froze. There was absolutely no way he could reach the lifts in time. "Go!" he shouted to Carradine and the rest, but the doors remained stubbornly open.

Roland stopped in his tracks. If the creature reached the service elevator before the doors closed, the Project was finished. It would make short work of Carradine and the soldiers—and while it might not be able to work the controls, once George Hanover initiated the lockdown, the elevator would be withdrawn automatically, carrying the beast into the bowels of the complex.

"Close the doors!" Roland shouted. "That's an order!" He saw Carradine slap a button, but the doors were shutting far too slowly. In his mind's eye, he could see the creature prying them apart again and savaging the men within. *Unless,* he thought suddenly, *it stopped to feed again* . . .

Without a second's hesitation, Roland ran toward the beast. "Sir Roland—no!" someone shouted behind him. But he ignored it; and it was, in any case, too late. The Devourer loomed over him, reached for him—

Then, like the flicker of a candle flame, the creature disappeared.

Danny, the Shenlu Chamber

T he spear pulled free.

At once the cavern was filled with the acrid smell of ozone, as snakes of static electricity wriggled along its length. The huge bearlike creature dropped deadweight from its cross, narrowly missing the three to fall with a thud on the cavern floor. Danny found himself holding the spear as the others jumped back. The weapon crackled and glowed. He dropped it hastily.

The bear thing rolled, then climbed to its feet. It seemed to grow taller as it did so. Within seconds it was a colossus, almost filling the huge cavern. Then the cavern itself shattered, leaving them standing on an open plain. Beyond the remnants of the cavern, a massive pentagram of fire burned on the barren earth. Within it, as if waiting for them, stood the tall, imposing figure of a bearded man. Despite the distortions of the astral plane, Danny recognized the fanatical, glittering eyes at once.

"My God, it's Farrakhan," he whispered.

It was like the scene Danny witnessed in the cellar, except a thousand times more terrifying. Beside Farrakhan crouched the living form of a grotesque stringed puppet, its twisted face instantly recognizable from a thousand newspaper photographs as that of the Skull.

Farrakhan raised his arms and began to chant as he had done in the cellar. His words reverberated like thunder across the open plain. Flames leaped high from the pentagram, and lightning arced from his open palms. It seemed that nothing could withstand him.

But the towering bear thing brushed aside the bolts of lightning as a man might swat a fly. It reached through the flames of the pentagram and seized Farrakhan in a taloned grip. He screamed, but the sound cut off abruptly as his chest ripped open. There was a flash of blinding light as the Devourer reached in for his heart, then stillness.

"It's disappeared," Danny said. He looked in bewilderment across the empty plain. The creature was gone, as were Farrakhan and the Skull. Even the fiery pentagram had vanished from the barren earth. He looked at Opal. "What do we do now?"

Michael said, "I think we go home."

[67]

Sir Roland, Blandings

It was a sunny morning for once, and Hector had organized a breakfast outdoors on his terrace. Sir Roland helped himself to orange juice and sat down with the *Times* to wait for the others. "See that?" he said when Hector finally appeared.

Hector took the folded paper. He frowned. "The thing about the politician and the actress?"

"Below it," Roland said.

"Ah," Hector said. "'Skull Top Aide Killed.' That one?"

Roland looked out across the garden. He sometimes wondered how Hector had managed to survive the war. "That one," he said.

Hector shook out the paper and began to read aloud. "'CIA sources claim that Hazrat Farrakhan, a top aide of Sword of Wrath leader Venskab Faivre (aka "the Skull"), has died in his native Lusakistan.'"

"We leaked the wrong place," Roland murmured. "No sense upsetting people by letting them know he managed to get into Britain."

"'Farrakhan's mutilated body was discovered in a mountainous region close to a suspected Sword of Wrath training camp. Indications are that he was savaged by a bear. No further details are available.'" Hector looked up and grinned slightly. "Pointless leaking further details since the ones you did leak are all wrong."

"It's true enough about his death," Roland said. "And the one detail we didn't leak was that his heart was missing."

"I see," Hector said. He walked over to the side table and poured himself a coffee. "Are you going to tell the kids when they come down?"

Roland nodded. "They deserve to know—it was all their doing."

Hector sat down. "Will it make a difference?"

"I think it will make a *big* difference," Roland said. "I think it may even mean the end of Sword of Wrath. Farrakhan was very much the power behind the throne, and now we're getting reports that the Skull is suffering from a mystery illness, which I suspect may have something to do with what happened on the astral plane. We've rounded up his sleeper cell—the ones who helped Farrakhan with the ritual—and we're questioning Uncle

Guy about his relationship with Avramides and Kanska. Opal's been great and young Danny really pulled through for us as well."

"You keeping him on as an agent?"

"We're sending him to Cambridge. When he comes down, we'll make him an offer he can't refuse."

"Poor fellow," Hector chuckled. There were sounds of movement inside the house. He pushed himself to his feet. "Sounds as if your daughter has gotten up. I just want a quick word with her before she talks to my nephew."

68

Opal, Blandings

"**I**s it true?" Opal asked.

Michael frowned. "Is what true?"

"That you're engaged to be married."

They were drinking coffee in the Blue Room. Opal was wearing a T-shirt and jeans, but Michael was still in his pajamas. Her father and Uncle Hector were on the terrace, lingering over the remains of breakfast.

Michael stared at her, stunned. "How did you know?"

"Your uncle Hector told me. Just now, actually. So it *is* true?"

Michael's mouth opened and closed like that of a fish. He put his coffee cup down on a side table, picked it up, then put it down again. "Yes, it is true. But he had no right to tell you—it was none of his business."

"Perhaps he thought it might be some of mine." Opal was experiencing a surge of dread. Even though an engagement would explain his odd behavior, she wasn't really sure she wanted all the details. But Hector had insisted she discuss it with Michael "for your own good," he'd said. And curiosity drove her now. She looked directly at Michael. "Are you going to tell me about it?"

Michael glanced through the French windows at the portly figure of his uncle on the terrace and looked, for a moment, as if he might cheerfully murder him. Then he looked back at Opal. "Did you know I was a direct descendant of the old kings of Mali?"

Opal nodded. "Hector mentioned it."

"Yes. I thought he might: he likes the idea that I'm a prince, for some reason." He drew a ragged breath. "The engagement," he said, "was something I entered into at the age of five."

Opal's mouth dropped open. "*Five?* You got engaged at the age of *five?*"

Michael looked flustered. "Well, obviously *I* didn't enter into it. Not personally, I mean. It was something the elders arranged. To keep the bloodline pure—the royal line."

Opal felt a small surge of relief. "Who . . . who did they engage you to?"

"A Dogon girl," Michael said. "Someone from a suitable family. She had no say in it, of course. Nor did I, for that matter. When she's eighteen and I'm twenty, we're supposed to get married."

It was incredible. "Why?" Opal asked.

"Why are we supposed to get married?" Michael glanced away. "The usual reason—to have children: an heir to the throne." He caught Opal's expression and added hurriedly, "Not that it makes any difference to anybody now. Mali's a republic. There is no question of reviving the old monarchy."

"But you still plan to marry this little girl?" Opal asked, appalled.

"She is not a little girl any more," Michael said. "She is just two years younger than I am." He looked uncomfortable. "She writes to me."

"She writes you letters?"

"Yes."

"What does she say?"

"That she doesn't want to do it," Michael said.

Opal was experiencing a mixture of emotions: shock, bewilderment, anger. But creeping through them was just the thinnest thread of hope. She took a deep breath. "And do you?" she asked. "Do you want to do it?"

"No." Michael shook his head vigorously.

"Then what's the problem?"

Michael shifted uncomfortably in his chair. "It's not as simple as that. This is a question of Mali tradition."

The thin thread snapped. "So you *do* intend to marry

her? You'll force her because it's Mali tradition?"

"No, of course not."

"Of course you won't force her, or of course you don't intend to marry her?"

"Of course I don't intend to marry her. Opal, I—"

"And does she intend to marry you?"

Michael shook his head again. "No. She's actually taken a fancy to some boy in Kalana. But until we undergo a release ceremony, we're still officially engaged. And we can't go through the release ceremony until I return to Mali. So at the moment the engagement still stands."

"So what has this to do with"—Opal hesitated—"me?"

Michael said miserably, "I didn't think it would be . . . correct to become involved with anyone while I was still engaged to another girl. Even if it was only a formality."

Danny walked in and headed for the coffeepot on the sideboard. "Sleep well, did you?" he asked cheerfully. "You two in good form after the adventure?"

"Oh, yes." Opal turned to him and grinned. "Feeling very fine indeed."

Author's Note

The book you've just read is, of course, fiction. But some of the most incredible aspects of the story are based on fact.

The CIA really did have an official remote-viewing (RV) program. By the end of the 1960s, the CIA discovered that both the Soviet Union and China had given high priority to ESP (extrasensory perception) research, and in 1972 CIA agents paid a visit to an American laser physicist named Hal Puthoff, who was conducting remote-viewing experiments with the help of a psychic named Ingo Swann. The meeting resulted in the establishment of the CIA's own program to train operatives in espionage using RV. The agency now insists that it has been closed down since 1996.

Since 1886 there have been hundreds of cases of out-of-body-experience (OOBE) documented by distinguished scientists and academics all over the world.

Various studies have attempted to establish how widespread the phenomenon might be. In 1954 Professor Hornell Hart discovered that out of 155 Duke University sociology students, 27.1 percent claimed to have had out-of-body-experiences. In 1967 Celia Green circulated questionnaires among undergraduates in two British universities. One yielded 19 percent who had had OOBEs, the other 34 percent. In a random survey carried out among one thousand residents and students from Charlottesville, Virginia, in 1975, 14 percent of the residents and 25 percent of the students reported OOBEs. If you average out the statistics collected above, nearly one in four readers of this book might expect to have an OOBE at some stage of their lives.

I also managed to leave my body on a few occasions, for what it's worth, and you can listen to an account of my experience at www.herbiebrennan.com.

Using sound to stimulate out-of-body-experience has been the subject of considerable experimentation. The Hemi-Sync was devised by the late Robert Monroe, an American businessman. It works to synchronize the left and right hemispheres of the brain.

What Sir Roland told Danny about psychotronics was true. There actually was an International Scientific Conference held in Moscow in 1968 during which Czech scientists announced their discovery of psychotronic energy, a carrier for telepathy, healing, and other odd phenomena.

The *Lancea Longini,* or Spear of Destiny, has been extensively researched, and several artifacts are claimed to be the spear that pierced the side of Christ while he was dying on the cross. Since 1424 one of these was held in the collection of Imperial Regalia at Nuremberg in Germany, but was moved to Austria for safekeeping when Napoleon threatened the city in 1796. It was subsequently sold to the Hapsburg Dynasty and held as part of their imperial regalia in the *Schatzkammer* (Treasury) collection in Vienna. Hitler took the lance back to Germany after his annexation of Austria, apparently convinced that it had magical powers, but it was returned to Austria by American General George S. Patton at the end of the Second World War. It is currently in the *Kunsthistorisches Museum.*

The *sohanti* exist too. They are a caste of the Songhai people, a group of three million who live along the great bend of the River Niger in border areas of Mali and two of its neighboring countries. The *sohanti* are witch doctors and enjoy a fearsome reputation as natural-born magicians.

Here's a sneak peek at the next
Shadow Project adventure,
THE DOOMSDAY BOX

Opal, the Montauk Carlton, Montauk

Opal awoke with a start.

For a long moment she couldn't work out where she was. The room was gloomy, but far from dark—a neon sign outside one window managed to throw a wash of color across the walls despite the curtains. Beyond the foot of her bed, she could see the outline of a television set looming over its own red standby light. Then she remembered: she was in the Montauk Carlton. She turned her head to confirm this and gasped in sudden panic. The space between her bed and the door was filled with alien white figures. Opal opened her mouth to scream.

"Miss Harrington," said the closest figure, and the only thing that stopped Opal from actually screaming was the fact that it was a woman's voice. "Miss Harrington, are you awake?"

Opal sat bolt upright, holding the bedclothes to her

throat. She was wearing only a short silk nightgown and felt extremely vulnerable. "Who are you? What do you want?" A hint of antiseptic wafted into her nostrils.

"Miss Harrington, you need to come with us. You have to get dressed at once."

"Who are you?" Opal repeated. She reached out and switched on her bedside lamp.

The woman was wearing a white suit of plastic material and some sort of headpiece that covered the whole of her face. Her eyes bored into Opal through transparent goggles. Three other suited figures—men to judge by their size—stood between her and the door. "We're from the Project," the woman said urgently. "Please, Miss Harrington, you must come with us at once. Have you had close contact with anyone since you left Colonel Saltzman? Anyone in the hotel?"

Frowning, Opal shook her head. "No, I came straight up to my room. What's going on?"

"We can discuss that on the way. We've alerted your father. Now can—"

"My father? What's my father got to do with it?"

But the woman and her companions were already pushing out of the room. "We'll give you privacy to get dressed," she said, "and talk on the way."

Opal stared for a moment at the closed door, then got up and headed for the wardrobe. A feeling of dread had settled in her stomach.

As she stepped from the room, they surrounded her and escorted her to the elevator, where another white-suited figure was holding the door. Opal had only the barest impression of the hotel lobby as she was ushered through to startled glances from staff and guests. There was an ambulance on the street outside. Opal stopped dead. "What's this? I'm not sick." But strong hands gripped her arms and she was frog-marched into the waiting vehicle. The woman and two of her companions climbed in with her.

As the ambulance pulled away, Opal looked from one silent figure to another and fought to keep calm. Eventually she said in her coldest voice, "This has gone far enough. If you want me to cooperate, you will have to tell me what is going on. Otherwise"—she fished her cell phone from her pocket and flicked it open—"I shall place a call to Colonel Saltzman and demand—"

"Colonel Saltzman is dead," said the woman beside her.

"What?"

"I'm sorry. I don't know any easy way to tell you this. The colonel is dead. Project Rainbow is now under the command of Brigadier General Tudor."

Opal stared at her, but the headgear made it impossible to read any expression. "Colonel Saltzman can't be dead. I was speaking to him only hours ago."

"Miss Harrington, I'm Dr. Amory—that's Major Helen Amory, Army Medical Corps, on assignment to Project Rainbow for the duration of the current emergency. Colonel—"

"What current emergency?" Opal interrupted.

"Miss Harrington, you and I will get on far better if you give me a chance to explain. Everyone here is cleared to hear what I have to say, and that may not be the case when we arrive, so I'd suggest you shut up and listen—okay?"

Opal shut up and listened.

"Miss Harrington," said Helen Amory, "I don't have the security clearance to know what Colonel Saltzman and his people were doing at Project Rainbow, but I've been told you and your friends were flown over from England to help. I also understand the CIA is involved here, as well as the army, maybe other agencies. Now, what I can tell you is this. Colonel Saltzman died just over an hour ago from a highly infectious disease. The disease is bacterial in origin, but resistant to our most powerful antibiotics. We tried seventeen of them on him, singly and in combination, and nothing touched his fever. We were still searching for an effective treatment when he died."

"He looked completely healthy when I saw him," Opal said, wide-eyed.

"It's one of the most virulent illnesses I have ever seen. It's also one of the most infectious. Two of the nurses who looked after Colonel Saltzman are now fighting for their lives. One of his military personnel—Captain Alison Woods—was with him when he collapsed. She is now showing early symptoms."

"I met Captain Woods," Opal said. "She was in charge of security."

Dr. Amory glanced out the ambulance window, then turned back to Opal. "We've set up quarantine units in the old underground base. It's only a matter of time before we find an antibiotic that works, of course, but in the meantime we must isolate everyone who's been in contact with the disease."

"That's where you're taking me?" Opal said, half a question, half a statement.

Helen Amory nodded. "Yes."

"I don't feel ill," Opal told her.

"And hopefully you'll stay that way. But it's vital we keep this from spreading, and you and your friends were in contact with the colonel."

"So you're bringing in the others as well?"

Dr. Amory nodded again. "Yes."

"Will I be given treatment?" Opal asked.

"Not unless you get ill. We've only managed to set up a few treatment units so far, and they're all in use.

The rest of the units are more like hospital wards, I'm afraid. Some of them were jail cells, dating from the time when Rainbow was first established. But we'll make you as comfortable as possible and you'll be fed army food, which isn't nearly as bad as you'd imagine."

"How long will you keep me isolated?"

"No more than a week," Helen Amory told her. "Unless you show symptoms."

"A *week*?" Opal exploded. "I'm supposed to fly home tomorrow—later today."

"If you're still symptom-free in forty-eight hours, it's unlikely you've been infected, but we need to be sure. A week to be on the safe side."

The woman was wearing an isolation suit, Opal realized abruptly. The very air she was breathing was filtered to remove bacteria. Opal had seen something similar in a movie about germ warfare. "And if I do start to show symptoms . . . ?"

Dr. Amory hesitated. "Hopefully we'll have found a cure by then."

After a moment, Opal said, "Do you know what you're dealing with yet? Some sort of superbug?"

"In a manner of speaking," Helen Amory said drily. "We're fairly certain Colonel Saltzman died of the black death."

Danny, in Quarantine,
Underground at Montauk

Quarantine wasn't as bad as Danny had expected. It was certainly a lot better than the nights he'd spent in the slammer during his bad-boy days. He had a private room, for one thing: comfy bed, little desk thing with a phone on it, chairs, flat-screen TV screwed into the wall. Nobody locked the door, for another. Thing was, the whole team was in quarantine, but isolation units were limited and they weren't in quarantine from each other. No point really. They'd already been in close contact. If one had it, they all had it. So you could wander down the corridor and visit your friends if you liked, just so you didn't try to leave the isolation unit. Leaving the isolation unit was something else. Wasn't just a lockdown either: there were *armed guards* on every exit. Yanks weren't shy when it came to lethal force. You had to admire them.

He was lying on the comfy bed using the remote to channel surf when Michael slipped furtively through the door.

"Knock?" Danny said.

"Sorry," Michael said, but gave no sign of going out again. He looked around for the nearest chair and sat in it. That's what irritated Danny about Michael: too self-confident by half. "Can I talk to you?" Michael asked. When there was no immediate reaction, he added, "About . . . something?"

Danny stared at him for a moment, then switched off the television and swung his feet off the bed onto the floor. About *something*? "Okay," he said cautiously.

"I'd like your advice," Michael said in his polite Eton accent.

"What about?" In the great scheme of things, *something* didn't convey a lot of information. Danny felt wary and vaguely suspicious. People didn't usually ask his advice. Especially African princes.

Michael looked uncomfortable. "You know when you join the Project, they give you a physical?" He hesitated, then added, as if Danny mightn't know what a physical was, "A medical examination?"

Danny nodded. "Yeah." The doctor who'd done his was cross-eyed with a hacking cough, a poor advertisement for his profession.

"Is it to make sure you're fit for the job, or do you think it's just, you know, an insurance thing?"

This was getting weird, Danny thought. "Bit of both, I expect. How should I know?" This had to be something to do with the plague, but when Michael decided to pussyfoot around a subject, he was a real expert. All the same, Michael was looking genuinely worried.

"Did you tell them the truth?" Michael asked. "About your health?"

Not just weird but downright bewildering. "No reason not to—I'm healthy as a horse. Tonsils as a kid, but that's about it."

"Did you tell the doctor about your tonsils?"

"Can't remember," Danny said honestly. "But if I did, it didn't seem to worry him."

"Suppose it had been something more serious. Like . . . diabetes or"—he licked his lips nervously—"something else. Do you think they'd still have taken you on?"

"You don't have diabetes, do you?" Danny asked.

"No, no," said Michael quickly. "That was just an example. What I meant was, if you *had* a serious condition, would they still keep you on?"

"Do *you* have a serious condition?" Danny pushed him. If he did, Danny couldn't think what. Never so much as heard him sneeze. He'd seen Michael in the shower, and he was one of the fittest-looking blokes he knew.

Michael flushed, then shook his head. "No, of course not. I was just wondering. You know . . . about Project policy."

"You've been with the Project a year longer than I have," Danny told him. "You have to know more about policy than I do." What was *wrong* with Michael? There had to be something, or he'd never have started this conversation. Maybe he was worried about getting sick and it had affected his brain. Danny opened his mouth to say something else, then shut it again as Fuchsia came in, waving a book.

"Boys," Fuchsia said. "I've found what they're all so worried about."

"I'd better go," Michael muttered. He started to rise from his seat.

"No, you stay," Fuchsia told him. "I wanted to tell Danny, but we all need to know this."

Michael sat down again, warily. He gave a warning glance toward Danny, as if asking him not to mention what they'd been discussing, not that Danny knew what they had been discussing in the first place.

Fuchsia said, "It's the black death."

"What's the black death?"

"What they're all worrying we might have. Opal told me. But the thing is, I've looked it up now." She waved the book she was holding. "It was the most awful disease that broke out in the Middle Ages. Listen to this." She flicked the book open and read, "'The plague that raged all over the land consumed nine parts in ten of the men through England, scarcely leaving a tenth man alive.' That was from the records of the Bristol and Gloucestershire Archaeological Society in 1883."

"It broke out in 1883?" Danny asked.

"No, silly," Fuchsia said. "They're an *archaeological* society. They were reporting on old findings. But imagine nine people in ten wiped out! That's worse than those awful African diseases like Ebola that everybody's frightened of." She waved the book at them again. "It broke out in China in thirteen-something and spread to Europe a couple of years later. They called it the *blue sickness* then. People used to catch it in the morning, and by the afternoon they were *dead*. It was totally the fastest disease *ever*."

"Yes, but that was before antibiotics," Danny said. "They can cure it now, can't they?"

"That's the thing," Fuchsia told him. "They used to think it was bubonic plague, which is pretty nasty and fast and deadly, but this book says scientists aren't so sure anymore. It broke out a few more times, the last of them in sixteen-something, then just sort of disappeared. So if it *wasn't* bubonic plague, it's a whole new disease we've

11

never tried antibiotics on, so they might work or they might not. And even if they did work, you'd have to move really, really fast and watch people, because if they caught it at night or something, they'd be dead before you'd think of giving them the pill. The early symptoms don't look serious, you see. The first thing that happens is you sneeze. Who'd think twice about that?" Her eyes were gleaming. "They made up a rhyme about it. You'll never guess what it was. . . ."

Michael said politely, "What was it?"

"'Ring a ring of roses, a pocketful of posies, a-tissue, a-tissue, we all fall down!'" She looked from one face to the other. "The old nursery rhyme is actually a plague song."

Opal came in then. All the color had drained from her face, and there was a frightened, haunted look in her eyes. "They're dead," she said. "Everybody's dead."